UNSEEN

Also by S.L. Stoner
in the
Sage Adair Historical Mystery Series
of the Pacific Northwest

Timber Beasts
Land Sharks
Dry Rot
Black Drop
Dead Line
The Mangle
Slow Burn
Bitter Cry

UNSEEN

A Sage Adair Historical Mystery
of the Pacific Northwest

S. L. Stoner

Yamhill Press
www.yamhillpress.net

Edition ISBNs

Softcover   ISBN 978-1-7320066-4-5
EBook   ISBN 978-1-7320066-5-2

Library of Congress Control Number: 2020910256

Publishers Cataloguing in Publication

    Unseen/ S.L. Stoner.

234 pages cm – (A Sage Adair historical mystery of the Pacific Northwest) 1. Northwest, Pacific—History—early 20th century—Fiction, 2. Detective and Mystery Fiction, 3. Action and Adventure—Fiction, 4. Progressive History—Fiction, 5. Indian History—Fiction, 6. Racism—Fiction, 7. Indian Reservations—Fiction, 8. Indian Boarding Schools—Fiction, 9. Native American-Historical Fiction

For

Connie Kay, Sarah E. Smith, Beatrice Mladenka-Fowler,
Claudine Paris, and P. Anna Johnson
Five Women Whose Positive Contributions to the World
Will Continue to Resonate Down Through the Generations

And

For George
Giver of Joy, Laughter and Love

And In Honor of

The American Indian Nations
Whose Resilience and Strivings
Teach Courage, Humanity, and Respect
For Those Things Greater Than Ourselves

"Man does not weave this web of life. He is merely a strand of it. Whatever he does to the web, he does to himself."

Seattle,
Suquamish and Duwamish Chief
(1786-June 7, 1866)

"The old Lakota was wise. He knew that a man's heart away from nature becomes hard."

Luther Standing Bear,
Lakota Chief,
(December 1868 – February 1939)

"You whites assumed we were savages. You didn't try to understand . . . Trouble is, white people don't listen."

Tatanga Mani, or Walking Buffalo,
Stoney Indian Leader
(March 20, 1871-December 27, 1967)

"Our ideas will become your ideas. We are going to cut the country's whole value system to shreds . . . we have a superior way of life. We Indians have a more human philosophy of life. We Indians will show this country how to act human. Someday this country will revise its constitution, its laws, in terms of human beings, instead of property. If Red Power is to be a power in this country it is because it is ideological. What is the ultimate value of a man's life? That is the question."

Vine Deloria, Jr.
Yankton and Standing Rock Sioux,
Writer and Teacher
(March 26, 1933-November 13, 2005)

FOREWORD

THE INTENT OF THE SAGE Adair stories is to use fast-paced, readable fiction to provide a history of the Pacific Northwest and the nation. These stories explore the viewpoint of the early 1900s Progressives. These people, their sacrifices, and bravery created America's middle class and a country once respected worldwide for striving to be at the forefront of compassionate human evolution. All of these gains are currently under attack by those promoting the greed-driven value system of the last forty years.

It is indisputable that U.S. history has been excessively rich-white-man-whitewashed. Consequently, each story works to show the ways in which the rich have historically preyed upon this country and its people. More importantly, the stories show how multi-racial, multi-ethnic, multi-cultural, and other people resisted this greed and fought to move the country closer toward social and economic justice. During the Progressive Era of the early 1900s, great strides were made in that direction. These stories try to share that history with the reader. This documented, but frequently ignored history, can give hope and inspire action—something that is needed during this time when greed, and thirst for power, by relatively few people, is hurting many in our country and the world.

The **Unseen** story offers a limited look at how white America has treated the Indian people. As a native Oregonian, I was taught absolutely nothing about the Indians who had lived for thousands of years on the land I walked. I knew Indians helped the Lewis and Clark explorers survive and I knew there was an Indian reservation in Central Oregon. That was it.

Because of their oral traditions, many American Indians already know the history upon which this story relies. Certainly, they know considerably more of their people's history than can be found in the following pages. As my own education shows, much Indian history remains invisible or misrepresented in the majority culture's historical renditions.

In preparing to write **Unseen,** I read at over 100 books and articles about Indian lifeways, reservations, boarding schools, and federal policy—in the Pacific Northwest, Oregon, and the nation. Many of these are firsthand accounts written by Indians and ethnologists that Indians have deemed credible. Whenever there was a conflict regarding fact or opinion, deference is given to the Indian account. A partial bibliography of these works is found on the Yamhill Press website at *www.yamhillpress.net.* That said, I am responsible for all errors.

The story uses the term "Indian" because the term "Native American" was not used in the early 1900s. Nor was the term "Aboriginal." Moreover, both historically and currently, organizations like the American Indian Movement and various Indian Nations tend to use the term "Indian" more than any other. I say that while recognizing that the Indians themselves have disagreed over what term to use. Personally, I favor the Canadian "First Nation" designation. It seems the most accurate and free of taint. Before Columbus, there were hundreds of nations on the North American continent and they were all Indian. They were the first.

This particular story focuses on what happened at the Elipeena reservation and boarding school. Let me be clear: There was no Elipeena Indian tribe. It is an imaginary tribe, with a made-up name. The made-up name means, "First Beaver" in Chinook Jargon (hereinafter "Chinook Wawa"). I am not qualified to provide an in-depth history of any Indian nation or tribe. You are urged to consult them directly.

With one exception, as noted in the "Historical Facts" section at the story's end, the description of tribal values, culture, and environment are taken directly from historical and ethnological accounts. Firsthand accounts are accorded precedence whenever the facts differ.

That said; please know that every corrupt, soul- and life-destroying act depicted in the story happened, not once, but countless times, on Indian reservations and in Indian boarding schools across the country.

Firsthand accounts of Indian boarding school life do not always agree. That makes sense because there were hundreds of schools, on and off the reservations. In some cases, the authors relate horrific experiences. In other instances, the authors credit their school with saving their life and/or as being a mainly positive experience.

The one certain thing is that the federal policy goal of assimilation was not in the best interest of the children, their families, or their people. The facts indicate that support of the assimilation policy was motivated by the whites' desire for Indian land and resources and by the government's desire to escape from treaty promises. Certainly, there were well-meaning and helpful whites implementing the assimilation policy but, ultimately, they were dupes. They were dupes because the fundamental motivation and primary force driving the U.S. Indian policy has been, and in most instances still is callous greed.

"I think the whole scheme of our management of the affairs of the Indian is a mistake. It is wrong; it is expensive to the Government; it is fatal to the Indians . . . The Indians of this country are down; they are down upon their backs and the white man is astride them and is at work taking from them everything they have."

Oregon Senator Harry Lane

ONE

THE MESSAGE CAME WHEN HE was sitting at the table beside the front window. Balancing the Mozart's Table restaurant accounts was Sage's least favorite task but, hallelujah, he was nearly done. He was restless, wanting to be out and doing. Beyond the restaurant's window, spring's warmth was edging out winter's chill. Crocuses had poked out from the dirt and daffodil spears had shot up overnight. That morning, after finishing the snake and crane exercise, the contented burble of Fong's carrier pigeons enticed him up the ladder and onto the roof. There the Daphne's' fragrance had swirled about his head, turning him woozy with its sweetness. Even his solitary rosebush sported nubbins of tiny buds.

For some minutes, he'd sat on the bench, simply drinking in the smell, relishing the bright coolness, and gazing at the hopeful green shoots in Fong's garden boxes. The pigeons' soft sounds eventually pulled him from the bench to wander over to their neat shed. Their food and water pans were full and their coops clean.

So, Matthew had already completed his daily assignment. No surprise there. The boy was a conscientious young man thanks to his innate intelligence and good character. He hadn't had it easy. The tragic killing of his brother, Matthew's false arrest for the murderer's subsequent death, and other challenges had scarred the boy but also strengthened him. At least, Sage had to believe that they had. Recently, Fong had taken the seventeen-year-old in hand, teaching him the fundamentals of the snake and crane martial art in exchange for Matthew's help with the pigeons. Fong, Matthew, and pigeons, all seemed happy with the arrangement.

Carriage wheels rattling across the cobblestones outside snapped Sage's attention back onto his task. He sighed. Tallying the bills and receipts was tedious in the extreme. And, there were many numbers because, as his mother was fond of saying, Mozart's was a highfalutin restaurant known for its fine food, wine, and high prices. Despite the latter, unless the weather turned nasty, its tables were seldom empty—whether at the dinner, tea time, or supper settings.

He dropped the pen and looked out the window at the sound of a robin's song, seeking the source. And, there they were. Two of them, one sporting a bright orange breast, the other more muted, both stepping along the overhead wires. Ah, the romance of spring.

"I swear. I've never known a man so easy to distract from doing a chore he don't like," came a chiding voice behind him.

He swiveled to look at his mother. Mae Clemens stood, hands on hips, a smile tugging at her lips and lighting her eyes.

"Don't nag, I'm almost done. But, you're right. It's the one job I hate every single month. Bookwork is torture. I'm glad I don't have to do more of it."

"How'd we do?"

Sage sighed, "As usual, we hauled the money in, hand over fist."

"Most folks would be doing a dance," she observed drily.

"Well, most folks need it. We don't."

She knew what he meant. A Klondike gold strike had filled his financial coffers, and now, that money sat there making more money. Mozart's was a sideline but a necessary one. It provided them with the cover story they needed. No one would suspect that the owner of the exclusive Mozart's Table was an undercover operative for the labor movement.

Mae fished a paper out of her apron pocket. "A messenger just delivered this. It's from Philander Gray. The boy said he'll wait for your answer." She handed it to him.

The message was terse: "I have an urgent need to speak with you. Please, if you can, come immediately. Otherwise, say when you can come. P. Gray"

Giving her the note, he stood, tossed the invoices, receipts, pen, and accounting book into a pasteboard box, tied the lid shut, and handed that to her as well. "I just have to do a final total on the columns. I've made all the entries. I better not wait. It's not like Philander to send that kind of message. And, it's Sunday. His wife always makes an extra special Sunday dinner. Given how much he loves food, it must be something mighty important. Tell the boy there's no answering message. I'll head out now."

She made no protest, just nodded toward the door. Philander Gray was an attorney who'd assisted their missions more than once. This was the first time he'd asked them for help.

Thanks to a horse cab waiting at the corner, Sage quickly reached Gray's office building. The building was relatively new and stood some blocks from the Willamette River. The disastrous flood ten years prior, in 1894, had effectively pushed Portland's central business district further west, beyond the river's reach at its highest flood level.

Sage strode past the elevator and took the stairs two at a time. Entering the third-floor corridor, he was surprised to see Gray standing in the hallway, looking in his direction. The lawyer shook his hand, thanked him for coming, but didn't smile.

"What's up, Philander?" Sage asked, wondering why the lawyer didn't usher him inside. Instead, Gray took his elbow and tugged him down the hall and into a windowed alcove.

"I need a big favor from you," he said in a low voice. At Sage's cautious nod, Gray continued. "I need you to be willing to let two other people know that John Adair," here he paused, obviously searching for words before saying, "That you sometimes work undercover using an alias."

Sage knew exactly what Gray meant. He used his birth name, "John Adair," in his role as Mozart's proprietor. Working undercover as an itinerant laborer he used the moniker, "John Miner." Only a handful of friends called him "Sage," and Gray wasn't one of them.

At Sage's frown, Gray hurried on to say, "They don't need to know you work for the labor movement. That's not what this is about. But they need help and you are the only person I know who can provide that help."

"What's this about?" Sage was hesitant but Gray's past trust and assistance had earned him a lot of credit in Sage's book. The time had come for Sage to return the favor though neither Gray's tone nor words implied he felt Sage owed him. After taking a deep breath, Sage plunged, even as he wondered what the others would say about his decision. "Okay, if you say they are trustworthy and can keep the secret, I'm in," he said. Hearing those words, Gray smiled for the first time.

"What's this about?" Sage asked again.

"I'll let them tell you," Gray said. "They're waiting inside for us."

Sage's eyebrows shot up when the man in the client's chair swiveled to watch them walk in. He was gratified to see an equal measure of surprise on Dr. Lane's face. The two men's recent and first encounters had been over the bodies of dead children. Sage thought the doctor a crusty, arrogant man while Lane did not try to hide his opinion that Mozart's owner was an effete rich man good only for the money in his pocketbook.

After a brief, sardonic smile at Lane, Sage turned his attention to the other man. He was a stranger and most probably an American Indian. He looked about middle-aged, with silver-streaked black hair neatly parted and braided. His jaw was square and his mouth long and narrow-lipped. The man's dark eyes were appraising though his face hid his thoughts. When he stood, he was about three inches shorter than Sage's six feet.

"John, I believe you already know Dr. Lane," Gray said before turning to the second man, "This is my client, George Red Hawk." The men shook hands but no one smiled before all turned their attention to Gray.

"Let's move over to my work area," the lawyer said, gesturing to a small square table at the other end of his office. Once seated, Gray gestured toward Lane, saying, "Harry, how about you give an overview of the situation?"

Lane hesitated, his narrow face with its Grecian nose looked skeptical, his lips seemingly glued together. Sage understood. After all, Lane knew John Adair only as a wealthy restaurateur who'd been briefly caught up in the hunt for a missing newspaper boy. Still, Lane must have mulled over his reasons for trusting Gray's judgment because he shrugged, cleared his throat, and commenced.

"Forgive me, Philander, if my summary seems a little lengthy, though I'll try to be short." He turned to Sage who sat immediately to his left. "I grew up down south in Lane County, near Corvallis. At that time, the area was home to several Kalapuya Indians. I was fortunate because they treated me like one of their own. I spent many happy days in their company and learned much from them. They are honest, hard-working, and spiritual people. I like to think that they came to trust me as much as I trust them.

"A month ago, they sent Mr. Red Hawk to me hoping I could find someone to help him with a personal legal problem. I brought him to our mutual friend here, Mr. Gray. Mr. Red Hawk lives on the Elipeena reservation south of Salem. Besides his personal issue, he also has serious concerns related to the reservation and its boarding school. He states there are serious problems at the school in particular. I believe him. So, I also contacted a personal friend who is rather high up in the Indian Service. A few weeks later, I received a letter from an Indian Service inspector."

Lane reached inside his suit coat and extracted a two-page document. Handing it to Sage he said, "This is that letter and it verifies much of what I've heard from Mr. Red Hawk. I think it will be quicker if you just read it."

Sage took the letter, though he doubted he could help solve a problem on an Indian reservation located some distance from Portland. All he knew of the Elipeena people was that they lived on the Cascade Mountains' western slopes, about eighty miles south, on the edge of the Willamette Valley. Still, he carefully unfolded the letter and read.

> My Dear Dr. Lane,
>
> I write you because I know of your longtime experience and deep sympathy for the Indians of the Willamette Valley. I am also aware of your friendship with the ranking Senator on the Indian Affairs subcom-mittee. I would be exceedingly glad if you will bring to the attention of Oregon's congressional delegation some of the reports I made to the Secretary of the Interior. I am hopeful that you will undertake the cause of the almost defenseless Indians. My statements below about the content of those reports can be verified by calling upon the Secretary for the originals.
>
> As you know, Congress, many years ago provided for the appointment of Indian Inspectors who were to be the confidential advisors to the Secretary and the President. The head of the division of Indian Affairs has read my reports. If the report related to schools it was referred to the educational division in the Indian Commissioner's office. If it pertained to finance, or land, he sent it to its respective department. Thus, as you will comprehend, mistakes, venal or otherwise, are referred to the man or men who made them. And, as generally happens, that always ends the investigation. Nothing is done.
>
> I have nearly served the full term of my appointment of four years, and whether I have done so faithfully is

best determined by my reports to my superior. But, throughout, I have been blocked so far as possible by the division heads at the Indian office.

I believe that publicity is the sovereign remedy for the undoubted ills that have become chronic in the management of Indian affairs. It is necessary for Congress and the public to know that, for more than one decade, Indian boys and girls have been crowded into unhealthy dormitories where their lives have been sacrificed. Know that Indian parents have been obligated to surrender their daughters into the care of incompetents who permit them to be debauched. . .

Sage paused, feeling hot anger flush his cheeks. He looked at Gray whose grim face confirmed the truth of the inspector's written words. "Mr. Red Hawk verifies the inspector's allegations and knows even more. Continue reading," he urged gesturing at the papers in Sage's hand. Only a couple of paragraphs remained.

Know too that the Treasury has been depleted to swell the coffers of contractors and others. The reports I have made as Indian Inspector reveal that conditions exist at many Indian schools and reservations which are a disgrace to the government of a Christian nation. But these reports have been conveniently suppressed.

One of the most serious situations exists in the Willamette Valley at the Elipeena reservation and boarding school. I have paper copies of the evidence I have gathered and will send it to you. It makes clear the perfidy and shame of the Indian Service as it has knowledge of this situation. In you, I place my trust and my hope that the Elipeena people will finally have fair play and justice.

Sincerely and hopefully yours,
William J. McConnell
Inspector, U.S. Indian Service

Sage re-folded the letter and for a moment said nothing, just stared at it where it lay on the table. His stillness belied the turmoil he felt. There was outrage that the so-called guardians of the Indians allowed such travesties. But, there was also puzzlement as to what he had to do with it. Suppressing the urge to blurt out both ideas, he asked, "Has Inspector McConnell's evidence arrived?"

Lane shook his head, "No, and that's a little worrisome. Inspector McConnell was in Portland when I received the letter. I promptly met with him. I told him I would consult Mr. Gray because he was already working with Mr. Red Hawk on a related problem, I thought the inspector should interview Mr. Red Hawk and Mr. Gray. McConnell explained that he had to return to the reservation. He is having difficulty getting trustworthy information from some reservation employees. Some of them are related to the reservation agent, a fellow by the name of 'Osborne Barnhart.'"

"I told him I would work on that situation since I had a trusted friend in the Indian Service. He left for the reservation after saying he'd send his evidence to me within a few days. He still had some facts to tie down. I haven't heard from him since but I'm expecting his evidence to arrive any day now."

Silence briefly reigned until Gray turned to the other man in the room. "Mr. Red Hawk, please tell Mr. Adair the concerns you have about the Elipeena School and the reservation."

The Indian stared at his folded hands before turning his dark gaze on Sage. When he spoke, his voice was low but clear. "About the school. Two years ago, Barnhart sent the Indian police to make my daughter and son go there. My daughter was eight. My son is now nine. I did not want to let them go but the agent told me that my family would not get its monthly $35 annuity check from the tribe's trust fund. My family needs that money because there is little work on the reservation."

He gave a heavy sigh and looked down at his hands once again. "Six months later, my daughter, she died at the school." His eyes still on his hands, he said something in a language Sage didn't recognize. Then he looked up at Sage, his eyes intense. "I asked questions of many people. Many things are wrong at the school. I am afraid for my son, Charley."

"You came to Mr. Gray to help get your son out of the school?" Sage asked.

Red Hawk shook his head. "No. We have many more problems. Some Indians own allotment land on the reservation free and clear. Agent Barnhart has no control over what they do with their land. But, most of us, our allotment land is held in trust. That means if we want to sell it or, lease it to a white man, we have to get the Agent's approval. Then the money goes to him and he is supposed to give it to us."

"He's not giving out the allotment money?" Sage asked to make sure he understood.

"For some, he gives part of it, yes. But certain elders have no family and their thinking is sometimes cloudy. They never get their lease money or annuity check some months. This winter, two old people died because they had no money. One of them, Jackson Spencer, was without money to buy warm clothes or food or wood to heat his house. He was too proud to tell us until it was too late. Barnhart gives people reasons why he keeps their money but, some of us, we never believe those reasons."

"So, you came to Mr. Gray to try to get the elders' money?" Sage asked, beginning to see the problem.

"Yes, first I went to Doctor Lane. I have a Kalapuya friend who says Dr. Lane's words match his actions. He is not like most white men. And now we are here, in Mr. Gray's office."

Red Hawk paused and then continued, "Also, I have a special problem. Barnhart wants me to lease my land to a white neighbor. That neighbor lets his cattle break down our fences, ruin our garden, and trample the places where we dig winter roots. The agent does not stop the white man's cattle from trampling our land. I made a complaint to the reservation court but they threw it out. They say the problem is not in their 'jurisdiction' because my neighbor is white. Instead, the tribal court ordered me to cut my hair."

Sage sent a questioning look at Gray and Lane's somber faces. Gray explained, "I met with Mr. Red Hawk, a few weeks ago. Osborne Barnhart refused him permission to leave the reservation to meet with me. He came anyway and Barnhart found out.

"Permission?" Sage echoed.

Red Hawk waited for a beat to see if Gray wanted to say more. When the lawyer kept silent, the Indian elaborated, "Indians must have a signed paper from the agent to leave the reservation. I came to talk with Mr. Gray without that permission. When Barnhart found out, he had the tribal court fine me and order me to cut my hair off."

"Tribal court?" Sage echoed. This was a world he knew nothing about.

Gray answered. "It has three judges, all appointed by Barnhart. Tends to do whatever he asks. It can only address minor infractions like theft and domestic disputes and reservation rule violations. I am still looking into the allotment problem, the trespass of the cattle, and now I've brought a case in federal court over the cutting of his hair. An Indian man's long hair has spiritual significance. I'm arguing that the order to cut his hair violates Mr. Red Hawk's first amendment rights. But first, I have to win the right to have the case heard in federal court because the law is confused about what court can even hear a matter that occurs on a reservation. That's because reservation Indians are not U.S. citizens unless they own their land outright and pay taxes."

Seconds passed with the only sound in the office the ticking of the wall clock.

Sage shifted uneasily before saying regretfully to Red Hawk, "I think the situation you face on the reservation is outrageous. It shouldn't continue. But, I have to say, I remain mystified as to how I can possibly help."

Gray leaned forward over the table and said words that knocked Sage back in his seat. "Actually, John, I think our only chance to rectify the situation depends entirely on you and your crew."

TWO

"Not citizens?" Mae exclaimed. "Why, that's crazy! They were here first! Every bit was theirs!"

His mother's response mirrored his own reaction but he didn't want to fan her flames. There were too many important things to discuss and decide. "I am sure the Indians would agree with you. But, Red Hawk's citizenship is Philander's problem. We need to discuss what role each of us is going to play."

The five of them sat in Mozart's dining room with drapes covering the windows and unlit gas sconces. Returning from Gray's the prior afternoon, he'd found tea time in full swing. A busy supper time followed so that, by the day's end, he was too tired to gather them together. Besides, about the time Mozart's closed, Lucinda's bordello business was reaching its peak. So, he'd sent Matthew to her and Eich with a request that they come at dawn the next morning. Since Fong and Mae were already at the restaurant working, he'd simply told them.

Ida's early morning pan banging sounded in the kitchen as he gazed at them with fondness. His "crew," Philander had called them. These four were the heart, though not the entirety, of those who took part in their social justice missions, like the last one fighting child labor. There were other people, dependable others, who also helped. But for this task, one that promised to be their most difficult, he needed these four. As he laid out the plight of the Elipeenas, their reactions matched his exactly. But he also saw puzzlement wrinkling their brows.

He hesitated, not entirely confident about how they'd react to Lane and Red Hawk's plan.

Mae spoke first, saying, "You might as well spit it out, Sage. Somehow, you men hatched up a scheme involving us or we wouldn't all be here at the crack of dawn. For sure, you wouldn't have hauled Lucinda here, knowing how late she goes to bed."

Mae reached over to pat Lucinda's hand. As always Sage silently rejoiced that his plain-spoken, Appalachian mother was fond of the woman who had recently refused to marry him. Few mothers would accept, let alone welcome, their son's involvement with a parlor house madam even if her house was the most exclusive in a city containing nearly five hundred of them.

Lucinda responded to the touch by covering Mae's work-worn hand with one of her own. She did look sleepy and tired. Still, she shot him an amused glance.

He cleared his throat. "Well, it turns out Dr. Lane managed to work a minor miracle through his friend in the Indian Service. His friend must be high up in the bureaucracy though Lane never identified him."

Sage paused then plunged into the heart of the matter. "Apparently, the reservation has an open position for a nurse's aide in its infirmary. Lane's friend managed to get the agent's clerk, who happens to be Barnhart's nephew, temporarily transferred to another reservation. The excuse was that the Service needed him to examine some questionable accounts." He glanced at his mother before continuing, "And, the dormitory matron, who happens to be the agent's sister, received a telegram calling her back to Washington D.C. for training." His pause let them absorb those words.

His mother huffed in exasperation, "I swear, Sage. You dole out information slower than a mine owner doles out wages. Spit it out. Tell us why we're here."

He grinned. "Okay, the plan is, Lucinda and I go to the reservation as man and wife." Out of the corner of his eye, he caught Lucinda's twitch. "She'll work at the infirmary as an aide and, lucky me, I get to muck about in the agency's records as a temporary clerk. You, my dear tender-hearted mother, will get to ride herd as a dormitory matron for about forty young boys, ages five to eighteen."

He turned to Eich and Fong. "The two of you will be our reserves. Fong you'll stay around town here, ready to jump in if we need help. You'd stand out too much down near the reservation."

Sage smiled at the ragpicker poet, "And you, Herman, if you don't mind, it would be nice to have you nearby. Fortunately, there's a small town on the reservation's border called Moolock. I am sure you can come up with an excuse for being there. You always do." Many times since they'd met, the poet had shown he could easily blend into the background, either as the familiar cart-pushing ragpicker or as an itinerant trader. Sage was sure Herman would come up with some kind of excuse for lingering around Moolock.

He leaned forward over the table and studied each in turn before adding, "Of course, all of that supposes you are all willing." He waited, fighting to remain open to the idea that they might reject the plan. If they did, he wasn't sure what he would do. Each role was essential. If they said "no," he'd still have to do something. Red Hawk's sorrowful face stuck with him, he couldn't let the man and his people down. He couldn't live with himself if he did. As the other four exchanged looks, he sat back and waited.

Lucinda spoke first. "Aren't you afraid both of us will be recognized? I mean, we're both fairly well-known."

Sage shook his head. That had been his initial thought as well. "We'll go down separately and get off the train south of Salem. Eich can pick us up in a trader's buckboard wagon and take us to the reservation where you and I will arrive as a married couple. The Elipeena reservation is fifteen miles east of the rail tracks, up against the Cascades. It is unlikely either of us will encounter a Portland acquaintance. Once we get there, we won't leave the reservation unless it's absolutely necessary."

Lucinda persisted. "I don't know enough to be a nurse's aide. Sure, I've nursed sick folk but there's more involved than that."

"You did a fabulous job with Prineville's smallpox patients," Sage assured her, "And, while Ma settles in at the reservation and Eich in Moolock, Doc Lane said he'll teach you what little you don't know. Lane said the doctor down there is so desperate for help he'll welcome anyone with two hands. He's made request after request."

"Is he one of the scoundrels?" Mae asked.

"That's the problem. Because Red Hawk doesn't know exactly what is going on, he can't know who's involved. There's one person at the school he trusts."

"Who?" asked Herman.

"He wouldn't say. He said it is up to that person to tell us. He didn't want that responsibility since, if it got out, that person would lose their job."

"Okay, then who can't be trusted?"

"It's very likely that the agent's relatives are part of the corruption. Red Hawk thinks others are involved as well—the teachers, other staff, the reservation police, the tribal court judges, and even the doctor. It's a mess," he added unnecessarily.

"Forty boys," Mae mused aloud, drawing Sage's attention. He expected to encounter the most resistance from her. After all, circumstances had forced her to surrender her only child to the mine owner when Sage was just nine years old. Faced with choosing between raising him in poverty with only a coal mining future and the mine owner's offer to foster Sage in a wealthy family with all its attendant benefits, she'd put Sage's future first. That meant she had limited experience raising children.

Not surprisingly, she read his mind because she said, with some asperity, "Really, you don't remember how we looked after each other's kids?" Her words jarred loose the memory of barefoot kids racing among the barely habitable shacks—his mother's window boxes a gay spot of color amid drabness. She didn't wait for his response. "I think I might enjoy the change. I'm mighty tired flashing my teeth at the rich folks here." She gestured around the dining room.

Sage turned to Fong who'd stayed silent the entire time. "Mr. Fong, some Moolock people are involved. Certainly one of the farmers thereabouts is. So, if we need to get information to you or Gray, we can't use the town's telegraph office."

Fong's face crinkled into a toothy grin. "You think my pigeons a good idea."

Sage nodded. "Maybe. I was thinking Mr. Eich could bring a couple down with him and end up selling them to my beloved wife."

Those last two words shot an unexpected thrill through him. Startled, he looked at Lucinda, noticing that she'd gone unnaturally still at his words. She stared back at him, her face a frozen mask. He hurried on. "Anyways that way, if we need to get word up here, we can send it with a bird."

The glint in Mae's eyes said she'd seen the exchange but all she said was, "Herman and I will go down first?"

Sage turned to Fong. "It will be okay with you, holding down the fort up here?" Sage wasn't sure he'd like being without Fong.

Fong flapped a dismissive hand. "No problem." Then he added with a sly smile, "Besides, always you find trouble and need me." The others laughed, knowing Fong was right.

Herman asked, "When do you want Mae and me to leave?"

"You today and Ma tomorrow. We'll have Homer run the restaurant in Ma's absence. Lucinda and I will follow in a couple of days."

Mae jumped in. "Homer will be delighted. He loves standing at the podium lording over things and wearing that fancy suit you bought him. It makes him happy as a bug pond frog. And, he likes the extra money too." Her metaphor made Sage chuckle because, with his small chin, protruding eyes, and long, thin-lipped mouth, their reliable waiter bore a striking resemblance to that pond-dwelling amphibian.

"Aren't all these strangers going to put the agent on alert?" Herman asked.

"Yes, but it can't be helped. He'll scramble around a bit trying to get his confederates to keep their eyes on us. But, they can't be everywhere. Besides, Lane says the Indian Service bureaucrats in D.C. have the nasty habit of yanking employees off the reservations without warning. So, he might be suspicious but he won't know for sure."

Inspector William McConnell's step was eager and light. After three days of rain, the sun shone and he was temporarily leaving the problems behind. Ahead he saw a field of tall bracken ferns and marveled at the sight. How his grandchildren would love playing beneath their fronds. He left the dirt road to follow the narrow path wending through their midst, feeling the fronds gently brushing his elbows.

Stepping from the bracken field into the forest, he paused and breathed deeply savoring the clean, earthy scent. It felt like he'd entered a cathedral. Stately trees rose skyward, their canopy dimming the late afternoon light except where narrow beams lit moss-covered tree trunks and limbs. Tightly packed white-blooming trilliums, flourishing sword ferns, and the leather-leafed tangle of Oregon grape covered the forest floor. The lush foliage muted all sounds to a reverent hush.

He gazed around searching for animals, but all remained unmoving and silent. At last, his stillness was rewarded and the forest awakened. A Douglas squirrel chittered from its perch on an overhead branch and the loud, heavy sound of a mallet hitting a distant tree said a Pileated woodpecker was hard at work. McConnell faced the sound but couldn't spot the bird's scarlet head.

The path ran straight, clear, and open, except for a scattering of easily-surmounted downed logs. He'd taken only a few steps forward when something dove past his head to disappear into a nearby evergreen. Stepping closer he stared up into the branches and wished he hadn't. He met the unblinking stare of yellow eyes that sent a chill skittering down his spine. He'd worked in the Indian Service long enough to know many tribes considered owls harbingers of death.

He sought to dispel the eeriness by addressing the owl, "Let's see. You are small, round-headed, and show no ears. Hmmm, maybe you're one of those Pygmy owls I've read about." The bird stayed mute and immobile. Its yellow eyes, mounted on either side of a tiny curved beak, stared unblinkingly at him. He shrugged and murmured, "Probably I only need to worry about the much bigger Horned owls . . ." before heading down the path.

He pulled a small notebook from inside his jacket, along with a stubby pencil. He might be on the job but nothing said he couldn't broaden his education on his way to the Red Hawk's allotment. Last time he'd take this path, he'd concentrated on not getting lost. Now he was certain of the way. Except for a single fork, this path ran straight to the tidy cabin in the woods.

This trip, he could focus on his surroundings. Only in the past few months had he begun to inspect the agencies. Until recently, his career with the Indian Service kept him in the Southwest, working as an industrial teacher in different boarding schools. He learned to appreciate the stark beauty of the Pueblo, Navaho, Zuni, and Ute reservations and come to admire the steadfast survival of the people.

But this land, it was completely different. Bountiful and lush beyond imagining, presided over by glistening snow-capped peaks, its beauty had got him thinking about where he'd like to retire. There were only a few years until that day. Recently, he'd become hopeful that Betty might consider abandoning Kansas as their home base. Maybe he could entice his son, daughter-in-law, and grandchildren to re-settle here as well. It was a new territory full of opportunity.

Ahead, the path wound between two huge evergreens rising at least two hundred feet into the air. Stepping closer, he noted that their trunks had deep furrows, separated by flat, broad ridges. He checked his notebook and knelt to study a cone lying at their base. Yes. It was egg-shaped, light brown, and sported three-point bracts. These were the Douglas fir giants prized by lumbermen. Still kneeling, he softly chuckled because, for a moment, he thought he heard his heart singing. Shaking off that fancy he made a few notes, thinking about what he'd put in his letter to Betty.

Ever since reading John Muir's writings, he'd wanted to know the name of every plant, tree, and animal he saw. Thanks to the Scot, he'd begun feeling a reverence when in nature's presence. And, he'd finally come to understand the Indians' spiritual connection to the land they'd known intimately for generations. This new understanding also brought shame for the derision he'd felt and expressed toward their beliefs in the past.

His musing abruptly halted at the sight of an unknown evergreen. This one had a long, slender, reddish-brown trunk. It too had deep furrows but its ridges were scaly. Stepping off the path, he lifted a small branch. Its needles were also different—shiny, dark green on the top but whitish below. He quickly thumbed through his notes. "Ah," he murmured, "Western hemlock." After putting a tick next to that entry he returned to the path.

That's it, he chided himself and picked up his pace. I keep dawdling and it will be dark before I reach the Red Hawk's place. He discarded that intention abruptly when a pungent, skunky odor assailed his nose. He turned this way and that, looking for the source. He spotted an evergreen's graceful, drooping branches about one hundred feet away. Could that be a red cedar?

Heedless of the spiky Oregon grape he plunged off the path. Cedars like water and skunk cabbages like water and the plant's yellow spears were reputedly in bloom. Soon he stood before an enormous, majestic tree. Its fluted base was easily fifteen feet around. He touched the tree, thinking of all the beautiful Indian bowls, ladles, and canoes carved from trees like this one. Speaking softly he told the tree, "I hope, ancient one, that the tribal elders continue to hold this forest sacred and off-limits to timber saws. Your beauty deserves to live out its days without harm." It felt rightly prayerful. Besides, there was no one to hear it except this tree and this forest.

Some minutes later, when he again stood on the path and was studying an unknown tree's purplish trunk and orange berries, he saw a man striding toward him. "Hey!" he called, "I was hoping to speak with you today!" These were his only words before a silver blade swooped from behind the other's back and drove into his neck. Notebook and pencil flew from his hand as his knees buckled.

Gloved hands snatched up the notebook and fumbled through its pages before tossing it aside. Next began a search of the Indian Inspector's pockets. A huff of relief escaped the attacker's lips at finding a packet of papers in an inside pocket. He opened them up long enough to read the first page. This was what he'd come for.

Straightening, he looked behind at the empty path. It was only when he turned back to face the way McConnell had come, that his eye was caught by the flicker of a small figure darting away between the distant trees. He dropped the bloody hatchet. He'd return for it later. Pulling a long knife from the scabbard on his belt, he started forward at a run.

THREE

"Boy Howdy, I could do with a little extra padding on my rear end," Mae exclaimed as the buckboard dropped into and jittered out of yet another pothole.

Eich laughed. He'd left Portland the day before, buying the buckboard wagon and goods in Salem before making his way to Moolock. When the morning train pulled up to the train platform closest to the town, he was there, waiting to pick Mae up. They'd set out immediately. Fifteen miles of bumpy road lay before them. "You might want to grab the blanket stashed below your seat and sit on it. We have an even rougher road ahead."

She groaned and did as he suggested. Turning to look at him, she mused about how those kindly and wise brown eyes softened his strong face. Today, the deep groove between his brows meant that he was worried. To distract him, she asked, "Have you seen the school and the reservation? What's the town like? Are folks friendly or standoffish?"

He sent her that lopsided smile that meant he knew exactly what she was up to. Still, he answered her last question first. "Well, the liveryman is happy I've rented the room above his stable and will be stabling my horse with him for the next month. He's letting me keep Fong's birds in the stable for a small fee. He's one talkative fellow. Apparently, Moolock sees few strangers. Usually, it's timber cruisers for the big lumber companies or contractors hoping to do business with the reservation. He's the one who was supposed to come get you but I talked him into letting

me do it. Told him I had to pick up some goods from the same train."
He nodded at the few boxes stacked in the buckboard's bed.

"As for the rest of the town folks, they seem friendly enough. But then, that's to be expected, the town's so remote that it seldom gets traders. As for the folks on the reservation, well, they're cautious and, according to the liveryman, desperately poor. I plan to give them what they need at a deep discount or in trade for whatever they have to offer—woven baskets, wooden bowls, ladles, and such. I've seen some of their work in the Moolock store. It would bring high dollars in New York City. Here, it's practically worthless.".

After a beat, he continued addressing her questions. "As for the school, it's about what you'd expect. Three stories high, all wood with narrow, double-hung windows. Barnhart invited me inside and gave me a tour after I expressed interest. He's an oily fellow, I didn't like him much. Said he could only buy school or reservation supplies from contractors. He softened that a bit by saying, there was no such restraint on his personal purchases. So, I expect I'll do a brisk business with him.

"Anyways," he said, using her trademark word with an affectionate smile, "the boys' dormitory is on the top floor, along with quarters for their matron." His smile turned into a grin, "That will be you, 'Mrs. Lofton'. The girls' dormitory shares the second floor with two classrooms. Their matron stays in quarters next to them. The reservation office, dining hall, and kitchen are all on the ground floor."

"Where does Barnhart sleep? And, the other staff? And how are just two classrooms enough?"

"My friendly liveryman tells me Osborne Barnhart, his clerk, and three teachers live in houses on the school grounds. And, the reservation infirmary is also in a small house on the grounds. The cook and the doctor both live away from the school. So, only you, the girls' matron, and the children will sleep in the school building overnight."

"Hmm, that might be a very good thing," she murmured.

"I don't have a good impression of Agent Barnhart," he said warningly and cast a glance at her. She was staring forward, her lips pursed. He knew what that meant. "Mae Clemens, you keep your nose out of that agent's office. That's why Sage is coming. You will be taking enough chances without unnecessarily taking on more."

Mae's lips tightened, but she repeated her question. "I don't understand. How can two classrooms be enough? I thought over eighty children boarded at the school."

"I asked that same question. It turns out they are split into two groups. Unlike the white children attending Moolock's public school, the Indian children receive only a half-time education. While one half is in class, the other is doing all the work around the school. The girls are charged with the cooking, laundry, and cleaning, while the boys are outside repairing, farming, and taking care of the lawn and flowerbeds."

"Are there any Indian employees?"

"Near as I could tell, the girl's matron is Indian and so is one of the teachers."

They bounced along the rough road in silence while Mae absorbed the information.

"Did you see the children? How do they look?" she asked.

This time it was Herman's lips that tightened. "They look underfed, raggedy, and sad. Just the opposite of Agent Barnhart."

Nearly two hours later, they rattled down Moolock's main street but didn't stop. There wasn't much to see. A small provision store, a saloon, the livery stable, a one-room clapboard church with a stubby tower, and a somewhat larger building that Eich said was the public school.

"Sure aren't many folks about," she remarked, having seen only one fellow dozing in a chair outside the saloon and a stray dog who slunk away down a narrow gap between buildings.

"Most folks hereabout farm on homestead land, on and off the reservation. They maybe come to town once a week."

At the town's far end, he gestured to a modest two-story house. "That's where the reservation doctor lives. He sees town patients as well as working on the reservation. Lately, he's had to spend nights on the reservation because the infirmary has two patients. My liveryman says he's none too happy about it. Something tells me, our married couple won't be seeing much of each other so long as the infirmary has patients."

Mae twisted to look as they drove past. A sign hung from a porch post. "Dr. Defler," she read. "What's your liveryman say about him?"

Eich shrugged. "He didn't know much—he has never been to him for treatment. He did say the doctor is usually out on the reservation. This makes me think the man might be diligent and on the up and up. But, at this point, who's to know?"

Mae nodded as her thoughts turned grim. Herman was right. Until they knew more, they couldn't trust anyone. She took a deep breath and mentally rehearsed the role she was about to play. The idea of taking care of forty boys was not the most worrisome part. Having to pretend she was something she wasn't, that's what worried her. One slip could ruin everything.

Eich pulled the horse to a halt beside the road. "There's something else. They found Indian Service Inspector McConnell's body in the woods yesterday morning. It looked like someone tried to take his head off with an ax. The weapon wasn't found and the tribal police are searching the reservation."

"Oh, my Lord. That poor, poor man. He was only trying to do the right thing." Tears glittered in Mae's eyes as grief for the loss of the well-intentioned man she'd never met washed over her. She realized that McConnell's murder explained the furrow between Herman's brows that she'd been wondering about since she'd seen him waiting for her on the train platform.

Eich tried one more time. "You sure you want to do this? I can say you heard about the murder and ordered me to take you back to the train."

For once, she didn't brush off his concern for her welfare. She gazed out across the adjacent farm field, noting the bright green spears of something or the other poking up from the dark, turned earth. Turning to look at him, she put her hand on his where it was holding the reins. "Herman, I'm not sure. I know I'm in a worse spot than the fish out of water. But, if I don't do it, I'll find it a mite hard to live with myself. Does that make sense?"

Those dark brown eyes watered and he dropped the reins to wrap his arms around her. "I'll stay near," he promised.

The lane from the road curved through the school's farm fields. Rough wood fencing marked the fields' boundaries. Soon, they were rolling under the leafing boughs of white oaks. She closed her eyes and breathed deep. This is me, this minute, I am wholly and solely me. This moment with this man beside me will be my touchstone, she promised herself.

Once out from beneath the oaks, the buckboard entered a park-like setting of neat flowerbeds and mown lawns. In its midst stood a three-story building around which they saw children for the first time. Alongside the drive, a herd of small boys bent over the flowerbeds, pulling weeds. One tossed a dirt clod at another and received an accurate counterattack. Seconds later another boy joined in. Mae had just enough time to think to herself, "This could be fun," before all three boys froze like statutes, only moving their heads to watch the buckboard advance.

She straightened her back and gave the three boys a civil nod as the buckboard rolled past. They didn't return it. Three men stood beneath the wooden portico at the head of the u-shaped drive. A smallish white man in shirt sleeves was haranguing the other two while flinging a hand toward the forested hills behind the building. Two men, both black-haired and dusky-skinned, nodded deferentially before rapidly descending the steps and heading off toward the distant evergreen-covered hills.

Then the buckboard was parallel to the porch steps and Eich was pulling it to a halt. The remaining man quickly donned the suit coat he'd been holding before hurrying down the stairs. "Mrs. Lofton, you're arriving much earlier than I expected. But, welcome," he said as he handed her down and lifted her suitcase from the buckboard bed. A single glance said the man's smarmy smile didn't match the measuring brittle of his eye.

Feet firmly planted, she nodded a dismissal at Eich and turned to the man. She dusted her skirts, straightened her hat, and said with some asperity, "How do you do? Yes, I'm Mrs. Louise Lofton. And who might you be to your mother?"

His mouth momentarily slackened before he caught himself and said, "Why, I am Agent Barnhart." Hearing the timidity in his voice must have goaded him into remembering his superior position because he straightened and added, "I am your boss."

She thrust her hand forward and unsmilingly said, "Why then, I am pleased to meet you, Mr. Barnhart. You do know that I had no control over the horse's pace?"

Barnhart flushed before gesturing to the stairs. "Please, come inside." He led her into a large central hallway divided by a wide staircase. A door off the hallway opened into a neatly organized two-room office containing file cabinets and tidy shelves. A single, cleared desk occupied the first room, next to a window. She looked at the empty desk chair and then at Barnhart.

"My, ah, my clerk was called away. The Indian Service needed his help sorting out a problem on another reservation. He'll only be gone for a short white—a few months or so. They're sending me an inexperienced, temporary, replacement. Supposedly he's a bookkeeper, though I don't know how he will cope. The Elipeena reservation and school don't run like businesses." The crinkle of concern on Barnhart's forehead seemed genuine.

"Where do you hail from, Mrs. Lofton?" he asked.

"Pennsylvania. I've only been out West for a few years. My son is here. Up in Portland," she said. "This was his idea. His or his dear wife's," she added, with a disdainful curl to her lips.

Barnhart's eyebrows rose in a silent question that she answered. "I've been staying with them. Some friend or other of his said there was a temporary job down here. My son thought I'd be a good fit. I couldn't exactly refuse." She clamped her lips shut, squeezed her folded hands just a little too tightly doing her best to make the domestic discord with her relatives obvious.

He cleared his throat. "Yes, well. We're fortunate you were available on such short notice. It is difficult handling forty young boys. The doctor's wife has helped out, but frankly, she's not cut out for it. Nerves, I'm afraid."

He led her from the office and they mounted the open staircase. Reaching the third floor he ushered her into the matron's quarters. "I believe you'll find this quite comfortable. There is this sitting room and a bedroom. We've stowed our regular matron's clothes but the remaining furnishings are hers. I hope you don't mind. I figured since you are here temporarily . . ."

He was seeking reassurance. She obliged. "This will be just fine, for the brief period . . . a very brief period, I trust."

He smiled before turning and gesturing to a closed door across the hallway. "In there is the boy's dormitory. Nothing fancy, but it does the job."

He headed toward the door. Turning to her he said, "Umm, well, ah. I'll leave you to settle in from your journey. The dinner bell rings at 5:00. I will introduce you at that time to your coworkers and your charges."

She followed him into the central hallway and listened as he descended the two flights of stairs. After the sounds faded, she crossed to the dormitory and eased the door open. After stepping inside, her eyes took a moment to adjust to the dim light that leaked in from behind the heavily curtained windows. Once they had, she saw what she'd expected to see. Iron cots, covered by gray blankets and flattened pillows, lined each side of the long room. A wide aisle ran down the middle of the room. Her eyes narrowed and her lips twisted. There was not a single spot of color or a solitary decoration on the walls. The air was a smelly combination of young boys' bodies and dust.

Eich halted the horse when it reached the curve just before the oaks. From this vantage point, the back of the school building was visible. He studied the outbuildings. Some were small houses for the staff. He eyed a small shed sitting about one hundred and fifty feet from the back of the building at a ninety-degree angle. It faced the matron's windows on the third floor. From this distance, he couldn't tell what, if anything, the shed contained. He'd have to explore later tonight. That decision made, he clucked the animal into motion. It set off at a brisk trot despite the very long distance it had traveled that day. He smiled. Both he and the horse were hungry.

FOUR

ONLY ONE PERSON RECOGNIZED SAGE as they traveled south. That was the black porter who Sage remembered from an earlier escapade. He'd met the man at the city's only black-owned hotel—one owned by Sage's friend, Angus Solomon. The porter had supplied a key piece of information during one of their first missions. Sage warmly greeted the man but said nothing about their earlier acquaintance. Likewise, the porter remained professionally polite until, just as Sage deboarded, one of the porter's eyes closed in a slow, deliberate wink, making Sage laugh and clap him on the shoulder.

Their rail stop was nothing more than a wide spot next to the track with a high platform and water tower for the train's steam engine. He and Lucinda were the only passengers who left the train—she from the first-class car, he from third-class at the train's rear.

They ignored each other until the caboose rounded the far curve and vanished from sight. It was an isolated spot. One where, in the absence of a deboarding passenger, the train stopped only if it needed wood or water or for a passenger or shipper wave-down. Weeds, trees, and farm fields were all they could see in every direction.

Once the chugging train was gone, the birds in a nearby alder copse broke into song. Sage and Lucinda moved together to stare up the rough road that led east. Sage turned to her, pulled a gold wedding band from his pocket, and held it up. She pulled off her glove so he could slide it onto her ring finger. They looked at each other and momentarily they were the only people in the world.

He smiled ruefully before teasingly saying, "Now I've got you!"

"Sage," she said warningly. "Don't make this any harder. You know we can't continue our work if we marry, and that would destroy you."

He hugged her shoulders. "I know Mrs. Lucy Adell. I'll behave."

She laughed and said, "And I shall be the proper wife, Mr. John Adell." Her expression sobered. "This will be the first time we've set up house together."

He smiled, "Are you scared?"

She bristled, "Probably a darn sight less scared than you!"

That comment so hit the mark that he could only laugh.

At that moment, rattles and creaks heralded the arrival of a buckboard coming toward them from behind the alders. Herman Eich's familiar figure perched on its single seat.

After exchanging greetings with a somber-faced Eich, Lucinda climbed up on the seat, making a cushion of the same blanket Mae had used. Sage wasn't as lucky. His seat was a wooden crate in the wagon bed. He pulled it up close behind them, grabbing hold of their seat's backboard as the buckboard began bouncing down the road. He, Lucinda, Fong, and Gray, already knew of McConnell's murder. Eich had sent the tersely worded telegram from a nearby office just before he'd met Mae at the rail platform. Sage immediately asked the question foremost on his mind. "Do we know any more about Inspector McConnell's murder?"

Eich swiveled on the bench to look at Sage and said, "Unfortunately, I have bad news."

Sage's gut took a plunge. "What do you mean? Did something happen to Ma?"

Eich shook his head. "No, no. She's fine but they arrested George Red Hawk late last night for McConnell's murder."

"What!" Sage's exclamation mixed surprise with disbelief. "No way George Red Hawk had anything to do with it."

"Well, I've never met the gentleman but the evidence is damning. The tribal police found a bloody hatchet buried beneath the stacked firewood alongside Red Hawk's cabin. Also, they found partially burned bloody gloves lying in his outdoor fire pit."

"What is Red Hawk saying?"

"I don't know. I never even saw him. I'm just telling you what I picked up around Moolock this morning before heading out to fetch the two of you."

"Why would Red Hawk kill the one man who was trying to fix the reservation's problems?" Sage wondered.

"He wouldn't," Lucinda declared before turning back to Eich. "Where's Mr. Red Hawk now?"

"Serious Indian reservation crimes are handled by the county sheriff—especially when it's the murder of a white man. So, he's being kept in the county jail though they'll move him to Salem for the trial."

"Philander needs to know where to find him," Sage said.

Eich nodded. "He should by now. That's why I was late getting to the platform. I had to travel a bit far afield to send the telegram off. Everybody knows everybody around here. I didn't want to send it from Moolock. And, it's a mystery who to trust even then, so my telegraph was in code, "Your product in county lockup warehouse." Hopefully, he'll know what it means."

Eich turned back to Lucinda. "So, I'm to give the birds to you? Fong taught you how to take care of them?"

She laughed and shooed that idea away with a hand wave. "The story is that I want them but Sage is the one who'll be feeding, watering, and cleaning their coops. That's the agreement."

"I will bring them out tomorrow evening after you've had a chance to get the lay of the land, talk to Mae, and such. That way, I can grab some time with you and figure out how we're going to message back and forth.

Nine-year-old Charley Red Hawk was hungry and shivering standing inside the tree. He'd eaten only what he could gather during these last two days and the April nights still chilled. His raggedy school pants and shirt offered little warmth. She would come. He was waiting in the place she'd told him to run to if anything bad happened. He squatted, wrapped his arms around his body, tucking cold hands into his armpits. Even now, with the spring sun hitting its bark, the tree hollow was chilly. He had to stay here because something bad had happened. It was so bad that his heart pounded against his ribs at the memory of it.

Squirrel chittering sounded. He held his breath, straining to hear. Two more times came the same call—three chitters spaced evenly apart. He waited for the pattern to repeat. When the next three chitters sounded he was relieved. He answered with three chitters of his own, slipped from the hollow, and moved toward the clearing, careful not to crush the plants underfoot and leave a trail. Just like his father taught him. It was difficult because the white man's hobnailed boots made it hard to step soundlessly.

He peered around a tree into the clearing. She was there, sitting quietly on a fallen log, sideways to him. Her lips silently moved in her upturned face. She was probably thanking the sun for its warmth and light. She often paused in their ramblings to thank trees, plants, roots, animals, water, and the sun—whatever spirit power caught her attention. She said honoring these things strengthened her spirit guide and brought her closer to the things she honored and needed. He didn't know if that was true since he was too young to have gone alone to face the rising sun and learn the nature of his spirit guide. That five-day quest would come in a few years. Still, during these last days, he'd thanked every green shoot and root before eating them.

No one lurked behind the trees around the clearing so he stepped into the sunlight. She stopped praying and without looking toward him, she patted the log beside her. He quickly sat, welcoming the arm she wrapped around his shoulders. She pulled him close into her small, compact body and murmured tender words in the Elipeena language that she'd taught him to understand. She spoke no English and used the Chinook Wawa only when she had to. His grandmother was a traditional Elipeena who practiced the old ways, teaching them to him and other Elipeenas' grandchildren. As a young girl, she'd married a Modoc from the Grand Ronde reservation that she'd met during hop-picking season. She'd lived at Grand Ronde until her husband died and she'd returned to her home reservation to be with her daughter, Charley's mother. After Charley's mother died at his birth, she had stepped in to raise him.

Tears he'd been holding back wet his cheeks. Glancing at his grand-mother's face, he saw tears also flowed down the wrinkles of her wide smile like streams follow gullies. Her comforting Elipeena prayer sounded softly in the clearing. "Thank you, trees and plants, for keeping my grandson safe and bringing him here to me. We honor you and your goodness." Her prayer finished, she waited for him to speak.

"Grandmother," he began in Elipeena. "I saw something terrible."

She nodded. "Those tribal policemen, they come for you."

He stiffened. "They must not find me."

She nodded again. "No, it is good that you hide yourself. Something is very, very wrong."

"My father . . . ," he began.

"The police have taken him away," she said. "You saw this?"

He snuffled and dipped his head before turning into her, wanting to forget everything and just breathe in her familiar scent.

She gently removed her arm from his shoulder. "You must not stay here, on the Elipeena reservation. You must go to your auntie and her husband, your Uncle Jack, on the Grand Ronde reservation. You must travel the trail your father once showed you, the one that stays far from white people. Do you remember that trail?"

At his nod, she reached down and lifted a burlap bag from between her feet. "In here is a blanket to keep you warm, some money, and food. You must be very careful. The tribal police are searching all the places for you. They searched our house and the trails and many other places. For two days now, they come to our house many times."

For the first time, her soothing voice faltered as she said, "I was afraid. Afraid they would find you or that big panther got you or a bear." She shuddered, hugged him tightly, and then smiled at him. "But, here you are and looking good but wearing the forest on your skin and clothes.

She opened the bag to pull out a pair of deerskin moccasins. These are much better for walking without leaving a sign," she said, holding them out to him.

He eagerly took the moccasins. "I hate these white man shoes. They hurt and I feel like I have wood chunks stuck to the bottom of my feet." He quickly unlaced and discarded the heavy shoes and slid his feet into the moccasins.

As she started to rise from the log he put his shoulder under her arm to help her up. He knew moving hurt her but her face stayed calm as she said, "You must head north. Remain within the forest until you can travel the shortest route to the Grand Ronde reservation. And, you must cross the valley at night, when the white people sleep. It will be hard. Maybe the journey will take three days. When you reach the edge of the Willamette River, find the place of Indian Joe. Give him the money I put in the bag to take you across the river in his canoe. He will keep your passage secret."

"Grandmother, when I came from school, I saw that man who was murdered . . ." he began, only to stop talking when she laid fingers across his lips.

"Do not tell me. If I do not know, I cannot tell. Elipeenas cannot lie." She stiffened, "The silence of the forest creatures says people are coming. You must go now." She picked up the bag and shoved it into his hands. She pointed north. "Run. Do not walk until you are over the ridge. I will try to make them stop and talk."

She gently turned him north, patted his back, and gave him a gentle shove. "Go!" she urged. And he went, running on tiptoe down the well-worn path, heading north.

His grandmother tossed the heavy hobnail boots far into the under-brush. Then she too stepped onto the path, though her shambling gait took her south. Her crippled legs dragged along the path, which was good in this instance because they wiped out any trace of a small boy's hobnailed boots. Minutes later she saw the two tribal policemen approach. She waited for them, leaning heavily on her staff.

These two were familiar. They were Elipeenas she had known since they took their first steps. She'd gone to each of their birth celebrations. They paused and dipped their heads respectfully as required when meeting a tribal elder. "Grandmother," one of them addressed her in their common language. "Do you know where your grandson is? The Agent is very worried for his safety."

She said, "I came out this way to look for him," she gestured with her staff, "but I see him nowhere here. I too am worried about his safety."

"Grandmother, he has been gone now for three days," the policeman persisted. "Are you certain he has not been staying at your house?"

She was able to answer truthfully, "He has not been in my house. I have stayed alone there since you took my daughter's husband away."

"We are sorry we had to take George, Grandmother. Because of the murder, the county sheriff made us search. You know what was found."

She pursed her lips and said nothing. She'd already given them a tongue lashing while they were clamping steel bracelets around the wrists of her dead daughter's husband. She'd pointed out that anyone could have used and hidden what was found beneath the woodpile. But stony faces met her words. She'd watched as they forced George Red Hawk to trot beside the sheriff's horse, pulled along by a rope tied to the saddle pommel. Her lips pressed tightly together at the memory. She wordlessly stared at the two tribal policemen.

"You us tell if your grandson see?" asked the younger officer who'd stayed silent up to that point. His Elipeena was crude, a sure sign no one had taught him the traditional ways. Her answer was a contemptuous sniff as she shuffled toward them, swinging her staff from side to side.

They stepped into the foliage to avoid her swinging staff and let her pass. "Elders," mouthed one in English and the other agreed by raising his palms in exasperation.

FIVE

MAE PLOPPED ONTO THE ABSENT Matron Daley's padded armchair and raised her feet onto the ottoman. Barnhart had kept her running since she'd arrived. The first night, he'd introduced her to all the children and her co-workers during the supper hour. Her nose wrinkled at the memory. The children seemed cowed as they sat before tin bowls of gray stew that she wouldn't serve to pigs. The dry bread of inferior flour was coarse and tasteless.

Afterward, Barnhart told her the staff ate together in a separate dining room nearby. He rotated supervision of the children's dining room among the staff with the assigned staff member relying heavily on the older children to control things. She was to supervise the dining room that week. It was also her responsibility to see that the boys made their beds, washed up before meals, and got to class or work on time. Once the boys were gone, she was to direct the girls in cleaning the school. Meanwhile, the girls' matron, Christine Many Feathers, would be supervising those girls assigned to laundry and seamstress work. It was only now, in the two hours before supper, that Mae was able to rest while the children studied in their dormitories.

Barnhart spent the last two days either in his office, house, or roaming the buildings and the grounds. Every so often he'd mount a horse and ride off into the reservation or toward town. A few rattles of the doorknob established that he locked the door office door behind him whenever he left.

Yesterday had been her first dining room duty. Barnhart said it was the best way for her to get to know all the children. The food was again, meager and tasteless. She wondered if government funds were so lacking that the school could afford nothing better. But then she remembered the barns and pens she'd toured. There were plenty of cows and pigs and silos of grain.

As for the children—they were too quiet and obedient. Maybe that was because she was a stranger and they didn't have her measure. Or, maybe, the regular matron trained them to be that way. Still, they could get rowdy. Hearing them carousing the night before, she'd slipped into their dormitory. She smiled at the memory. The simple pillow fight between the older boys had sputtered out as, one by one, they registered her presence.

She didn't chastise—merely went to the little ones' bedsides to make sure all were warmly tucked beneath their blankets. She'd felt eyes tracking her every movement. Once the younger boys were snug, she walked to the far end of the room where the older boys slept. By this time, they'd also settled in their beds but dark eyes in mulish faces watched and waited. They obviously were expecting a lecture on proper behavior. But, she had something else in mind.

Keeping her voice low, to not disturb the younger ones, she said, "Boys, I understand that Indians like to tell stories."

At first, no one responded, but then a sixteen-year-old named Joshua spoke up. She'd observed him receiving deference from the other boys so he was likely their leader. "Our elders tell us many stories," he said cautiously.

She grinned, "Good! Because I am part Irish and part French. In my father's Irish family many are storytellers. So, I thought that tonight, I would tell you the short story of the Old Crow and the Young Crow." This pronouncement caused the boys to exchange wondering looks and sit up in their beds.

Before she began, she frowned, and asked, "Why are the curtains in this room always drawn? Why aren't the windows ever open?

And, again, it was Joshua who answered. "Matron Daley wants it that way. She says it prevents disease."

"Well! I can't agree with her. Do you mind if I open the curtain a bit and crack a window?"

When the boy shrugged, she went to the nearest window, tucked the curtain behind the sill edge and lowered the top pane of the double-hung window. Taking a seat at the end of one of the boy's cots, she'd told them the story.

> Once upon a time, an old crow had a young son. His son was of an age where he needed to leave the nest but the old crow feared for his son's safety. So he said to his young son, 'Sometimes you will see a two-legged animal come into the field where you are eating. When that happens, observe him carefully. If he carries a stick, fly away quickly because the stick makes a loud noise and will send pain and death into your body.'
>
> "A gun! The stick is a gun," one of the boys interrupted eagerly. Mae smiled her approval even as the other boys shushed him—one going so far as to sternly instruct, "Do not interrupt your elder." Though uncertain how she felt at being called an "elder," Mae smiled and continued:
>
> The old crow wasn't finished with his lesson. He next said, 'Watch to see if the two-legged bends over and takes a stone from the ground. If he does, you must also fly away quickly because that two-legged can knock you from the sky with that stone.
>
> Now, through this all, the young crow was nodding. To show he'd listened carefully, he said, "I understand. If the two-legged comes with a stick or bends down. I must fly away quickly." The old crow puffed out his chest, proud that he had taught his son well. Then the young crow asked. "But father, what if the two-legged has put a stone in his pocket?"
>
> For a moment the old crow said nothing, and then he flapped a wing and said, "Off you go now for you know more than myself!"

Silence greeted the story's ending. Mae looked at the boys who shifted uneasily. "Now, I understand that Elipeena stories often have a lesson. It so happens that Irish stories also have lessons. What do you think is the lesson of my crow story?"

Again the boys shifted uneasily and looked toward their leader. Joshua swallowed and said tentatively, "Even an old crow can learn something new?"

She softly clapped her hands in delight and the boys all relaxed. "Yes! That is exactly right! I told you that story so that you will understand that I am like the old crow and you are like the young crow. While I am supposed to teach you things, there are also things I can learn from you. I don't know what it is like to be an Elipeena or to live here, in this school, or on this reservation. So, we will take turns. Tonight I told you an Irish story. Tomorrow night, after the little ones are asleep, you can tell me an Elipeena story." That said, she slapped her hands on her knees, stood, and after nodding at them, walked down the aisle and out the door.

This morning, as the older boys filed past on their way to another dreadful breakfast, she'd received more than one shy smile. And, what little trust she'd gained the night before had come in handy. She'd stood on the porch, watching half the boys leave for work in the fields, barn, and forge. As she turned to go back inside, her attention was snagged by a small figure sitting on the bottom step, his arms wrapped around himself, clearly crying his eyes out. Just then Joshua headed past her. She grabbed his elbow.

"Excuse me, Joshua. But that little boy down there, I don't recognize him. Who is he?"

"That is Nika Leloo Quirt. I just saw his grandmother go into Agent Barnhart's office." Seeing that Mae remained puzzled, Joshua explained. "She says she has no money to feed and clothe him and that she is too sick now to care for him. She wants him to live here at the school."

"He looks like he's only four years old. Is he an orphan?"

Joshua nodded. "Yes, his parents are no longer. His grandmother loves him very much but she also has no people."

"Joshua, will you please sit with him? Give him comfort? I'm going to find out more."

The boy looked torn, glancing first at the sobbing boy and then over his shoulder, into the school. "I will get a mark against my name if I am late to work."

"What do you mean, 'a mark'?"

"Well, five marks and I do not get bread with my dinner for a week. Ten marks and I get no dinner at all. There are many ways to get marks. Being late is one of them."

"Are there other punishments? Worse ones?"

"Boys have been tied to a post all day. Some have been whipped with a switch."

"Good Lord!" Mae exclaimed. "I will tell Agent Barnhart I ordered you to stay behind."

"Thank you," the boy said and quickly went to sit beside the small child, putting an arm around him and speaking softly into his ear."

Mae entered the school and strode to the office. Inside she found Barnhart talking to an elderly woman wearing a faded long skirt, frayed along its bottom edge, and a tattered blanket wrapped around her shoulders. "Excuse me, Ma'am," she said to the woman before turning to Barnhart. "The young lad, Nika Leloo, is crying his eyes out. I told Joshua to stay behind to keep him company."

Barnhart frowned. "That is totally unnecessary. The boy is going to be staying here with us. In no time at all, he will get used to being here. Besides, he will be able to visit his grandmother once a month. All the Elipeena children can visit their families one day a month, though they must return to the school before nightfall." He'd directed his words at the grandmother who looked stricken, tears filling her clouded eyes beneath their reddened lids.

"Ma'am," Mae addressed her. "Is there anything special your grandson likes to do?"

The woman nodded. "He likes to sit on my lap while I comb and braid his hair and sing to him. And, he likes to sleep with this. His mother made it for him before she left us." She leaned down and pulled a tiny ragdoll from a cloth bag. The doll had black threads woven into little braids falling from beneath a miniature leather headband. She passed the doll to Mae who remarked, "My, what fine stitching,"

That was the right thing to say because the woman straightened and said. "The wife of my son learned to sew at this school. She was very good but there is no seamstress work on the reservation. All the girls in this school learn to sew," she added, and her face returned to its sorrowful lines.

Barnhart abruptly stood and said, "Mrs. Lofton, a word? Out in the hallway?" Although he phrased the words as a question, his tone made it a command. She turned and left the office, still holding the doll. He followed, closed the door firmly, took her by the elbow, and rapidly steered her into a far corner.

"First, you will tell Joshua to get to work. Second, as soon as that woman leaves you will take that boy to the bathroom. There, you will cut his hair off down to the scalp and you will scrub him until his skin turns redder than it already is. After that, you will coat him with kerosene to kill any lice he might have. You will stuff his clothes into a bag and toss them into the garbage pit. You will then dress him in one of the spare school uniforms and take him outside to work in the garden. And, his name henceforth will be Timothy Quirt. Do you understand me?" he demanded.

She let her eyes spit fire but she merely gave him a thin-lipped nod of acquiescence. "Good," he responded and turned away. She started to follow until he stopped and turned back to point at the doll and say, "And, throw that crude thing onto the burn pile!"

Later, she felt heartbreak as she watched the tearful grandmother hug the little boy and tenderly stroke his cheeks. Unlike her own threadbare clothes, the grandmother had dressed the boy in fine buckskin trousers, a nearly new calico shirt, and beautifully beaded moccasins. He's too young to understand, Mae thought as she relived her pain at surrendering her nine-year-old son. Sage hadn't understood either and their parting had haunted her— for years she'd never stopped seeing his tear-stained face staring at her from the back window of the carriage—the first such ride he'd ever taken.

"Buck up girl," she told herself as she descended the stairs and gently pried the boy's tiny hands from his grandmother's legs. "I will watch out for him," she said as she touched the woman's shoulder. After a quiet thank-you, the woman began her slow walk down the driveway.

The boy started wailing and Mae lifted him in her arms, knowing even more painful experiences lay ahead for him at her hands. She gently shushed him, wishing she knew some Elipeena words of comfort. Joshua had told her that four-year-old Nika Leloo spoke no English. So, Mae could only pat his back, repeat his Elipeena name, and make shushing noises. Carrying him up the stairs she thought, I might have to cut his hair but I will not throw his clothes away. And, I will not burn his doll.

SIX

"Tell me, Mr. Adell, how is that you are already acquainted with the new matron, Mrs. Lofton?" Sage hadn't expected such a challenging question first thing. "Why, I'm not," he managed to stutter out, hoping his surprise would be mistaken for puzzlement. "I believe she said, at dinner, that she came down from Portland. We've been staying in Olympia. Why would you think we are acquainted?"

Barnhart stared at him a moment before saying, "It just seemed that Mrs. Lofton was particularly friendly with your wife."

Sage shrugged, "You know, that's how some women are. They take quick measure of the other woman and decide immediately that they like each other. Other women always seem to take to my Lucy."

Barnhart looked unconvinced but simply gestured to a desk by the window that held a stack of ledgers. "That's your desk. Those are the various account books you'll be working with. Go ahead and look them over. When you've done that, let me know and I'll come and explain the entries for each. I believe my neph . . . our clerk, Otis Daley, left them in excellent order." Barnhart turned on his heel, entered his inner office, and closed the door firmly behind him.

Sage sat, sighed, and opened the top ledger. Instead of numbers, he found the name of an individual at the top of the large page. Below the name were various dated entries, most in beautiful handwriting. It took a while for him to figure out that this book contained entries about the various Indians on the reservation. Paging through, he frequently saw the school name "Chemawa' followed by a notation of "grad", "left", "runaway", or "sent home". There were a lot of entries that said, "ill health", "infected eyes", or, "lung ailment." Quickly he flipped through the pages until he found the name, "George Red Hawk." That entry he studied, noting a "Chemawa grad" entry as well as several favorable entries:

> Is particularly kind and devoted to his mother-in-law who is somewhat crippled. Wife was mentally above average but succumbed to childbed fever after birth of son. Noted for his grace and skill in the annual root gathering dance in which he assists the old Indians for whom the dance is a semi-religious rite of thanksgiving and also an occasion for the collection of coin. Keeps traditional ways, works cutting timber, and in seasonal hop fields. Provides well for family. Well respected.

Scanning down the page, Sage noted that the last two entries were written in another, less legible, hand.

> Has turned dissipated and surly, disorderly and riotous since daughter's death. Is leaving reservation without permission. Has refused to follow Indian Court judgment regarding hair cut.

The final entry was harsher in judgment:

> Of very bad reputation. Untrustworthy, troublemaker, lazy. Lives on allotted trust land, refuses to cultivate it. May have to take control of allotment. Has nine-year-old son attending boarding school. Red Hawk seems to be a bad influence on son. Home life may be unacceptable."

A chair scraped the inner office floor, signaling Barnhart was on the move. Sage quickly thrust aside the ledger and grabbed another. It was open to a middle page by the time Barnhart craned his head out of his door and asked, "Do you have any questions, yet?"

"I will be making entries in each of these five books?" Sage asked.

Barnhart leaned over him to see which book Sage was examining. "Yes. And, you'll be drafting correspondence for my signature as well. By the way, Adell, see that absolutely all letters sent by anyone in this school to anyone in the Indian Service are first reviewed by me," he said, inserting steeliness into his command.

Sage widened his eyes and said, "But of course, Agent Barnhart."

Barnhart turned and pulled the inner office door shut, using a skeleton key to lock it before heading toward the hallway. Looking back at Sage he said, "I have to check on the new matron and a few other things. I'm not sure she's going to work out. She has a pretty sassy attitude for someone who's never been a matron before."

Sage glanced down to hide his smile. Oh, if you only knew. "Sassy" is putting it mildly.

Barnhart waved at the ledgers. "Continue your review of the books and then take a look in the file cabinets so you'll know how to find things. I'll return soon." He didn't close the outer door when he left.

Better to sneak up on me, Sage thought to himself before looking down at the book he'd so hurriedly opened. He was appalled. It appeared to be monthly entries detailing Indian health problems on the reservation. A quick scan of a few pages showed many lung and eye infection entries and a surprising number of suicide deaths.

The doctor and his wife warmly welcomed Lucinda Collins, now known as Mrs. Lucy Adell. Both of them looked tired and strained, their faces hollowed by sleeplessness. The wife's fluttering hands said that she, in particular, had reached the end of her rope.

Their obvious distress calmed Lucinda. Seldom was she in the role of savior and found she liked it. The doctor, Harold Defler, had shooed his wife, Beatrice, out the front door of the small house serving as the reservation's infirmary. Once she'd left, he turned to Lucy. "My wife has been invaluable, these past weeks. We've taken turns staying here day and night because we have two patients who cannot be left unattended. Beatrice is not a strong woman." He gave Lucinda an appraising look before saying, "You, on the other hand, look both healthy and strong."

Lucinda nodded, "I'm rarely sick. I can't remember the last time that I was."

The doctor rubbed his hands together, saying, "Good, good!" before asking, "Do you have any nursing experience, Mrs. Adell?" He rushed on to add, "It's fine if you don't. I'd like it very much if you did but I can teach you."

Lucinda smiled, already liking this overly tired, obviously kind man. "Please, call me 'Lucy.' I have limited experience. I nursed smallpox victims in Central Oregon, so I know how to change bandages and beds, take temperatures and pulses, give baths, and administer various pills and salves."

Doctor Lane's instructions had been thorough. He'd also allowed her to attend his examinations and demonstrate her nursing skills. He'd been more than complimentary. She'd liked the crusty doctor, especially once she saw his tenderness with his poorer patients. As they worked together, he'd had no inkling that his temporary student was the proprietor of Portland's most exclusive parlor house. He wasn't the kind of man who'd visit bordellos.

Dr. Defler's relief brightened his face as he clapped his hands together. "All right then, Miz Lucy. Before I introduce you to our two patients I will show you how we do our charting and tell you a bit about what we're facing. As long as we have people staying with us overnight, you will have to stay here. You'll be left alone quite often—at night, six days a week, and also, sometimes during the day because every few days I have to leave the infirmary to treat patients at my town office or in their homes on the reservation. Poor Beatrice has been filling in during my absence. She'll still do that on your day off or if you've had an especially hard night but otherwise, you'll be on your own. That small cot in the corner is where you can sleep."

Lucinda kept her face agreeable although she was dismayed at how little time she'd be spending with her "husband" in that tiny house they'd been assigned. Also, her responsibilities sounded a bit daunting. Still, many a time, she'd handled the smallpox patients on her own. "I can do that, sir," she assured him.

He smiled and gestured at two charts lying atop a small desk. "These are the charts of the infirmary's current patients. You will be responsible for entering their vitals and recording any changes in their condition." He heaved a sigh. "This one is a six-year-old, Patty Blake. She came to the school underweight. Unfortunately, she never gained weight, in fact, she's lost some. And now, her lungs are congested. We'd need an x-ray machine to make sure, but I fear she has tuberculosis. She's an orphan and has no relatives. Agent Barnhart ordered me to send her somewhere, like a fostering Indian home, to die." Bitterness twisted his lips as he added, "If she dies here on the school grounds we have to enter it in the school records. If she dies at anywhere else, well, that isn't a black mark against the school. All the boarding schools do it."

"Yet, she's still here?"

Defler's face turned mulish. "I told him she can be cured and that I'll not send her somewhere to infect another Indian family. Plus, they likely wouldn't have the food she needs if she is to recover. Almost everyone living on this reservation is destitute."

Lucinda thought back to food she'd choked down the night before when she'd dined with Mae in the children's dining room. There'd been no fruit or vegetables, only sparse chunks of tough meat in the thin stew and coarse bread. No wonder the child had lost weight.

Defler wasn't stupid. He'd caught her considering look. "Don't worry, we eat better here than they do at the school. I make sure Barnhart supplies us with fresh vegetables and good meat—the same as what he and the other staff eat and like what he sells."

Lucinda looked puzzled as she echoed, "Sells?"

Disgust twisted Defler's lips. "He claims he sells the farm products because the school's operational budget needs more money." The doctor looked down, noticed his fist clenched atop the chart, and relaxed his hand.

"The important thing is that Patty gets fresh air and good food. I keep her bedroom window cracked open for fresh air. Same in this room," the doctor explained. "I've repeatedly told Head Matron Daley that she must let fresh air flow through the dormitories, but no, she keeps both rooms closed up tight as a dungeon. Today, I was gratified to see that temporary matron fling open the boys' curtains and raise the windows. The girls' matron has done the same."

"I thought the girls' dormitory had a different matron, a Miss Many Feathers," Lucinda observed.

"It does, but Daley calls the shots for both dormitories. The girls' matron, Christine, is new, and one of only two Indian staff members. I suspect she doesn't think her job secure enough to challenge the reservation agent's sister. Barnhart will transfer her out in the blink of an eye if his sister demands it."

Their discussion ended, Defler gave her a brief tour. There was the front room, the kitchen, and two very small bedrooms. In one lay the little girl with the suspected TB. Her window was slightly open and thick quilts covered her sleeping figure. The other bedroom held an elderly Indian man who was also sleeping. Defler said the relatives of the man, Gerald Wolf, lived too crowded and poor to look after him. Still, they visited him regularly.

Once he and Lucinda returned to the infirmary's main room, Defler told Lucinda, "There's really nothing we can do for Mr. Wolf. He's fading fast and sleeps most of the time now. So, be prepared. Change him and be kind to him and feed him if he'll eat. Let his relatives visit him, no matter what the hour. Otherwise, there's nothing more we can do," he repeated.

Mae straightened and pushed back a hair strand that had escaped from her bun. She was working right alongside the girls and had been surprised at the amount of dust and dirt beneath the boys' beds. Apparently, Matron Daley was slipshod when it came to cleanliness.

Movement at the door caught her attention. Barnhart stood there, a frown on his face. She nodded at the girls and asked them to continue cleaning. As she walked toward him, he abruptly gestured her out of the room and into the hallway.

Great, another lecture, she thought to herself. She wasn't wrong. "Mrs. Lofton, why are the windows open in this dormitory? It is not hot outside."

She wrinkled her nose and said, "Well, it's stinky inside. I don't think that room has been aired for ages."

"You're wasting building heat."

"It's better than letting bad air accumulate. The children tell me there's some who've come down with TB. The latest medical advice for preventing that disease is plenty of fresh air. Why, they just opened a sanitarium in Portland where all the patients live outside, in tents, for over half the year, just so they can get fresh air."

Barnhart's eyes narrowed but all he said was, "And, another thing. Our matron does not get down on her hands and knees and scrub alongside the children. It is undignified. It sets a bad example—breeds disrespect."

"Well, maybe she should have. This room is filthy. These girls can't clean the whole thing by themselves. We haven't even touched the toilets, yet. I have to begin as I intend to end and that means the rooms on all three floors are going to be spic and span." She stared at him, daring him to order otherwise.

Red suffused his face and he snapped, "That dormitory is a darn sight better than their parents' filthy hovels." When she continued to stare at him, he added, "Well, then, you better get back to it. See that the room is back in order by study hour." He turned on his heel and headed downstairs. She smiled sourly at hearing his hissed murmurs drift up the stairway in his wake.

SEVEN

CHARLEY RAN, LANDING ON HIS toes first, just like his father had taught him so he could run longer and leave fewer signs of his passing. Were they coming after him? Had Grandmother delayed them long enough? He stopped, hands on knees, and tried to breathe quietly, his ears straining. There! A crow's warning squawk sounding in the forest behind him. He needed to abandon the path soon.

He straightened and began running, his eyes searching for the deer trail that wound up the hillside. Even though his heart was racing and he was sweating, he shivered, remembering the two runaway boys. The government had taken them from a desert reservation on the other side of the mountains where they'd lived with their parents. The tribal police chased after them into the mountains. It had been a fall day when gray clouds hung low above the valley. As desert boys, they could not read the weather coming from the ocean. They only knew that they wanted to go home.

That night, a snowstorm buried the Cascades beneath a white blanket. Snow caught them far above the tree line. Days later, a hunter following deer tracks in the snow, found them curled together as if sleeping. Charley would never forget their mothers' wails when they came to take their bodies home.

That would not happen to him. He'd only climb into the mountains far enough to escape his pursuers. Ahead, there was water glinting between the trees. That was the shallow pond where his family harvested wapato. It had been their patch for many generations. They tended it carefully, taking only what they needed, and leaving the strongest mother plants to send out life-giving runners.

Without slowing, he felt inside the burlap sack Grandmother had given him. His fingers touch a knife and scabbard, his father's gift to him on his last birthday. Reaching the pond's edge, he used the knife to quickly dig beneath the arrowhead-shaped leaves. He cut the white root loose from the muck, swished it clean, and dried the knife on his trousers. Then he stowed both knife and wapato root in his bag and took off running.

Minutes later he reached the edge of the Red Hawk allotment. Ahead lay a patchwork of Indian and white man's lands. He paused and listened. Behind him, he heard a crow's call sounding closer this time. He had to leave the path.

He scanned the hillside. Somewhere around here a deer trail led upward. Then he remembered. His father had dragged a heavy log across the trail's opening. He studied every log and finally spied bristly deer hair snagged on one nearby. That was it! He stepped over the log, careful not to scuff its mossy coat, then he leaned back over and smoothed the ground to hide any foot signs.

It was hard to tell with the tribal police. Most of them were not traditional Elipeena, like his father and grandmother. But one of them had kept up with the traditional ways and he was a good tracker. Charley climbed upward, moved cautiously so that he broke no plant nor stepped on moist earth. Finally, he crawled onto the rock ledge his father had recently shown him.

In a few years, this was to be his vision quest place just as it had been his father's. A large pile of rocks leaned against the ledge's back wall. His father stacked the rocks years ago while awaiting his spirit guide's appearance. Charley knelt beside the pile and ran his hand softly over the soft moss that covered the stones. He closed his eyes and silently prayed that his father's panther spirit guide would protect him from capture.

His prayer finished and feeling at peace, he crawled on hands and knees to the ledge edge and peered down from between the leaves of a small bush. Far below ran a long stretch of the main trail. Once again, the crow cawed a warning as it circled above the path but level with Charley's eyes. For a brief moment, it swooped in small circles, almost stationary in the air, as if checking whether Charley was paying attention. He looked into its black eye. Then, sounding a final caw, it swooped down into the trees and was gone.

At that moment, two tribal policemen stepped into his view. There was no mistaking their brown, wide-brimmed hats, and brown canvas coats. One of them was intently eyeing the ground. Darn, it was Victor, the policeman he feared most. Charley held his breath as they reached the opening to the deer trail. He slowly exhaled when they walked past it. Five minutes he waited and they did not return.

He had to go higher, to the meadow that wrapped around the hill and ran north. It was his only chance. He backtracked south along the hillside until he reached a rocky streambed that cut the mountainside. The spring runoff was wetting the rocks but he carefully picked his way among them and grabbed shrub branches to pull him up the steepest places. Whenever his foot rolled a stone, he stopped, and returned that stone to its original position, dirt side down. Although the tracker might believe the step of deer or elk or bear had dislodged the stone, Charley could not take the chance. So his father had taught him.

At last, the land leveled and opened up to a windy sky. The sinking sun colored the sky's western rim gold. He'd reached the meadow. A flash of movement caught his eye and froze him mid-step. A hundred feet away, the yellow-green eyes of a mountain panther stared into his eyes before it turned and slipped into the trees.

Charley bowed his head, thanked the big cat for not attacking, for protecting him, and promised no panther would ever know death at his hands. He turned and thanked the stream for carving his path to safety. He looked upward into the scudding clouds and thanked the crow for its warnings.

He started walking north, keeping to meadow's edge, stepping from tree to tree, frequently pausing to peer forward and behind, and hoping that he wouldn't see the tribal officers' brown uniforms. With luck, they'd think he was already heading west across the valley floor where roads made the going much easier.

Sage was leaving the tiny, one-bedroom house just as Lucinda was coming in. He wrapped his arms around her and asked into her golden hair, "Did you get any sleep?"

"It was my first night. I was afraid to sleep. I must have checked on my patients at least twenty times," she said and yawned against his shoulder.

"How were they?"

"The old man never woke the entire night. I think Dr. Defler is right; he's slipping away, although I did get him to sip some broth in the early evening. I think he only did it to please me, not because he was hungry. As for the girl, she has those fever red cheeks I've seen before with consumptives. So, I think the doctor is right. She's got TB. But she did eat, not only in the evening but also in the middle of the night. I was able to sit her on the commode. The old man, well, I had to change his sheets."

"I'm sorry. I think you got the worst end of the deal this time," he said.

She stepped away and looked at him with those ever-changing cornflower blue eyes that, at this moment, held wonder. "You know, Sage. I find pleasure in caring for them—in giving them comfort."

He felt a rush of warmth toward her but all he said was, "Well, I'm glad. Get some sleep while I go beard the lion in his den."

She nodded, kissed him quickly, and said, "Be careful, Mr. Adell. Your loving wife wants you to stay in one huggable piece."

Sage laughed as he went out the door but all merriment faded as he entered the boarding school. He arrived early, hoping to do some snooping before Barnhart turned up. No such luck. Sage didn't use the office key Barnhart had grudgingly given him because the closed outer door was unlocked. Quietly stepping inside, Sage saw that the inner office door was ajar and he could hear a raised voice beyond that door.

"I don't understand! I thought you were a renowned Indian tracker. How can you not find a nine-year-old boy?" said Barnhart.

A low rumble sounded in response but it had no calming effect. "Did you search his house? Did you talk to the grandmother?"

Again the rumble, and again, a querulous response from Barnhart. "And you believed her? You and that Elipeena claptrap about never lying. You're a naïve dolt to believe that!"

Another low rumble and this time, Barnhart switched from hectoring to commanding. "Get off the reservation and look in the valley. You have my permission. If the sheriff asks, tell him you're looking for a runaway. He'll believe that. Describe the kid but don't tell him the name. If you value your jobs, you'll find that boy today!"

Barnhart sounded genuinely concerned and, for the first time, Sage wondered if perhaps the agent actually cared about the children. Maybe they had the reservation agent figured all wrong.

At the sound of scuffling feet, Sage crossed to the hall door, opened it quietly, and then closed it loudly. He was on his way to his desk when

Barnhart appeared in his office door. "What are you doing here so early?" he demanded, not suppressing his foul mood.

"I thought I'd use the extra time to familiarize myself with a few things. Everything's still pretty foreign to me and I don't want to make a mistake. Your regular clerk's work is very organized and tidy. I'd like my work to be the same."

"Humph," Barnhart said. Then he turned to gesture at the people in his office and stepped out of the doorway. The two Indian men who edged past him were short in stature but imposing in their neat police uniforms. Their faces were impassive but Sage noticed that the older of them had a white-knuckled grip on the brim of his hat. The man saw Sage's glance and slapped the hat onto his head, casting a dark look in Sage's direction as he passed.

Barnhart issued a final command at their retreating backs. "I mean it. Find him today!"

Sage let his curiosity show when Barnhart turned to him. He asked, "Were those men tribal police? I didn't realize reservations had their own police force."

"Yes, they are. We had a runaway the other day and those two incompetents have been unable to find him."

Sage said nothing which spurred Barnhart into further explanation. "The boy's only nine. A hunter found our last two runaways dead. So, I'm worried about the boy. There are mountain lions, grizzly bears, and whatnot out in that wilderness."

This time, Sage's continued silence spurred Barnhart into action. He pointed at a stack of papers on Sage's desk. "Those are the invoices we've received since our permanent clerk was called away. Put them in date order, enter them in the proper ledger, and prepare the related bank drafts for me to sign," he directed before turning on his heel, entering his office, and closing his door.

Damn, Sage thought, I missed my chance. Am I ever going to get the opportunity to search that office? Maybe, if his mother pulled off the plan they'd hatched late last night when they'd met on the side of the school building hidden from Barnhart's windows.

He heard the children tromping downstairs for breakfast. Half an hour later, he looked out the office window and saw boys heading to the fields and outbuildings. Noises in the hallway outside the office meant the other children were heading up to the classrooms and their work duties. "Any time now," he said under his breath.

As if summoned by those words, the outer door was flung wide and Mae stormed past, winking at him before adopting an alarmed expression. She didn't knock before hurriedly opening the door to Barnhart's office and saying, "We've got a disaster on our hands, Agent Barnhart. Water's spilling everywhere, I can't stop it!"

As they hoped, urgency made Barnhart careless because he charged out of the inner office in his shirt sleeves. Seconds later, their footsteps were rapidly climbing to the third floor.

Sage wasted no time. He strode to the outer door and shut it. Next, he stepped through the open door into Barnhart's office. Initially, he felt disappointed. A desk, filing cabinet, and bookshelves took up most of the space. It was only after he'd stepped to the desk and began searching its drawers that he noticed a small safe, tucked into the corner and draped with a decorative cloth. After quickly searching the drawers he turned to the safe. Lifting the cloth, he tried the dial and found it locked. Damn.

Sage was calmly organizing the invoices when Barnhart stormed back into the office. He looked at his open door and then at Sage but said only, "Stupid woman. One of those little monsters stuffed a towel down the toilet and then flushed it. You'd think she'd have been smart enough to figure it out. That damn woman is more trouble than she's worth!" he exclaimed before entering his office and, once again, closing the door.

"Now, what's in that file cabinet and why does he need a safe in his office?' Sage murmured.

EIGHT

Eich hallooed from the clearing's edge and listened for the woman's answering call but heard only distant songbird chirps and trills. The cabin looked abandoned. Despite the slight chill in the air, no smoke drifted from the chimney. As he waited, he surveyed the homestead. The well-built cedar-log cabin was simple but well-caulked, as was a nearby outbuilding. Both gleamed mellow gold in the spring sunlight. A small, open-sided shed, attached to the house, was empty, its firewood contents were strewn about the ground as if tossed aside in anger. He hallooed again and, when still no one answered, he crossed the clearing to the door. Stepping onto the covered porch, he found the front door ajar. Cautiously, he pushed it open until the front room was in full view. He saw a loft and two doors opening off the rear wall. A kitchen filled one end while a stone fireplace anchored the large room's other end.

But the cabin's simple beauty was marred. Someone had made a mess of the place. Chairs and a small table were overturned, the kitchen shelf's contents lay all over the floor, and the ax head buried in one of the wall logs felt threatening.

"Is anyone here? I come as a friend," he called out. When silence answered his question, he carefully picked his way across the littered floor to open the closed doors and found bedrooms. The same human tornado that had hit the front room had blown through these two rooms as well. He climbed the ladder until he could see into the loft. Here too, he found a mess. The narrow bed and a scattering of boy's clothes indicated the loft was where the younger Red Hawk slept. Back on the main floor, Eich took a final look around, shaking his head at the wanton destruction.

When he left, he secured the latch. His quick check of the outbuilding and the outhouse yielded more mess but no body. That had been his biggest concern. He had to believe that the destruction had happened after Red Hawk's mother-in-law had left. He needed to find out whether she was safe somewhere.

Eich set off in search of the missing woman. Leaving his buckboard at the cabin, he headed down the footpath that led to the school. He knew someone had murdered McConnell on this path. Soon he spotted a wide section of the path disturbed by scuffing and with broken plants on both sides. He stopped and sensed a lingering of the man's terror. He shivered, even though the sun's rays felt warm on his back. A faint noise in the undergrowth broke his paralysis. He held his breath, looked around, and listened, before deciding it had probably been a weasel, squirrel, or some other small creature. Still, he stepped off the path, feeling drawn in the direction of the sound.

A few steps in, he noticed something man-made poking out from beneath a sword fern. Moving closer he saw that it was a small notebook. He picked it up and read the name "McConnell," on the inside of the cover. Hoping he'd found McConnell's inspection notes, he rapidly paged through. Instead, he realized that he held the personal notes of an amateur naturalist. As he read the man's wonder-filled words, grief washed over him. Nature's variety and beauty had enthralled McConnell—a man not unlike himself. He would have enjoyed befriending William McConnell.

The raucous shack-shack-shack of a stellar jay snapped his attention away from the notebook and thoughts of its author. He slipped the small notebook into an inside pocket and headed back up the trail to his buckboard and his hunt for the missing grandmother.

Eich bypassed the neighboring white man in his field and instead, rolled on toward the Red Hawk's nearest Indian neighbor. Reaching a hut, an abode not nearly as well-built or tidy as the Red Hawk's, he spotted an elderly man sitting on his stoop, turning his face up to the sun, his white-clouded eyes gazing into its brightness. Again, Eich stood at a distance and called "hello".

"You that trader man, I been hearing about?" came the answer.

"Yes, sir. My name is Herman Eich."

"Well, trader, come closer so I can see your shape."

Eich moved to the bottom of the stoop and set his goods crate on the ground.

"I can't buy nothin' since I got only but a few cents," the man told him with a smile that revealed astonishingly white teeth.

"Well, what do you need, exactly?"

Eich's question triggered a harsh laugh. "Just about darn near everything. That scoundrel agent is way late giving me my annuity. I am lucky though. I have a good son. He works up near Portland and he sends me money when he can. So, I get by. Not like some." His lips turned down as sadness swept across his face.

"You have lost a friend?"

"Yes, Jefferson Spencer. Him and me was kidnapped off the reservation when we were just little fellows. They took us to a white man's school far away. It was a terrible time but it made us good friends for all our lives."

"Mr. Spencer also didn't get his annuity money on time?"

"Huh! That agent never pays on time and when he does, it is not the right amount. He sure enough cheated Jefferson because, in his last year, my friend got easy to confuse."

"You mean you are supposed to be getting more than Barnhart gives you?"

The old man's sightless eyes stared across the yard at the forest. "The treaty says one amount, the agent says less. Neither one is enough."

"Well, it just so happens I traded with one of your neighbors and I've got more venison jerky than I can use. How about you take some of it off my hands?"

The old man's face looked skeptical. "Exactly what do you want in return?" he asked.

Eich chuckled. This was one sharp fellow. "Well, I need help with two things. I was just at the Red Hawk's place. Someone has turned it upside down. I need to know who to tell. I understand the grandmother has trouble getting around and with Mr. Red Hawk in jail . . . well, she needs someone to put things back in place. So, maybe you can tell me who I should talk to. And, secondly, for my peace of mind, I need to know that she is somewhere safe."

For a very long time, one filled with bird song, the old man said nothing, his face expressionless. Finally, he lifted a wrinkled finger and pointed. "Two cabins down the road thataway there is a place. You'll be seeing a broke-down wagon in the yard. Tell them about the messy cabin." He turned his cloudy eyes toward Eich. "Grandmother is safe, we are taking care of her," he said with a confidence that made Eich believe him. That said, the man's lips clamped shut, signaling it was pointless for Eich to ask further about the grandmother's location.

Eich set off down the road, the elder's dignified "thank you" was payment enough for the jerky and the few other bits and pieces he'd left on the stoop beside the sightless old man.

It was more a shack than a cabin. The detritus cluttering the small clearing was that common among the impoverished who threw nothing out on the off-chance that it, or parts of it, might be useful in the future. Here too, Eich found a person sitting on the front stoop in the patchy sunlight. She, however, was busily weaving an elaborate cedar basket. She sent him an inquiring glance even as she kept weaving the strands of spruce root.

"That's a beautiful basket. Have you others like it for sale?" he asked.

She paused her weaving and, again, looked at him inquiringly. He realized she hadn't understood his English words. The liveryman in Moolock had taught him a few simple phrases of Chinook Wawa, the shared trade language among Pacific Northwest Indians. He tried it out, knowing his pronunciation was poor. "Makook opekwan?" he asked, pointing at her weaving.

For the first time, she smiled, her dark eyes dancing. "No opekwan. Seahpo," she said and pointed at her head.

"Ah, a hat! Halo mika opekwan makook?" He'd seen some of the Elipeena baskets and thought them exquisite. He saw a potential trade in the offing if she had baskets for sale.

She nodded and stood to enter her home. Reaching the top step she called out in Elipeena and a small boy, no more than four, ran around the house's corner. She said something to the child and he immediately mounted to the top step and turned to face Eich. She disappeared inside leaving the boy to silently study Eich, his eyes moving from the top of Eich's head to his boots. Once the boy's survey appeared done, Eich said. "Hello?" The boy merely stared at him in that disconcerting expressionless way of very young children.

The woman appeared with her arms around a stack of baskets and rescued Eich from the awkwardness Eich felt at the boy's scrutiny. She stepped past him to a wooden table set beneath a white oak's newly sprouted bright green leaves. She carefully set each basket out for his examination.

He was amazed at their fine detail and beauty. Some were loosely woven, obviously intended for gathering. Others had a tight weave that meant they could hold water and even be used to cook food. She'd decorated many with dyed bear grass woven into patterns. He did not know the Elipeena or Chinook word for beautiful so he smiled widely, said, "beautiful," and put both hands to his heart in the hope she would understand.

She did because she gestured at them and said, "Mika makook." He nodded vigorously to indicate he did, indeed, want to trade. He studied the baskets in earnest, all the while thinking how much they'd bring in New York City. He wondered if he could find a way to sell them for her since, in the East, there was a growing demand for authentic Native basketry.

Finally, he pointed to the smallest basket. This one would be for him and it had to be small since his lean-to was very small. He glanced at her and caught a look of disappointment.

He lifted his pack and began laying its contents out on the table next to the baskets. She looked interested and so did the young boy standing at her side, his eyes level with the tabletop. She pointed at some buttons, a needle, and fingered a length of red material before sighing as if knowing that the cloth's addition would unbalance their trade. The little boy's hand reached for a spinning top and she said something sharply. The little boy snatched his hand back, his eyes filled, but he did not cry.

Eich shook his head and she frowned. He knew how much that basket would bring if sold in a fair market. The price she asked didn't come close to its value. He took the length of red cloth, another of blue, and stacked them. Then he added a small frying pan into which he piled the buttons, a packet of needles, and finally the spinning top. He pushed the items toward her.

She looked sharply at him and then gestured to the whole selection of baskets, her wrinkled forehead making her puzzlement clear.

He gave his head a vigorous shake and picked up the smallest basket. She gave him a disbelieving look before her face became thoughtful. He knew she probably thought he was an idiot but he didn't care. He had to follow the dictates of his conscience. This woman was a true artist whose work would command a much higher price if she was somewhere other than on a remote Indian reservation in the West. He would feel like a thief if he paid any less.

Finally, she shrugged. She took the basket from him, put it in a slightly larger one, and handed both to him. When he raised a hand to protest, she shook her head. So, he shrugged and stowed them in his crate with the remainder of his goods. This time, when the small hand snaked forward toward the top, she smiled and said something softly in Elipeena. The boy grabbed the top and ran off.

She walked Eich to the road's edge. Reaching it, he remembered his original reason for the visit. He pointed back the way he came. "Red Hawk?" he said.

She nodded.

Using gestures he mimed knocking on the door and discovering turned over tables and cleared shelves. At first, she looked confused then her face turned angry. "Mesahchie man!" she exclaimed and mimicked his wild gestures.

He nodded vigorously, though it wasn't until later, when he asked the liveryman, that he learned "Mesahchie" meant "evil".

Like many good people, when confronted with evil, she sadly shook her head and huffed her exasperation. She patted his arm and nodded while rattling off something in Elipeena that sounded definite and reassuring. Once atop his buckboard, he waved and rolled off, quite certain that someone would soon clean up the mess at the Red Hawks'.

Charley was glad of the sun, even though it was sinking. He'd made his way northward for several miles until he was far outside the reservation's border. Once he descended from the heights he'd feared striking out across the valley in the daylight. Folks hereabouts knew that a lone Indian boy meant a runaway from the school. They'd caught and returned more than one boy for the small reward Agent Barnhart offered. His three days of running and hiding had left him too tired to make the trek the night before. So, he'd spent the night and next day hunkered down in the foothill forest.

Darkness had fallen and he stood at the forest's edge, studying the stars sparkling above the wide valley. At last, he spotted the solitary light his father had taught him to use as a guide. As long as he angled so that the star kept on his right shoulder, he should reach the river near where Indian Joe used a small boat to ferry people across for an equally small fee. His was the only Indian-operated ferry on that section of the river.

Clutching the burlap bag to his chest, Charley stepped out from under the trees. Soon, he was tromping across the white people's plowed fields. As he did, he recalled his father saying that when the white man first saw this valley, he thought he'd found a heavenly garden. The white man never knew it was the valley Indians who had created the paradise with their careful plant culling, burning, and tree falling. A paradise the white man promptly destroyed.

His father had pointed to meadows that once grew an abundance of camas roots and berries, to swamps that once yielded a plentitude of wapato, and to woodlands where game had bedded and nuts had fallen from the trees. All of it was gone. His father once said, "In the old time, before the white man, our people had enough food. It was so plentiful that those who lived here were known to love peace because hunger never forced them to raid. They would defend themselves, but they never made war." Charley liked knowing that about his ancestors.

On their journey to visit their Grand Ronde relatives, his father made the land tell stories by pointing out places where he had once hunted and harvested. He'd explained that the Elipeenas never owned the land. That all they ever claimed was what grew or roamed on specific patches of land. Every Elipeena knew where his family could harvest and hunt. That had been the Elipeena way before the white man came and said white people owned the earth and everything on or in it.

His father said the white man's trade goods separated the people from the earth. Many had broken their sacred promise to those things that gave them life. He talked about Beaver, an animal whose spirit was loyal and trustworthy. In olden times, the Elipeena had killed Beaver but only for the pelts they needed and only after thanking Beaver for his sacrifice. Then the white man came and soon, Beaver was no more and the Indian had helped to make him vanish. His father said for that, the Indian had "shem,"—shame.

These memories carried Charley past farmhouses, into and out of ditches, and through rare stands of white oak. At last, just as darkest night made walking harder, he reached the river. Eagerly he looked for a familiar landmark and felt proud when he recognized a bluff. The star had guided him well and he raised his palms in fervent thanks.

Carefully, he made his way along the river, avoiding its swampy places. At last, he spotted Indian Joe's small docks, one on each side of the flowing water. Stealthily, he picked his way among the reeds and trees until he found a hidden spot behind Indian Joe's outhouse. There he sat down to wait.

Early morning throat hacking jarred Charley from a light doze. He peeked around the outhouse and was relieved to see Indian Joe coming down the path in the gray of dawn. He crept forward and put his ear to the outhouse wall. When the sounds of leave-taking began, he knocked lightly on the wall and waited. Hinges screeched as the door swung open. Seconds later a man cautiously peeked around the corner. He grinned when he saw Charley.

"Charley Red Hawk, aren't you a sight for sore eyes!" he exclaimed. Indian Joe was not an Oregon Indian. Some thought he'd come from the Flatheads of Montana. Others said he'd come from the plateau country of the Dakota tribe. Indian Joe would never say, thereby gifting everyone with many enjoyable hours of speculation. Indian Joe spoke only English and none of the local Indian languages.

"Well, Red Hawk boy. They tell me you are runaway."

Charley remembered his father saying Indian Joe was to be trusted so he stood his ground instead of giving in to his urge to flee. "Yes, I ran away but for good reason."

"Tribal police came late yesterday looking for you."

That didn't surprise Charley. For a moment he said nothing, wondering what question he should ask.

"They ask if I seen you," here Indian Joe let a long pause elapse before he chortled and said, "I tell them you come through yesterday morning, heading for the Siletz reservation." The man turned anxious. "That okay? You are not headed to the Siletz are you?"

Charley relaxed and grinned. "No, I am not heading to the Siletz. That was very smart of you to say that. Did they head in that direction?"

Indian Joe shook his head. "No, they are hiding in the trees on the river's other side, keeping eyes on my place. No surprise. Every time there is a runaway, I send them in the wrong direction. Maybe they catch on to my trick."

Charley twisted his lips as he pondered how to evade the two tribal policemen. Indian Joe understood because he said, "They will soon leave. When they do, we will get in boat and row downriver to a place where they cannot find your tracks—all rock. It will be closer to the Grand Ronde reservation so better for you."

Charley was surprised that Indian Joe knew of his destination and was so willing to help. Indian Joe also understood this thought because he said, "Your father is one very good man. He helped me in the past. It is only right I help his son. His son is just as clever as him, I'm thinking. I know about the uncle who lives on the Grand Ronde," he added and gently pushed Charley toward the woods. "You go hide in trees. I bring you food soon."

NINE

THAT SILLY MAN THINKS HE'S so clever, Mae stood at the window, teacup in hand and watched Eich slink across the field in the graying twilight. Still, she'd felt touched the first time she saw him sneaking into that unused outbuilding. "No wonder he looks so tired," she murmured.

Eich rolled up every day to show the staff gewgaws and whatnots. Since he always had something new to offer no one had questioned at his diligence. Some merchant in Moolock had to be happy as a pig in warm mud over the trader buying so many goods for resale. Usually, it was Barnhart and his favorite teacher, Weldon Willingham, who bought.

When Eich wasn't hovering around the school, he was wandering the reservation, giving folks more than he got and winkling out whatever information he could from the tight-lipped Elipeenas. She worried about him. Eich wasn't a young man, close to sixty, just three years older than her. All his running around and sleeping in an unheated, uncomfortable shed all night, was a bit too much even for a younger man.

It was time she talked to the others about it. That wouldn't be too hard since Agent Barnhart frequently absented himself. Getting to talk to Lucinda was more difficult. She seldom saw her since the poor girl was working every night and sleeping most of the day. Mae sensed that Sage was unhappy about not seeing more of his "wife".

Mae swallowed the last of her tea. It was time to chivvy her boys into the washroom and down to supper. Barnhart evidently had taken against her because, contrary to his initial promise, there was no rotation of dining room duties. It looked like he intended to keep her supervising the children for the duration of her temporary service. She didn't mind. She liked these children and being with them was a darn sight better than looking at his greedy mug while she ate.

Still, the thought of yet another night of the watery, tasteless stew was enough to turn her stomach. Her lip curled in disgust. She'd snuck into the kitchen and found shelves loaded with good flour, meal, fruits, vegetables, and cured meat. She figured the decent provisions went to Barnhart and his favored ones on the staff because she'd never seen them served to the children. She suspected the good food also went elsewhere. More than once she'd seen Barnhart load his buggy with crates that could only have come from the kitchen. Once, he'd looked up at the third-floor windows just before he drove off and scowled when he caught her watching.

Now, as she gazed out the window she caught sight of movement in the trees that edged the nearest field. Probably Christine Many Feather's beau was waiting for her. Every evening, the young matron ate quickly before slipping away from the staff dining room and scurrying across the field and into the woods. Sure hope that gal knows what she's doing, Mae thought. She got on well with the Cherokee woman. Once Mae began voicing disgust at how the children were treated and fed, Christine warmed up to her and talked about her man friend, Jeremiah Hunter and their plans to get married.

When Mae had offhandedly questioned the boys about Jeremiah, she learned he was industrious. He worked cutting timber for a white man but he was saving up to open his own sawmill. He'd also completed his schooling at the Indian Industrial Training School near Salem.

There were four other staff members at the school. One was the industrial teacher, Adolph Brunner. He ran the farm and was supposed to be teaching the boys and the men on the reservation farming, welding, animal care, and other farming skills. She only saw him in passing but didn't like how tired the boys were after working in the fields. He drove them hard, even though they were just children—and, underfed ones at that.

Mae had her suspicions about the slovenly white cook, Katy Devon. First of all, she was no cook. Everything Devon made for the children tasted worse than it had to. Mae shuddered at the thought the woman was teaching the girls how to cook. But worse, the woman had to know that there was better food stored in the kitchen yet she did nothing to see that the children got some of it. If she'd been in the cook's shoes, she would have quit before allowing the children to be so ill-fed. To Mae's mind, that meant the cook must be benefitting from Barnhart's shenanigans.

The other two staff members were teachers. Weldon Willingham was a white, lanky, sour-faced, old puss who didn't seem to like his students. He, however, was quite cozy with Agent Barnhart. More than once she'd caught him skulking in the hallway outside the boy's dormitory, no doubt spying on her for Barnhart.

The other teacher was an Ojibwa Indian from Minnesota by the name of Virgil White Cloud. The children flocked around him, always smiling in his presence. He seemed to like them in return for she'd often see him in friendly conversation with one or another outside his classroom. Even better, she'd overheard him arguing with Barnhart, their heated voices echoing up the stairwell. White Cloud was protesting the discipline meted out to one boy who persisted in speaking Elipeena to his classmates. He was insisting that the boy had a right to speak his tribal language which, if Barnhart only understood it, he would realize it was grammatical, elegant, and completely devoid of slang or swearwords. Of course, White Cloud's protest fell on the Agent's deaf ears. But, to his credit, the conversation ended without his backing down.

Mae turned from the window, put her teacup in the tiny corner sink, and headed for the door. Time to get a move on.

They waited until midnight before converging on the reservation infirmary. Luckily, it stood on the far side of the school building, opposite the housing. Still, Lucinda had all the curtains pulled and only a single oil lamp lit when they slipped in, one by one.

Mae carried a flour sack and when Lucinda hugged her, she said, "Careful girl. I've got eggs in this sack. Don't want to break them."

Eich, Sage, and Lucinda gave her questioning looks. She looked embarrassed. "I never thought I'd take to pilfering at my age but, dagnabbit, those kids need more food." She handed the sack to Lucinda, "So, Lucinda girl, I have a big favor to ask. That sack's got cornmeal, eggs, and a chunk of lard. Tomorrow, could you bake up a passel of cornbread? It's got to be enough for both dormitories."

"I'll do my best. There's two big pans in our kitchen and we've plenty of firewood for the cookstove," Lucinda said.

That bit of business over, Sage took charge. "Okay, let's compare notes. What do we think is going on at the school and on the reservation? Exactly what is Barnhart up to? And, who else is involved?"

Eich went first. "Around 1885, the reservation was divided up into what the Elipeenas call "allotments", and what we'd call "homesteads". These allotments are around 160 acres or smaller. Each adult was assigned an allotment. Oftentimes, that allotment was the poorest land on the reservation—hilly, swampy, timber-covered—not very suitable for farming.

"Even worse, the Elipeenas did not get the title to their own allotments. Instead, the government holds them in "trust." Only after twenty-five years, if the agent deems the person "deserving", will that person get the title. Until then, the Elipeena must have written approval from the agent to lease his allotment to another person. But, even with that approval, the lease money goes directly to the agent who then doles it out to the Elipeena. I am told Barnhart usually takes a "cut" and delays paying the lease money out."

"What makes someone "deserving" of a title to their land?" Lucinda wondered aloud.

Eich frowned. "Near as I can tell, they have to be living "white", whatever that means, and obedient to the agent."

"Red Hawk said something about his elderly friend dying because he never got his annuity money," Sage said. "What is that?

Eich stroked his full beard thoughtfully before leaning forward to say, "When the U.S. government took parts of the reservation land and sold them to white people, the government promised to pay every Elipeena adult a certain amount each month. That's what folks around here call their "annuity". It's a pittance, but the money is crucial for their survival. In the case of Red Hawk's friend, Barnhart probably kept all of the man's annuity money. From what I heard, that man was a bit senile in his last years. Barnhart might also be shorting the amounts he gives others.

"People are pretty angry about the annuity money and the loss of tribal lands. They say the government agents used bribery and coercion to get the tribe's agreement for the land sales. Nowadays, Barnhart controls the timing of the annuity payouts. It's a big stick that he uses to control folks."

The other three frowned as they absorbed Eich's information. Finally Sage commented, "Red Hawk said Barnhart wanted him to lease his land to a neighboring white farmer but Red Hawk was refusing. He said there were plants on his land that the neighbor's cattle would destroy. I wonder if Barnhart withholds folk's annuity money to force them to lease their land."

Sage thought back and then said, "I have a ledger book that supposedly shows the date and amounts of the annuity and lease payouts. Barnhart pays the Elipeenas in cash and then gives me a list of what he's paid out. I wonder just how accurate his list of numbers is."

"Well, one thing I've learned is that the Elipeenas believe lying is the worst sin," Eich said, "So, that makes their words pretty trustworthy. I think I have made friends with a couple. Maybe they will tell me exactly what Barnhart has paid them. If the amount does not match the numbers in the ledger, we can do a more complete survey."

"If you start asking, be awful careful. Something tells me that's the trail Inspector McConnell was following when he was murdered," Sage said.

Lucinda was the next to speak. "I think Dr. Defler is a good man. He is distressed about his lack of medical supplies. Sometimes, he buys stuff with his own money." She pointed at the cabinets lining one wall. "The Indian Service sends money to Barnhart that is supposed to be used for medical supplies and medicine. But, if you open those doors, you'll find the cabinets nearly empty. And, our two patients would be eating poorly except Defler tells me that when he demanded better food, he backed it up by threatening to file a complaint with the Indian Service. He doesn't think much of Barnhart—though he could be faking that, I guess." She frowned and added, "I'm afraid Defler's getting ready to quit out of frustration."

"So, Barnhart could also be skimming the medical funds. For sure, I can see what comes in from the government. Does Defler track what he receives?"

Lucinda raised and dropped her shoulders before saying, "I will try to find that out. I haven't searched his desk. But, he's asked me to help out with some of the reports, so maybe I can turn up something."

Sage was nodding but in his head, he was thinking how tired Lucinda looked. "How are your patients?" he asked.

"The little girl is improving and she's much livelier. She's gaining weight and her breathing is easier. As for the old man, well, it's just a matter of time. Dr. Defler has told the family. One of them sits by his bedside every day."

Mae harrumphed, her arms tightly folded across her chest as she said, "Well, I am doubly darn sure that scoundrel Barnhart is thieving the food the children raise. I've inspected that kitchen. There's lots of good food but they never get to eat any of it. I think that it either goes to some of the staff members or Barnhart sells it." Mae then went on to tell them about the stew glop, coarse bread, and Barnhart taking crates from the kitchen.

Sage said, "Interesting. The food is decent in the staff dining room where Lucinda and I eat. It sounds like the children are the ones he's cheating. It will be hard to confirm that he's selling the school's food. Do you think the industrial teacher, Adolph Brunner, is involved?"

"Wouldn't surprise me," Mae said in disgust. "He works those poor children hard. One other thing. Brunner also oversees the equipment the Indian Service buys for the school and for the Elipeenas he's supposed to be helping. Maybe there's something crooked there."

Eich spoke up. "I've seen the equipment he provides the Elipeenas. It's used, cheap, and antiquated. I wonder what purchases are shown in the records."

"Well, that's another investigation I'll need to make," Sage said drily. "It seems like anything involving money on the reservation might also involve some kind of swindle. You know, speaking of money... I am supposed to send a monthly student census to the Indian Service. Barnhart gives me the changes to make in the names." Sage's lips twisted. "Can you imagine, the government only provides $167 per child a month? That's supposed to cover staff wages, food, and other needs like wood for the boiler."

Mae asked, her tone thoughtful, "Just how many boys were listed on the last census?"

Sage thought back and then said, "As I recall, there are nearly fifty."

"Well, that's darn funny because I count noses every night and there are only forty. I bet the same thing is true in the girl's dormitory. I'll ask Christine Many Feathers how many girls she has in her dormitory."

"That's probably why Barnhart is so frantic to catch that runaway," Sage said.

"What runaway?" the other three choroused.

Sage shrugged. "I never heard his name. Just heard Barnhart getting all hysterical with the tribal police because they hadn't found him."

"Well, I think I've made friends with one of the older boys. His name is Joshua. I'll ask him who's missing," Mae said.

Sage stood up, "I guess we all know what we have to do next. I sure wish we could find out what Barnhart is keeping in his safe."

"Probably all his illegal booty," Lucinda commented.

"Unfortunately, he's always careful to lock it whenever he leaves and I'm no safecracker. I guess we'll have to leave the safe to whatever inspector we get to come here."

As they began readying to leave, Mae's voice stopped them. She told them how Willingham seemed to be spying on her for Barnhart.

"I bet you're right because the two of them are thick as thieves. Willingham's always in Barnhart's office with the door closed," Sage said.

Eich cleared his throat. "I don't like it that you are alone in that building at night, Mae."

She looked at him, her face showing a mix of tenderness and exasperation. "Yes, Herman I know you don't. And, I don't like it that you are sleeping in that dirty, unheated shack to keep an eye on me."

He looked shamefaced but made no excuse. Mae turned to Sage. "We've got to get him out of that shack. What do you think about sending for Matthew? We can say he's your nephew and you can pay Barnhart to have him stay in the dormitory and work alongside the other boys. That way, if something does happen, he'll be on hand to run for help. I think he'll also get more information out of the children than I can."

Sage looked between the two of them and said, "Herman, if we can get Matthew into the school, will you start sleeping in your room above the livery stable instead of in that outbuilding?"

Reluctantly, the ragpicker poet nodded. "I'll agree but I don't like being so far away in town should something untoward happen."

Sage nodded. "I understand. But we need you at your peak if we're going to get the answers we need from the Elipeenas."

They quickly planned the particulars of Matthew's arrival. Eich and Mae left first, leaving Sage with his "wife." After they left, Sage remarked with some satisfaction. "Guess one of Fong's pigeons will be flying home to summon Matthew. And," he grinned, "that will mean less pigeon poop to clean up."

TEN

"I am sorry it took so long, Charley. Those tribal police didn't pull up stakes until an hour ago. I don't know whether they hung around because they didn't believe me or because they don't want to find you," Indian Joe said, once Charley was fully awake.

Charley stretched, dusted off the few twigs attached to his clothes, and said, "I needed that sleep. It is the first I've had a full belly in many days. It helped me sleep better. I thank you, Uncle."

"Well Charley, it just so happens that "uncle" is the magic word. That Agent Barnhart sent a telegram to the Grand Ronde reservation in case you went there. So the Grand Ronde tribal police are also looking for you. Your Uncle Jack worried you would head into a trap so he came here. He turned up on the riverbank on the other side. Lucky he saw them Elipeena tribal police and hid until they left. He followed them a ways and then came back to wave me across. He said he's here to take you someplace safe. He's your mother's brother, isn't he?"

Charley nodded even as he felt a chill moment of panic. If he couldn't go to his relatives at the Grand Ronde, where could he go? He swallowed his fear and thanked Indian Joe once again. "You sure are going to a lot of trouble for me."

Indian Joe gave him a big grin. "Boy, your father once went to a lot of trouble for me. So, I'm glad I can pay off that debt. Being beholden is not a place of comfort."

As night fell, turning everything gray and black, they set out in Indian Joe's big rowboat. They drifted downriver beneath a moonless sky, with the stars tucked behind clouds. Many river bends later, Indian Joe guided the rowboat to a place where it looked as though molten rock had flowed into the river and froze. He'd been right. There'd be no tracks left where they landed.

Indian Joe whistled and Charley's Uncle Jack stepped out of the shrubs to snug the boat's rope around a boulder. Reaching Charley, he clasped the boy's shoulders with his strong hands. Even in the dimness, Charley saw his uncle's tight lips and the grim lines of his face. "Glad you are here, boy. Can you handle a long trek tonight? We cannot go to the reservation."

At Charley's nod, his uncle turned to Indian Joe. "Thank you, Joe, for your kindness to my sister's boy. Our family will not forget it. I must apologize but I cannot say where . . ."

Indian Joe threw up a hand. "No, do not say where you go. If I do not know, I cannot tell. Though if they ask me I might just tell them some big city downriver, like Portland town," he said, with his gap-toothed grin.

The uncle laughed. "Yes, tell them that. Trying to find a boy in that mess of people would eat time. Especially, since he will not be there."

Indian Joe untied his boat and was soon rowing upriver along the riverbank. Once he had rounded the bend and was no longer in sight, Charley's uncle went into the shrubs and returned with a small canoe and two paddles.

Charley's mouth dropped open in surprise. "You carried that all the way from the reservation? Why that must be thirty miles."

His uncle laughed. "No, I traded with a Kalapuya man who lives nearby. He liked my deerskin coat, the one your aunt decorated with beads. His canoe's small but it is sturdy. Come. We have a long way to travel. The river and its flow will shorten the journey."

Once aboard, Charley sat in the back and watched his uncle's smooth, powerful strokes. The clouds drifted east, making it easier to see the river's main channel. Deer abounded, raising their heads from the water to watch the canoe pass silently by. Soon they'd be heading to their bed-down place. Charley greeted each one with a silent assurance of safety this night. He now knew how it felt to be hunted. To the comforting sound of his Uncle's paddling, he let himself recall the horror that had sent him on this journey.

It was late morning when Matthew jumped from the train, eager as a young pup. Spring sunlight made his auburn hair shine and his skin glow beneath a sprinkle of freckles. He'd grown at least five inches taller since his arrival in Portland two years before. He'd turned up at Mozart's with his spirit shattered by his brother's murder at the hands of a railroad bull. Eich hadn't known him then, but he'd heard about Matthew's subsequent jailing for that same bull's murder.

Eich greeted the young man with genuine affection. Not only was Matthew an admirable person but he'd also aided their endeavors more than once. "I hope you won't mind taking an early lunch and sarsaparilla at the hotel," Eich said. "Attorney Gray has arranged for me to see a fellow in the county jail. After that, I've got to buy supplies before we set out. On the ride to the reservation, I'll fill you in."

Eich saw that questions were fighting to get out but Matthew held his tongue—a measure of his newfound maturity. Mr. Fong's martial arts training has given the boy more confidence and self-control, Eich thought.

After dropping Matthew at the hotel, Eich easily found the brick jail, with its iron-barred windows. A surly desk man greeted Eich, showing resentment at having to heft his key ring, unlock a door, and lead Eich down to the cells. The man slung a ladder-back chair before Red Hawk's cell and departed with an admonishment that Eich should hand the inmate "nothing" and the warning that he'd be back in fifteen minutes.

Eich studied the expressionless face of the square-jawed man who rose from the iron bunk. Once Eich quietly explained that Gray had sent him and that Eich was working with Adair to find Inspector McConnell's killer, Red Hawk stepped closer. He still said nothing, simply waited. Eich next stated the purpose of his visit. "Your son has run away from the reservation school. Your mother-in-law has disappeared, and someone tore your house apart. We don't understand what is going on and thought you might have an explanation."

Red Hawk briefly closed his eyes before turning to walk over to the barred window and stare up into the patch of blue sky. When Red Hawk crossed back to Eich, he quietly asked, "What else do you know, Mr. Eich?"

"Well, some of what I know might be reassuring. I spoke to a blind, elderly man who lives down the road from you. He said your mother-in-law is safe. He wouldn't say where she was. As for your house—a woman down the road, one who weaves baskets and hats, let me know that someone will straighten and lock things up at your house."

Red Hawk's stance relaxed slightly but his voice held urgency when he asked, "And, my son? What do you know about my son?"

"Ah, well. It was not until early this morning that I learned he had run away from the school. We know that Agent Barnhart has the tribal police looking for him. They are now searching off the Elipeena reservation."

"The Grand Ronde reservation—that will be where he heads. I did not see him before my arrest. I thought he was safe at school."

"Yes, we thought that too. But apparently, he ran away about the same time someone murdered Inspector McConnell."

Both men were silent, thinking about the implication of that timing. Red Hawk put their fear into words. "Sometimes, Charley sneaks home to see his grandmother and me. What if he saw something? What if he saw Inspector McConnell's murderer?"

"That's what we wondered. If he did, it would clear you."

"If the murderer saw him, he will kill Charley," Red Hawk said, panic surging in his words.

"That means we have to find Charley before the tribal police do," Eich said.

Red Hawk nodded. "He will go to my wife's sister's farm on the Grand Ronde reservation. That's what I told him to do if there ever was trouble. I showed him how to go to his Uncle Jack's. I never thought he'd have to do it. It is such a long way for a nine-year-old."

Eich was silent, thinking about leaving Mae in that awful school. Sure Sage, Lucinda, and Matthew would be there. But still . . . He took a deep breath and made a painful promise, "I will find your son."

Hope flickered in the man's eyes. "The husband of my wife's sister is called Mr. C. Jackson in English. Everyone on the reservation knows him as 'Captain Jack'. Do not ask a white man where to find him. Only ask an Indian. Most of them will keep silent. Just to be sure, do not mention Charley. Once you find Jack, tell him that I said, 'She Who Brings Flowers wove stars into her basket.' Then he will know he should help you."

"Here's the letter you're to say is from your mother," Eich said, pulling a paper from his jacket and handing it to Matthew as they bounced along a rutted road. Matthew unfolded the paper and read aloud, "Dearest John, I must go to Seattle to nurse sister Hetty. She has a severe case of influenza. Please take care of Matthew until I return. Your loving sister, Elmira."

"The plan is that you'll sleep in the boys' dormitory across from Mrs. Clemens' room, except she is called Mrs. Lofton here. If something untoward happens, you can alert Mr. Adair and Miss Lucinda. They are posing as husband and wife with the names of John and Lucy Adell. He's working as the reservation's clerk and she's working in the infirmary. Mrs. Clemens is the boys' matron."

When Matthew asked what might be going on at the boarding school and reservation, Eich quickly filled him in. When he finished, Matthew asked, "What can I do to help, other than keep an eye on Mrs. Clemens?"

"Foremost, make sure she stays safe. Barnhart doesn't like her and one of the teachers is spying on her. The other thing you can do is become friends with the boys and pick up what information you can. You'll be going to school and working alongside them in the fields. There's one Mrs. Clemens says is the natural leader, a boy named 'Joshua.' Maybe you can befriend him."

When Eich and Matthew presented themselves at the agency office, Sage jumped up to say with surprise, "Matthew! What are you doing here? Did something happen to Elmira?" He shot a meaningful glance at the open door to the inner office.

Matthew played his part well. "Aunt Hetty's real sick up in Seattle. Ma went to take care of her," Matthew handed the note to Sage, saying, "She wants me to stay with you while she's gone. If that's okay?" he added anxiously.

Before Sage could reply, Barnhart was standing in the inner office doorway. "Mr. Adell? What's this all about?"

Sage made a show of reading the note penned in Eich's elegant hand. He handed it to Barnhart saying, "It appears my sister has temporarily sent my nephew into my care."

Barnhart read the note and wordlessly handed it back to Sage who rushed on to say, "Do you think he could room with the boys, go to school and work with them? I'll be happy to pay for every day he's here." That offer put a gleam in Barnhart's eye as Sage had known it would. After all, those payments would be off the books and go straight into Barnhart's pocket.

Still, Barnhart's agreement was grudging, "Well, we can give it a try." He turned to Matthew and said, "If you cause any problems, you're gone on the next train. You understand?"

After Matthew dipped his head submissively, Barnhart turned to Eich, his tone hearty. "Well, what new items have you for sale today, Mr. Eich? I must say, I am beginning to look forward to your visits."

"Ah, I have some particularly elegant cravats," Eich answered as he followed Barnhart into the inner office. "Though, today is your one chance since I soon will be leaving these environs for a while."

Sage raised an inquiring eyebrow at Matthew who gestured toward the door and mouthed the word, "Outside."

ELEVEN

MATTHEW STOOD BESIDE JOSHUA AS the Indian boy patiently taught the white boy how to work leather. Ordinarily, Mae wasn't supposed to be outside, watching the boys at their morning tasks, but Brunner was off to Moolock, and Barnhart had assigned her the task of "keeping the boys under control." Christine Many Feathers was left overseeing all the girls as they worked at their tasks of sewing, laundry, and cleaning the school.

Matthew's quietly respectful and open attitude seemed to have won Joshua over. The fact Matthew had taken sad little Timmy Quirt under his wing, also seemed to help. Joshua was partial to the little boy who still cried himself to sleep. Mae vowed that next visiting day, she would take Timmy to see his ailing grandmother.

She'd been careful to treat Matthew as a stranger. She wasn't worried about the boys tattling. She'd never met such a group of closed-mouth youngsters. At the same time, their parents had also raised respectful, thoughtful, and well-behaved children. White parents could learn a thing or two from them.

No, it was that the sneak Willingham she had to fool. But, here in the barn and away from Willingham's spying eyes, she felt less restrained, especially given Joshua's friendliness towards Matthew.

"Joshua, you seem to have a knack for leatherwork," she commented as she stepped closer to the two boys. He flushed and flashed a grin. "I like working with my hands but making and repairing harnesses is a waste of time. It won't be long now until everything is motorized. I sure wish Mr. Brunner would let me learn to work on the tractor motor. It's always breaking down."

She recalled seeing that tractor churning across the school's fields. It looked like a relic of bygone days. "Doesn't the Indian Service give Agent Barnhart money to buy new farming equipment? I thought one of Brunner's jobs was to teach Elipeena men how to farm their allotments. Seems like he'd need a decent tractor to do that."

Joshua twisted his lips to one side as he paused, obviously weighing his answer. Finally, it came, "Well, I once saw a John Deere 4630 tractor. It was a beauty—green with yellow-rimmed dual tires on the back and two chrome exhaust pipes sticking up in front of the glass cab. It was brand spanking new."

Mae was struggling with how to get to the nut of the matter when Matthew picked up the inquiry. "Wow, did you see it in town?"

"No, it was right here at the school," Joshua said as he stabbed an awl through the leather to make a hole for the harness buckle's tongue.

Matthew and Mae exchanged a look over Joshua's bowed head. The boy's silence felt heavy and his stabbing angry.

At Mae's nod, Matthew cleared his throat and tried again. "Gee, I'm sorry I missed seeing that tractor. How long ago was it here? Where is it now? Maybe you and I could go look at it?" He turned to Mae to say, diffidently, "If that's alright with you, Mrs. Lofton, I mean?"

Joshua tossed the awl down on the bench and said, "Nah, it isn't on the reservation anymore. I saw Farmer Brunner showing it to that inspector fellow someone killed. Once he was gone, so was the tractor."

Later, after Barnhart drove away in his carriage, she'd left Joshua in charge at the leather shop and headed for the school. Slipping into the office, she quietly closed the door as Sage looked up from his ledger books.

Mae glanced around the office. "Where's Barnhart heading?" she asked in a near whisper.

Sage shrugged and also kept his voice low. "Good question. He said he had a meeting on the reservation."

He glanced out the window and said, "I watched his carriage turn to the northwest when he reached the road."

"What's up that way?"

"The building for tribal police and court. Nothing fancy. It looks to be a one-room operation," Sage said.

"Do you think they're still searching for Charley Red Hawk?"

"Well, I know Barnhart's still steaming mad about the police not finding him, because I heard him yelling at those two tribal policemen when I came in this morning."

"Do you think George Red Hawk is right? That his son is hiding out on the Grand Ronde reservation?"

"I don't know. I guess we have to wait for Eich to tell us. Something tells me that these folks will draw close if one of their own is threatened—especially if the fellow doing the threatening is a white man with a bad reputation—like Barnhart."

"Speaking of a bad reputation," Mae began and quickly told him about the missing tractor.

"Well, that is peculiar," Sage said. "I guess they could have sold it and pocketed the money. At this point, nothing would surprise me. Sounds like Adolph Brunner is in on the graft. I'll see if I can find anything in the files about a tractor."

He reached inside his coat to pull out two papers that he handed to Mae. "Those are lists of the names on Barnhart's student census. One list has the girls' names, so you may not be able to check them. But, at least you can check on the boys' names. Be careful who you ask."

The wooden floorboards outside the office creaked. Mae put a finger to her lips and swiftly crossed the room, flung open the door, and stepped into the hallway. She saw no one but a whiff of man odor lingered in the air.

She returned to the office and closed the door behind her. "I think that skunk, Weldon, was trying to hear what we were saying," she said before adding, "Good thing we were talking low."

"Except that, in itself, might alarm Barnhart. You better get back to the boys. You know what to say if asked?"

Grim-faced, she answered, "Yup."

The old man passed during the night while his family's murmured prayers caressed his ears. Lucinda stayed out of the room except to offer hot drinks during their vigil. The loving sounds from the other room were soothing as she dozed off and on beside the little girl's bed. From yesterday's conversation, Lucinda knew that the doctor was turning anxious over the child's rapid improvement. "These boarding school kids need better food. Cooping them up together just increases their risk of infection. Little Patty is still too weak to fight off anything else that might sweep through. I've lost more than one child to measles," Dr. Defler said.

He was sitting at his desk, his face sad as he added, "When a child at the school takes seriously ill, Barnhart insists they be sent home to their families or somewhere else. More than once, I've seen that sick child die because of the home's overcrowding, lack of sanitation, and insufficient food. And usually, before dying, that child gives TB to everyone else in the family. The poverty on this reservation is worse than anything I saw in New York City.

"But Patty's an orphan; she has no home, no relatives, so there was no place to send her. Typhoid took her mother, father, and baby brother. We nearly lost Patty to typhoid as well. So, the only place she can live is at the school. Right now, Agent Barnhart will let me keep her here until she's better because he doesn't want to see the school's death rate increase. But, recovery doesn't mean she's strong enough to survive in the school's close quarters and poor food. He doesn't understand that. He insists I return her to the school when she's better. And, that day is rapidly approaching."

"That man they arrested, Red Hawk, didn't his daughter die here at the school?" Lucinda asked.

"Measles. It was a simple case of measles. But the Elipeenas don't have as much resistance to the disease as do whites. She wasn't the only child who died. It swept through those crowded dormitories and most of the children caught it. Three of them died. She was one of them."

Lucinda pushed a little further. "Do you think that is why Red Hawk killed Inspector McConnell?"

His response won her over completely because his face was stern as he looked directly at her and said, "George Red Hawk killed no one. He's considered an upright, honorable man by those who know him. So, don't go repeating that slander. His arrest is a mistake. He didn't do it."

That was yesterday. Lucinda stirred and jumped up to hurriedly begin searching the papers on the doctor's desk. There was very little time before he'd arrive. Tamping down her feelings of disloyalty, Lucinda read yesterday's report on Patty Blake that Defler had sent to Barnhart and saw that the doctor had lied for the good of his patient. The report stated the little girl remained "critically ill and needed continued confinement at the infirmary." She felt a rush of affection for the frustrated doctor. He'd said the Elipeena reservation was his first Indian Service posting. She hoped it wouldn't be his last.

She peered out the window, noting that Defler still wasn't in sight. Shifting through Defler's correspondence, she quickly made a list of the equipment and medicines he'd asked Barnhart to obtain from the Indian Service. The plan was that Sage would see if Barnhart had followed through on Defler's requests and whether the reservation had received the supplies. If it had, it would be her job to learn whether those supplies had made it into the infirmary's cupboards.

Once Lucinda had the list tucked into her apron pocket, she sat down on her cot. It had been an exhausting night. She straightened her spine, told herself to "buck up," and went into the small kitchen to make coffee. Her workday wasn't over because Defler had asked her to stay for his morning eye clinic, saying, "You've got a gentle hand, Lucy. We've got to swab out a lot of eyes and administer copper sulfate. I'd appreciate you staying a few hours longer come morning." She hadn't been able to resist either the compliment or his appeal.

From the kitchen window, she saw Defler's buggy turn into the drive. The morning sun lit his slumping shoulders and her heart twisted. She was going to increase his despair with news of the elderly man's death. She hoped he'd not be angry that she'd let the family take the body away. She'd had no way to send word to him and, besides, there was nothing he could have done. Though he'd known Mr. Wolf was dying, she was sure Defler would feel sorrow at his passing.

She pushed her list deep in her pocket and composed her face. When Defler entered, she gently told him the news and watched his face fall.

He sighed and said, "I'm sorry we lost him. I'm glad his family was here. I wish I'd been here. It wasn't right for you to have to deal with that. Did they take Mr. Wolf's body?"

She nodded. "They asked and it seemed proper to me. I've already changed the bedding and cleaned the room. I hope that's okay."

Defler patted her on the shoulder and said, "I wish you could have known him. Gerald Wolf was wise, kind, and had a wonderfully dry sense of humor. You saw how much his family loved him. This winter was just too harsh. The Elipeena treaty requires the annual issuance of thick winter coats and blankets. Instead, Barnhart gives them the cheapest and thinnest stuff on the market. These elders have a hard time of it during winter's damp cold."

He heaved a sigh and turned businesslike. "I see that you've gotten everything ready for the eye clinic," he said, gesturing to the supplies she carefully arranged atop the treatment table. As if on cue, a timid knock sounded. The first patient had arrived.

The next hours were busy as a steady stream of people let her bathe their seeping eyes so the doctor could administer drops of medicine. Men, women, children, the young and the old, all quietly filed through the door, sat in the chair, and bore the treatment without complaint. Lucinda had seen isolated incidents of this eye disease before. But, never had she seen so many cases in one place. Sometimes her own eyes filled with unshed tears at their angry red lids. When they finally closed the infirmary door, Lucinda was bone-weary—not just from her labors but also because people's suffering tired her.

"Does that copper sulfate work?" she asked, pointing to the bottle containing a blue solution.

The doctor shrugged his shoulders. "With a few people, it seems to. What works far better is prevention—making sure people have clean water and healthy living conditions. Those two things are rare on most Indian reservations and on this one in particular. There's more trachoma on Indian reservations than on New York's Ellis Island. Like most of the Indian-killing diseases in this country, that's where trachoma comes from, Europe." He looked away and muttered bitterly, "There's too damn many blind and dying Indians."

As if to punctuate the doctor's anger, a cry sounded in Patty's room. Abandoning Defler to his bleak thoughts, Lucinda hurried to comfort the little girl.

TWELVE

"How'd you get away?" Gray managed to ask between mouthfuls of food. Sage marveled at how the man could shovel the food in and still stay skinny as a green bean.

Sage gave a flippant wave of the hand. "I told him I had to meet my lawyer here in Salem over a real estate deal. That caught his interest. The thought I might be dabbling in real estate made him look at me like I had potential. Or, else he was contemplating cannibalism."

Gray laughed. "You don't like him much."

"You know, at first, he seemed okay but as I delve deeper into the reservation records I'm coming to intensely dislike Barnhart." Sage leaned forward. "How's Mr. Red Hawk doing?"

That question triggered a conflicting reaction in Gray who shrugged even as his forehead wrinkled. "He's very worried about his son. As it stands, the case against him looks bad. We know the evidence was planted but how do we prove that? And, how do we convince the jury who will hear the case? I don't need to remind you, white male jurors are very closed-minded when it comes to people of different skin hues."

"Why isn't he being tried in the reservation's court? I thought that there's a tribal court with judges. From what Eich and Lucinda tell me, no one on the reservation believes Red Hawk killed that inspector. He's got a good reputation. The agent's ledger has many notations saying that Red Hawk is a 'good Indian.'" Sage went on to warn Gray about the recent notes stating the opposite. "The handwriting changed. I think they were written recently, probably after William McConnell's death."

Gray pushed his empty plate to the edge of the table, signaled for more coffee, and spoke only after the waiter left. "I'm new to the field of Indian law and I have to say, I've never seen such a convoluted mess. It's irrational and repugnant. That's how I got involved in the first place. But, I'll try to explain the jurisdiction issue."

Gray swallowed some coffee and leaned forward. "A major crime like murder is outside the tribal court's jurisdiction. They can only deal with minor crimes like theft, minor assault, contract disputes, liquor violations, public disturbance, and such. Even then, tribal courts can only rule on cases that take place on the reservation, and only if the dispute is between two Indians. If a white man's involved then the matter goes to state or federal court."

"Which is it, in Red Hawk's case—state or federal?"

"We're still haggling over that but I am certain we will end up before a federal judge because Red Hawk isn't a citizen—he's a dependent of the federal government."

"You've said that before and it strikes me as ludicrous since his people have lived in the Willamette Valley for eons. Why doesn't that make him a citizen with all the rights of a citizen?"

"It has to do with the fact that an Indian reservation has the status of a quasi-nation under the control and jurisdiction of the federal government. If he owned his allotment instead of it being held in "trust," we could argue he's a citizen because he pays property taxes to Oregon. Or, if he lived off-reservation, had a white ancestor, and we could show that he has been "living like a white man," the court might consider him a citizen. But, as it stands, the law sees him as a 'ward of the government'—as if he's a child."

Sage thought of the intelligent, dignified man he'd met in Gray's office and could only shake his head. It was clear from the way Gray was biting off his words that he was also disgusted by the state of Indian law. Sage felt a surge of sympathy. Normally Gray took pleasure in the law's logic and he relished using that logic to win cases. Apparently logic was absent when it came to the field of Indian law.

Gray wasn't quite finished explaining. "That question of citizenship is initially what got me involved. Red Hawk wants to stop his neighbor from encroaching on his allotment and destroying his traditional resources, roots, berries, and etcetera. He went to tribal court, since the violation was taking place on the reservation, but the tribal court said it had no jurisdiction because the neighbor is white. When we filed in state court the judge threw it out saying the state is without jurisdiction because the crime is occurring on the reservation. When we tried to file the lawsuit in federal court, the neighbor's lawyer argues that, because Red Hawk is not a citizen, he can't bring the lawsuit. That's where it stands right now. We have to argue the matter before the federal judge just to get the case heard."

"But, that all changes now that he's been charged with murder? The murder case can be heard in federal court?"

"As I said, the federal government does claim jurisdiction over major crimes on Indian reservations and it doesn't matter whether the defendant is a citizen or not."

For awhile each sat silent, immersed in his thoughts. Then Sage said, "I better fill you in on what we are discovering about Agent Barnhart and the reservation." It took another coffee refill before Sage finished listing all the ways Barnhart looked to be cheating the federal government and the Elipeenas.

Gray had been studiously taking notes. When he glanced up, disgust was writ large across his face. "So, you're finding that Red Hawk's claim about withheld annuity monies is just the tip of the iceberg?"

Sage nodded. "We're discovering more of that iceberg every day. Of course, now our task is to start compiling the evidence and getting it to Harry Lane. I presume he's the appropriate person?"

"I'll be back in Portland tomorrow and ask him as soon as possible. How do you propose to get it to him? Send it up with Eich?"

Sage shook his head. "Nope, can't do that. Eich's off the reservation, on the other side of the valley. Red Hawk thinks his son fled to the Grand Ronde reservation. He told Eich that he fears Charley witnessed the murder. If so, it explains why the boy ran away from school. It also explains why Barnhart is so desperate to find him—it suggests that Barnhart's involved in the murder. Anyway, Eich promised Red Hawk he'd find the boy and make sure he's safe."

They fell silent again until Sage said. "I think I need Mr. Fong here. He can take messages and the evidence up to you in Portland. And, given the scale of corruption we're finding, I am starting to worry about Mae and Lucinda's safety. Oh, and I forgot to tell you, we've brought Matthew down. He's making friends with the boys and keeping an eye on Mae."

Gray laughed. "Well, it's only right Mr. Fong come here. I bet he's irked at being left behind."

Sage had to laugh as well. "I am sure he is. But, I'll be damned if I can figure out how to insert a Chinese man into Moolock or onto the reservation. He can't skulk about in the woods. It wouldn't be healthy and he'd be noticed."

As Sage spoke a calculating look swept across Gray's face. "I think our Mr. Red Hawk can solve that little conundrum. Mr. Fong's cheekbones suggest an Indian connection. He could claim he's distantly related to Red Hawk." Sage knew exactly what Gray meant. Fong had the more prominent cheekbones of his Northern Chinese ancestors. It was unlikely the Elipeenas would fall for a "part-Indian" ruse but the whites might.

Gray looked thoughtful. "I've had more than one Elipeena send me letters saying they want to help. One of the most insistent has been Red Hawk's brother, Albert. I'll ask Red Hawk to write to him and request that Albert welcome their 'cousin, Wong.'"

Gray pulled out his pocket watch, started, threw his napkin on the table, and stood. "Wait for me in the hotel lobby. I am late for my meeting with Red Hawk. I'll get you that letter. Then we'll figure out how to get word to Mr. Fong."

Sage waved a hand and laughed. "Worry not. I have the perfect courier for that." As he watched Gray hurry from the restaurant, he mentally patted himself on the back. He finally had an excuse to get rid of the last little poop machine under his care, although he did find its lonely burbling a comfort at times.

"Say, I hear that Barnhart sure wants to find that runaway. What's his name?" Matthew asked as they stood in the hallway between classes. He already knew Charley Red Hawk's name but at the group's last meeting, they'd agreed that he'd get more information about the runaway if he pretended ignorance.

"Shh," cautioned Joshua. "We can't talk about that here."

Matthew lowered his voice, "Because of that sneaky teacher, Mr. Willingham?"

"Him and others," Joshua said. "Wait until our free hours. We'll go outside."

They parted, with Matthew heading to Willingham's history class. He had found the education here to be woefully behind that of Portland's schools. But, that was no surprise, since six-year-olds were learning alongside sixteen-year-olds in classes that ran only half a day. Mr. Willingham was a terrible teacher; ignorant and unkind to his students. In contrast, he found the Ojibwa teacher, Mr. White Cloud, to be as excellent as any teacher he'd ever had. When he'd pointed out that difference at their nightly meeting, Mr. Adair had an explanation.

"According to Dr. Lane, the Indian Service has been exceedingly slow in adopting civil service protocols. People are still getting their positions because of political patronage. That's how Barnhart got to be the agent here—some senator is his friend and a member of the former president's party. Barnhart, in turn, got his family and friends hired. That also seems to be the common practice.

"But things might be changing because President Roosevelt insists more Indians be hired. That's probably why Christine Many Feathers and Virgil White Cloud got their positions. Roosevelt also wants the Indian Service to fully implement civil service procedures. He's insisting on 'cleaning house' and doing away with the political patronage. Lane told me that corruption is rampant on the reservations and has been for decades."

He eyed Matthew before saying, "Try getting to know White Cloud better. See if you can tell where his loyalties lie. We may need him as an ally down the road if you decide he's trustworthy. It's my understanding that he's a relatively new appointment."

Matthew beamed in surprise. For Mr. Adair to trust his judgment in such an important matter was something new. He silently vowed he'd live up to that responsibility.

❀   ❀   ❀

Matthew met up with Joshua after supper. The Indian boy quickly led them away from the school toward the woods at the field's edge. Once they passed into the trees, Joshua struck off at an angle, taking a winding route and finally halting in a clearing where debarked logs encircled a rock-lined fire pit. "Wow, this is great," Matthew enthused with complete honesty.

Joshua looked uncomfortable and blurted, "Matthew, can we trust you? I mean, trust you not to tell Barnhart or anyone else about what I tell you?"

Matthew pondered the question. Joshua felt responsible for the other boys and did everything he could to keep them out of Barnhart's notice.

It made sense that Joshua was reluctant to tell a relative stranger anything that might boomerang back on the others.

"Maybe we should sit a minute," he said gesturing toward the logs. As they took seats, Matthew was undergoing an internal tussle. He'd not been authorized to share their mission with anyone but, in this moment, he needed to win Joshua's trust.

"Look, Joshua. I also need to tell you things you can't share with anyone. Not your parents, not your trusted friends, not anyone. Can you hold that trust as well?"

Joshua's dark eyes widened but all he did was nod solemnly. Matthew sighed and then took the plunge, albeit a small one. "My mother is not taking care of a sick sister. Uncle John asked her to send me because he needed my help. He's discovered that bad things are happening here at the school and on the reservation. I know that Charley Red Hawk is the runaway. My uncle and I are certain that Mr. Red Hawk did not murder the inspector. We think Charley knows something about it and that he's in danger."

Astonishment flitted across Joshua's face during Matthew's long explanation. Once Matthew finished, Joshua gazed at the treetops and said nothing. Matthew didn't press him. The one thing he'd quickly learned was that Indians tended to think long and deep before they spoke. So, the two boys sat on their logs, one eying the treetops, the other eying the thick woods around them.

Joshua finally cleared his throat to say, "This clearing is where we boys hold our top-secret councils. Here we can speak Elipeena to each other without punishment and eat our traditional foods." He toed the cold ashes at their feet. "Many a wapato root has been cooked in these embers; many camas bulbs have been boiled in these flames."

He turned to look directly at Matthew. "You said that you and your uncle think Charley is in danger?"

Matthew nodded.

"That would explain why the tribal police have been coming to the school so much. They questioned each of us boys but we said we knew nothing about Charley's whereabouts. Because Barnhart picks who gets to be a tribal policeman we do not trust them."

Joshua continued, "We don't know much. Charley snuck away from the leather shop late that afternoon to head home. His father left the reservation to go see a lawyer fellow in Portland. Charley was worried about his grandmother being alone. She has a hard time getting around.

He wanted to fetch water and firewood for her and come right back. We expected him to return before supper but he didn't. Next thing we know, Barnhart's calling him a 'runaway.'" Joshua raised empty palms. "That is all we know. We are also afraid for him."

"Is there any place on the reservation where he might hide?"

If anything, worry darkened Joshua's eyes even further. "Every day, I sneak away to look in those places and I can find no sign of him. He's not here."

THIRTEEN

Eich slowed the buckboard to look down the path Inspector McConnell had walked on his last day. As birds twittered and the undergrowth rustled, he thought about the man who'd loved trees and felt grief at the loss of him. He would have liked the inspector.

He reached the Red Hawk's and found a tidy yard and locked up cabin. He went on down the road, first visiting the blind man and then the basket-weaving woman, to tell them he'd be gone for a while. Both expressed regret at his leaving and gave him parting gifts: the old man a carefully wrapped parcel of venison jerky, the woman a beautifully carved ladle. Not for the first time, Eich noted that poor people were often more generous than wealthy people.

Returning to his buckboard and, with trepidation, Eich turned the wagon away from the boarding school and reservation. As the buckboard jittered and bounced, he fretted about abandoning his friends, old and new, to a bad situation. Still, Charley Red Hawk needed finding and so Eich headed steadily northwest. This time, he was crossing the valley on an oblique angle. His destination was the coast range's fir-clad slopes. His immediate goal was a distant ferry landing opposite the town of Independence. He knew there was a closer ferry, one run by someone called "Indian Joe," but it couldn't handle horses and wagons.

Eich marveled at the valley's lushness, green sprouts burst from every tree, bush, and field. There were a few stands of maple and fir but, mostly, the valley was a patchwork of tidy fields, many edged with manmade ditches to capture and channel the abundant rainfall.

He knew he was nearing Independence when he spotted fields of tall wooden poles connected by wire strands. With some justification, Independence called itself the "Hop Capitol of the World". Small green shoots were already poking from the hop yards' rich dirt. By summer's end, these fields would hold tall columns of hop bines drooping beneath the weight of pale green flower buds. He saw several hop driers, tall barn-like structures with drying kilns on the ground floor, and sturdy ramps to the second floor, where the hops were spread to dry in the kilns' rising heat.

The ferry crossing at the Willamette was busy and he had to wait in line for a place on the ferry's small deck. Once he paid his 20 cents and boarded, the ferry's steam engine began hauling the boat along a steel cable anchored to the river's banks. As the ferry drew near Independence, he studied its sturdy brick buildings, including a three-story one sporting a Queen Anne tower topped by a spire.

Minutes later his buckboard rolled down the main street in the late afternoon sunlight. Although spring rains would mire the dirt streets, he noted that the sidewalks were concrete, with ramps sloping into the street—a sure sign of a prosperous community. Today, both the sidewalks and streets were dry and crowded with people going about their business or engaged in friendly conversation. Overhead wires ran between wooden poles, putting Independence at the forefront of small-town electrification. Not surprisingly, given the hop yards, several saloons fronted the street.

He tied up outside a local provision store and once again used Sage's money to fill his buckboard with sales goods. Then he drove the horse to a stable, got assurance of the overnight security of his goods, and headed for the hotel with its octagonal tower. Once there, he climbed to the second-floor lobby and booked a room. After washing his face and combing his hair and beard, Eich descended to the street and bought a newspaper. Spying a likely restaurant, he entered.

He'd just begun eating an excellent roast beef dinner when the word "Injun" caught his ear. He glanced at the two prosperous-looking men sitting at a nearby table. From their conversation, he gathered they were hop farmers. Keeping his eyes focused on his newspaper, Eich strained to hear what the men were saying.

"Hell, yes, I'm going to hire me an Injun crew," one of them declared. "They're reliable, work harder, and complain less than those white folks you bring in. The Indians will keep working until it's pitch dark and I can pay them 90 cents per pound—ten cents less than what you pay the whites."

"What about all the hullabaloo they raise?"

"Heck, truth be told, I look forward to it. I like seeing them greet their relatives and watching their midnight dances and horse races and looking at the stuff they bring to sell. It makes the farm interesting for a bit. My wife and kids like it too."

"Hiram, you are one strange bird," came the other man's head-shaking response.

Eich smiled to himself, remembering his own experience with hop-picking Indians who had been traveling from Central Oregon to the Willamette Valley. They'd been eagerly anticipating their reunion with friends and relatives. They'd been interesting, kind, helpful, and generous.

❈   ❈   ❈

The next morning, Eich found the clay road leading to the reservation boundary mired from overnight rain. he let the horse slowly pick his way. He knew he'd crossed into the reservation when two men stepped into his path, with one raising a halting hand. Both were tall, of substantial build, and black-haired with dark honey skin. They wore dark blue police uniforms with big brass buttons, wide leather belts, and matching small-brimmed hats.

"Sir, welcome to the Grand Ronde reservation. May I ask your business here?" one asked politely.

"I was hoping to do some trading among the residents," Eich answered—completely truthful in part.

"Do you have a permit from the Indian Agent to conduct business on the reservation?"

Eich's brow wrinkled, "Why, no. I did not know I needed one. How do I obtain one?"

By this time, both men had advanced to the side of the buckboard. They weren't threatening but they were business-like and alert for any aggression on his part.

The older one explained, "You proceed down this road until you reach agency headquarters. It is located near the church and the school. But the Agent is gone from the reservation for a few days. Dr. Duncan, the reservation's doctor, is in charge but he's not in his office at present. He's off tending to a patient. You should wait for him, with your wagon, at the church." The tribal officer's face softened as he continued, "I believe you will find Father Bucher at the church. He always welcomes visitors."

The two officers stepped back and with a nod and a "thank you," Eich rolled westward. Many things suggested that the people on this reservation were a bit more prosperous than the Elipeenas. The road, itself, bespoke of greater resources being available to the reservation's inhabitants. A high center ridge and runoff ditches on both sides made it more passable than the off-reservation road he'd just traveled. A few of the houses and barns in the clearings seemed solidly-built and many looked new. Most of these had gardens, penned hogs, cattle, and had plowed and fenced fields ready for spring planting. Even the dogs charging his wagon looked better fed, unlike the Elipeenas' scrawny pups.

Still, shabby huts outnumbered the better homesteads. Built out of gray, unpainted vertical boards, they seemed to contain only one room and few, if any, windows. Most of their yards sported ramshackle sheds, small gardens, and a chicken or two.

He soon spotted the agency compound. It sat in a small valley, amid plowed fields, and was sheltered on all sides by wooded hills. The clapboard church's steeple made it easy to spot. It wasn't very big, having a footprint of only thirty by sixty feet at most.

Eich tied the horse to a hitching post, passed between white picket fences, and down the plank sidewalk. He was mounting the wooden steps when the church door swung open and a small white man in a priest's collar stepped out wearing a welcoming smile. "Greetings and blessings upon you, stranger," he said, holding his hand out to shake.

"Father Bucher?" Eich asked.

"That's me alright. From the looks of that wagon, you must be a trader needing a permit to sell on the reservation. Now, I know Dr. Duncan is absent from his office so you best come inside for a spot of coffee. He'll be passing by, see your wagon, and stop in. You needn't worry about missing him. Come on in," Bucher said with a slightly Germanic accent.

"I've just come from the Elipeena reservation across the valley," Eich explained as he followed the priest into the wooden building. It contained little; a few handmade benches before a crude lectern, a simple wall cross, and, beneath it, an altar table holding only two brass candlesticks and a small vase of spring wildflowers. The simplicity gave the room beauty. Eich thought it fitting that the church lacked the usual ornate Catholic trappings. Impoverished people didn't need their noses rubbed in wealth they'd never see in their own lives.

Bucher led him down the center aisle to a small door at one side of the altar. Stepping through, Eich found himself in the priest's living quarters. It was small and more Spartan than the church. He saw two ladder-backed chairs, a scarred table, and a small oil heating stove sitting atop a cookstove. The priest's bed was two planks atop two crates with a thin pillow and faded blanket. Two fruit crates nailed to a sidewall held a few food tins, two plates, and three cups. Eich thought the priest's living quarters made his own lean-to home look sumptuous.

"Please, sit down. I'm Father Bucher, but you can call me Felix. Tell me, are you Catholic in your faith?"

Eich shook his head. "No, Father. I am Jewish and my name is Herman Eich."

"Ah," Bucher said and sat down. Eich waited for the proselytizing or worse but it didn't come. Instead, Bucher said, "I have known many a good Jew in my lifetime. You are most welcome here. Tell me, which of Life's churnings tossed you upon our shores?"

Eich smiled at the turn of phrase and readily answered, "I was trading over on the Elipeena reservation and some of those folks advised that business might be better here on the Grand Ronde. Given what I've seen, I'm thinking they may be right. Some people's farms look more prosperous here. Though, I was surprised to learn that I have to get a permit to sell my goods to them."

Bucher was nodding eagerly. "Well, our dear people are still poor but, from what I've heard about the Elipeena reservation, there is a big difference between the two."

"Why is that, do you suppose?" Eich asked.

"It's not my place to say, but I will tell you that our Agent is very, very protective of people on the reservation. That's why you need the permit." While speaking, the priest poured out coffee that looked thick enough to float a spoon. "This might be a bit cool," he advised. "I only fire-up the stove for an hour a day, just long enough to boil my rice and coffee."

They drank in companionable silence until Eich asked, "I notice there is only a Catholic church here. Why is that?"

The question elicited a rueful shake of the head. "Former President Grant is responsible. He assigned every reservation to a church denomination thinking that the religious would handle education and charity. This reservation, here, was given to us Catholics. He assigned the Siltez to the Methodists. The Siletz is our nearest reservation. Since people on the two reservations are related to each other, either through tribe or marriage, you can imagine the problems that has caused. Not to mention the problems the Indians face if they want to belong to a congregation that has not been assigned to their particular reservation."

"What's happened to the native religion?"

A moue of distaste crossed the priest's face. "They're still holding their heathen dances and ceremonies. The agent has done his best to suppress them but they've just learned to hide what they do from us whites. Hedging their bets regarding the hereafter is what I think.

"The doctor will tell you that he has the same problem. He hollers and lectures his patients but it doesn't seem to matter. They'll still go to their black arts healers. The agent has threatened to withhold Indian Service supplies from folks but that didn't seem to work either. Those Indian healers claim they can take away pain and pull out disease. When people get sick, the drums come out, and they start dancing and singing. I guess it's an improvement that folks at least try to follow Dr. Duncan's instructions as well."

"Do the Indian healers ever seem to cure anything?" Eich asked.

The priest shrugged, "Some folks claim they've been healed. Who knows? I've seen some inexplicable things happen on this reservation."

Just then, they heard the sound of a door closing and footsteps headed in their direction.

Bucher smiled widely. "Ah, that will be our Doctor Duncan."

FOURTEEN

AFTER A ROUND OF PLEASANTRIES, Eich bid the priest goodbye and mounted his buckboard to follow Duncan's buggy to the agency office. Inside, papers covered every surface. The absent agent could do with a clerk of Sage's caliber, was Eich's immediate thought. The doctor motioned Eich toward a chair, offering no apology when Eich first had to clear the seat of ledger books that he piled on the floor.

"As Felix must have told you, I am standing in for the agent. Before I give you a permit, I need to make a few points perfectly clear. First, if there is even an ounce of liquor on that wagon, I will seize the wagon's entire contents and have you thrown in jail. Second, if I find you are overcharging the people, I will revoke the permit and the police will escort you off the reservation. Now, I understand that they have to pay a bit more than they would in town but, only a little bit because I know you buy your goods in volume so you get a discount on the price. Do you understand those conditions?"

Eich assured Duncan he understood and would comply. The man relaxed enough that Eich felt like he could ask a few questions. "Which tribe of Indians is on this reservation?"

Duncan huffed in exasperation before saying, "I see you don't know this reservation's history." He waved a hand toward the land outside his window and said, "There are at least 27 different bands of Indians on this reservation which means they originally spoke six different languages and innumerable dialects within those languages. Some were force-marched here from their original lands in 1856. Many of them died on that march. You and I may not know that history, but believe me, the people on this reservation do. How could they not? It was their grandparents, their lost way of life, and their lost lands."

Eich sat back, appalled at the dire upheaval those people had experienced. Then he forced his thoughts back onto his mission. He needed to know what questions would help him find Charley. To do that, he needed to understand the reservation better. So, he began with an easy subject, "Why are the reservation roads as good as they are?"

Duncan smiled ruefully, "That's one of the things the reservation's Indian legislature has done right. Every allotment holder has to pay a road tax and, if they are young enough and healthy enough, they have to spend a few days a year working on the roads."

"It sounds like you have problems with the legislature."

That brought a shrug from Duncan. "They could be more active in taking steps to see the Indians assimilate better. They are strict about alcohol but other than that . . . Problem is, they're elected rather than being appointed by the agent. Some of them are traditionals and that causes the problem."

"Father Bucher mentioned some traditional ceremonies and practices are continuing."

"Ignorance is always a problem with Indians," Duncan said.

Eich suppressed the challenging comment that came to mind. This man had to believe Eich was wholly on his side. "So, how are the reservation people surviving these days?" he asked instead.

Duncan passed a weary hand over his face. "They have the typical problems of most Indian reservations: poverty, ill health, susceptibility to epidemics. Over the years, they've lost their way of life. We whites have left them with almost nothing with which to make an entirely new one. Their tendency to cling to the old ways makes it even harder for them to assimilate. Of course, predatory and racist whites are also a big problem." The doctor's narrowed look following that declaration sent a message and Eich smiled to show the message had been received.

With those words, Eich relaxed. Dr. Duncan was not nearly as bad as Osborne Barnhart. According to Barnhart, the Elipeenas were responsible for every bad thing that happened. "I saw several plowed fields, and sturdy houses," he said encouragingly.

Duncan smiled. "They are making progress. This past summer, quite a number of the Indians purchased cows, horses, harness, wagons, and such. The crops, owing to a favorable season, also turned out well, with everybody having good grain and an abundance of hay per acre."

"Is there a lot of leasing to white farmers?" Eich asked, knowing this was true on the Elipeena reservation, though lease monies were one of the ways they suspected Agent Barnhart robbed the Elipeenas.

Duncan shook his head, a hint of pride on his face. "Very little leasing is done on the Grand Ronde. Quite a number of the people have taken an interest in farming and have made substantial improvements on their allotments. Those who want their allotments cultivated prefer doing it themselves." He leaned over the desk, his manner eager. "What is especially gratifying is that all the harvesting was done by the Indians with their own mowers, binders, and thrashers that they purchased with their own money. They received no help from the Government whatsoever. A great many also have gardens, raising potatoes and other produce for their winter needs. And, they are even operating their own grist and lumber mills."

He twisted his lips, "Unfortunately, a considerable portion of the tillable land was allotted to Indians who are now too old and physically unable to farm their land. Many have no children and they are unwilling to lease so their land lies idle. Well, not exactly idle, since they harvest traditional foods, roots, berries, nuts—things like that, to share among themselves."

Duncan brightened and now there was no mistaking his pride. "During the past year, ten houses were built, also five barns; and it should be remembered that all the work is performed by Indians. They fall trees on their allotments, haul the logs to the mill, help the sawyer, who is also Indian, to cut the lumber, haul it to their allotments, and then, either by themselves or with the help of other Indians, build the house or barn, whichever it may be. Of the fifteen buildings erected this year, not a day's work was done by anyone other than Indians, and these buildings compare very favorably with the houses and barns erected by white men in the area, making a good appearance and being very substantially put together."

"That is exactly what I observed when driving in." Eich said and added, in the hope Duncan would provide valuable insight, "The Grand Ronde presents a striking contrast to the conditions on the Elipeena reservation. I have trouble understanding why the two reservations are so different. Here you have some poor housing and some idle land but not nearly as much as on the Elipeena reservation where that's practically all one sees."

Duncan sat back in his chair and folded his arms across his chest as he considered his response. "Yes, I visited the Elipeena reservation once.

I am acquainted with Dr. Defler, the medical man over there. Good man, Defler. He has an impossible task."

Eich allowed the silence to lengthen to good effect because Duncan continued, "You know that the Elipeena agent position is an appointment?"

Eich nodded. Duncan continued, "I came here to Grand Ronde as its medical doctor without patronage from anyone. So, my appointment bypassed the usual political appointment scheme. That's not the case with the Elipeena reservation's agent. My understanding is that he had no Indian Service experience before being awarded the position. I gather he's some shirttail relation of a political bigwig."

Duncan held up a hand, saying, "I don't want to give you the wrong impression. Things aren't all that rosy here either. As I said, there's a lot of poverty and we just came off a measles epidemic last fall. Every child in the reservation's boarding school came down with it." A weary smile flitted across the doctor's face, "We didn't lose a single one of them. Still, the parents want a day school. And this last epidemic drove home the fact that having the children sleep in dormitories guarantees the spread of disease."

"Do the people here ever sell their land?" Eich had wondered why so few Elipeenas held free title to their land.

"Nah, those who have patents on their allotments tend to hold on to them. Recently, though, the Indian Service sold off some of the reservation's unallotted lands for a pittance per acre, shrinking the reservation from eight by twelve miles to eight by ten miles. Unfortunately, the town shopkeepers have been extending credit to the Indians in anticipation of the land sale proceeds. That's where the money for some of the Indians' improvements has come from. But, that credit is worrisome. The land sale should have brought in money to pay off the Indians' debts but it hasn't. The Indian Service is sitting on it and I suspect the amount will be a lot less per person than people think."

"What do you mean? Where did the money go if not to the Indians?"

Duncan raised his palms in the universal gesture of "who knows?" and said, "Over the years, I've seen tribal money go into Indian Service trust accounts but precious little of it seems to come back out."

Once he had a permit and was riding his buckboard, Eich didn't start asking about Charley's uncle right away. He had his name, C. Jackson. He figured pleasant conversations would eventually reveal the man's location. At least, that was his plan. Permit in hand, Eich rolled along the reservation's back roads, some of them not as well-maintained as the one leading to the agency grounds.

He thought about Duncan as his buckboard jittered over the potholes and jolted into and out of deep grooves. The doctor was typically dismissive of the Indian's point of view. Such white arrogance caused problems everywhere. Still, Duncan seemed an improvement over Barnhart. Maybe he and the reservation agent didn't view this reservation as a way to line their own pockets. But who knew? He'd been fooled before. Duncan's enthusiasm for folk's progress toward self-reliance was a good sign. If corruption was the goal, then creating dependency would make it easier. He'd seen that on the Elipeena reservation. But, poverty seemed endemic here as well, especially among those too old or ill or otherwise unemployed.

To his credit, Duncan sided with the parents who wanted a day school instead of the boarding school. He claimed that he'd been fighting for a reservation day school for the little ones and wanted the high school students to attend the public school in town. When it came to education, Duncan's position was 180 degrees opposite that of Barnhart's. Eich suspected that was because the Elipeena boarding school enriched Barnhart and his friends.

Eich reined in his horse at the first house he saw. He waited on the buckboard seat. The smoking chimney said that someone was home and would have heard him rattle up. Sure enough, the front door edged open to let a middle-aged woman peer out, a toddler clutching her leg.

"Good day, madam," Eich called, "My name is Herman Eich and I have some provisions for sale if you might be interested."

Suspicion slowed the woman's steps as she advanced toward the wagon with the young child riding her hip. A large yellow dog stayed protectively at her side.

"May I get down and show you the items I have for sale?" he asked.

At her silent nod, he carefully dismounted and went to the back of the wagon and began pulling the weather-tight crates forward. "I have sewing notions, various staples like sugar, flour, pepper, clothing, small hand tools, seeds . . . so many things that I can't name them. Is there something, in particular, you might like to see?"

She shrugged before asking, "Dress cloth? How much?"

He quoted a price that caused her brow to wrinkle. "Something wrong with it?"

He laughed and said as he pulled it from a crate, "No, no. It is of fine quality. I just got it at a good price."

She fingered the cloth and, for the first time, smiled. "Five yards, please." After making the exchange, she asked if he would like some coffee. He declined, explaining that he was just starting out but promised he would return the next day.

As the buckboard rolled down the road, he saw a young girl appear from inside the house. The woman grabbed her arm, said something, and gestured toward the woods. Eich saw the girl take off running. He suspected she was going to alert others to the new trader in their midst, one whose prices were much better than they'd find in town.

Of course, he was right. By the time he reached the next house, a woman was already standing on her porch. He spent the next hours making brisk sales and declining innumerable offers of coffee. During his visits, he couldn't help but notice that certainly, these folks were very poor. Still, most seemed less desperately situated than the Elipeenas. There were pigs, goats, cows, and most had gardens already planted. At each house, Eich introduced himself and asked the family's name.

It was not until the sun touched the coast range that he heard the Jackson family name. Unfortunately, only a teenage girl greeted him. She spoke English well, in contrast to many elders who'd used the Chinook Wawa he'd heard on the Elipeena reservation.

Unfortunately, the Jackson girl wanted only some flour and sugar and seemed to be in a hurry to make her purchases and end the conversation.

"I have some fine tools here that maybe your father would like to see?" he pressed.

She shook her head. "My father is not here presently."

"Maybe, I should come back later today. Is he off at work and returning this evening?" Eich asked. Her answer was discouraging.

"No, he is not expected later," she said firmly, before turning and trotting toward her front door.

Eich's hopes plunged. Where was that blasted uncle? The girl's nervousness suggested something wasn't quite right at the Jackson homestead. Maybe it meant her father was with Charley but Eich dared not ask that. It could be that the uncle had left the reservation without a permit. He'd forgotten to ask Duncan whether the Grand Ronde agent strictly enforced the traveling permit regulation. If it so, and Jackson was absent without a permit, the girl would say nothing about her father's whereabouts and he couldn't blame her.

"I'll be back around tomorrow, in case you need anything else," he called after her. The front door closed but not before she sent a nod back over her shoulder.

FIFTEEN

"I UNDERSTAND THAT LOFTON WOMAN was in here yesterday. What did she want this time?" Barnhart's tone was offhand but there was an edge to his question.

The agent's voice startled Sage since he'd thought him settled behind his desk in the inner office and hadn't heard him get up. He casually dropped his forearm across the list he was making as he turned toward Barnhart, twisting his lips in a show of disgust. "Oh, that! She came in yesterday, shut the door as if she had state secrets to impart, and demanded I immediately produce soap for the bathrooms." He shook his head. "As if I'd keep buckets of soap in my desk drawer!"

"So you find her troublesome too?" Barnhart asked.

"Well, she certainly doesn't lack for confidence," Sage responded drily but with an inward chuckle at knowing his answer applied to Mae Clemens as well as to Mrs. Louise Lofton.

"Humph, that's putting it mildly," Barnhart said before disappearing back into his office. Sage had just breathed a quiet sigh of relief when Barnhart again popped his head around the doorframe. "I need to dictate a letter. What are you working on?"

Sage jumped up, "Nothing important. Just putting some files in order." he said as he stepped away from the desk to forestall Barnhart coming close enough to see what Sage was working on. He had the medical file out and was comparing Defler's supply requests to those Barnhart made to the Indian Service. He was also comparing Barnhart's requests to the shipping documents that showed what the Indian Service had sent. Lucinda planned to inventory the cupboards and ask Defler a few carefully phrased questions to determine whether medical supplies shipped to the reservation ever made it to the infirmary.

It was nerve-wracking to work on the project while Barnhart was in the office but the timing had turned urgent. Fong carried a message from Gray when he arrived to stay with his "cousin" on the reservation. Gray wrote that the judge had scheduled Red Hawk's trial for just eleven days away. That meant they had very little time in which to discredit Barnhart as a witness and find McConnell's killer.

When Sage entered Barnhart's office he took the chair across from the agent who said, "I need to dictate a letter that you'll send to the Indian Service with a copy to the prosecutor in the Red Hawk case," he informed Sage before leaning back in his chair, closing his eyes, and beginning to dictate.

> Dear Commissioner Leupp,
> I write to inform you that Inspector McConnell's murderer has been arrested. He is an Elipeena by the name of George Red Hawk. He will be tried within the next ten days. I am to be summoned as a witness for the prosecution. I regretfully inform you that my testimony will result in Red Hawk's conviction since I have nothing positive to say about him and I have found a witness who saw Red Hawk in the vicinity of the murder shortly before the body was found."

Sage must have twitched at this last declaration because Barnhart paused and opened one eye to stare at him. Sage allowed his curiosity to show on his face but the agent's only response was to say, "The prosecution has asked me to keep the witness's name confidential so I will not be putting it in the letter nor will I be telling it to anyone else," This last was said somewhat repressively to communicate that Sage was included in the "anyone else" category. Sage bent his head to his pad and waited for Barnhart to continue.

> I ask that you use all the influence at your disposal to see that a conviction is obtained. Only then will Inspector McConnell and his poor family receive swift, full, and final justice. Sincerely, etcetera, etcetera.

Dictation concluded, Barnhart sat up straight and said, "See that you get that ready for my signature immediately. I will be going to Moolock in an hour or so and will mail it then."

❀   ❀   ❀

Mae had debated how best to find out if there were more children on Sage's lists than lived at the school. She finally decided to couch it as an attendance list when talking to the boys. She still wasn't sure how to broach the question with Christine Many Feathers.

That task was another reason why she was entering the boys' dormitory just before mandatory lights out. Not that the lights mattered. She'd changed the curtains so they covered only the bottom half of each window and let light in from the outside. It was also time for the story session. Tonight one of the boys would be telling an Elipeena story.

The older boys were quietly joshing each other and didn't stop when she entered the dormitory and advanced on their corner. She took that as a sign that they no longer feared her and that realization gave her pleasure. Still, she had to get their complete attention.

"Before we start with the story, I have a favor to ask you boys," she began. Once they settled down and were looking at her expectantly, she continued, "I have a list of the boys who are supposed to be attending school. But, the numbers don't match up with the number of boys staying here in the dormitory. I want to read some names and you can tell me what you know about them. Are you willing to do that?"

They all nodded, clearly intrigued by her query. She began reading down the list of names she hadn't recognized. Some of the boys were actually in the dormitory; she just hadn't learned their names. Those she crossed off. Then she came to Tyler Taylor. At that name the boys exchanged looks and one said, "Tyler died a year ago from TB." There were four other names where either the child had died or left school long ago or where they'd never heard of the child.

Sage said that Barnhart had sent these names to the Indian Service just the last month. What these absent children meant was that Barnhart was falsifying the school census to get more money from the Indian Service—$167 per month, per child. Over time, that would add up. Given the poor food, clothing, and such, she was certain Barnhart wasn't using the extra cash for the children's benefit.

The boys waited quietly to see if she was going to comment. They were to be disappointed because she silently folded the list, stuck it in her pocket, and said brightly, "So, who is going to tell us an Elipeena story tonight?"

It was another of their midnight meetings and Lucinda was scanning the list of shipped medical supplies and equipment that Sage had handed her. "I know I've never seen some of this equipment and if these supplies came in, Dr. Defler would have had to run through them lickety-split because we are way low on some of them and others just aren't in the cupboards. What are these numbers beside each entry?"

"Those are the dates of the shipping receipts. We can assume that's the date the supplies came in. As you can see, I only checked the last three months."

"Oh, boy. There's no way he could have used these supplies so quickly. Where did they go, I wonder?"

Mae snorted. "Into the back of Barnhart's buggy and off to someone willing to pay for them without questions," she said.

Fong's dark eyes were alert as he followed the conversation. "My new 'cousin' say on reservation, many people must go away for jobs. When gone, Barnhart take their land, lease it out. They never see money. He also show me government blankets agent give out." Fong raised a finger, "They so thin, I put finger straight through."

Sage shifted restlessly. They'd find his next bit of news discouraging. "Barnhart has changed the official records. He tore out the original ledger page describing George Red Hawk. Fortunately, I read it before it disappeared. He's replaced it with an entirely new one that makes Red Hawk out to be a long-time drunk, wife beater, layabout, thief, and liar. I'm sure he intends to present it in court."

"Whoa," exclaimed Fong. "That not what people say. They say Red Hawk man with virtue. Mix of old and new. They say he chief-like."

Sage held up a hand, "What you heard is true. That's what the entries said on the missing page."

"My new 'cousin,' Albert, also say Red Hawk thorn in Barnhart's side after old man die this winter. He say, nobody think Red Hawk kill inspector. Everybody know he helping inspector."

"Can't the Indians testify to that at the trial?" Lucinda asked.

"It's going to be an all-white jury. There's little chance they'd credit the words of Indians. Gray tells me that judges always let prosecutors tell the jury that an Indian's testimony should not be believed if it conflicts with a white man's."

That brought another derisive snort from Mae. "That's darn funny. What I've learned from the boys' stories is that the Elipeenas think the greatest sin is to tell a lie. You sure can't say that about the white folk's tribe."

"Well, there is that Italian story about Pinocchio and his nose growing," Sage said.

Mae scoffed. "That story is nothing compared to the Elipeena stories. Their stories about liars end in shunning or gruesome death. These boys take it to heart, believe me. I've never caught a one of them lying. If they don't want to tell the truth they just clam up rather than lie."

She turned to Sage. "What about the tractor? Where is it?"

Sage shrugged. "I took a chance and asked Barnhart about it. I told him I'd found an Indian Service transmittal letter about the tractor misfiled."

"What did he do?"

"Looked startled, then mad, then smarmy. Claimed an Indian farmer is using it somewhere on the reservation. He didn't say exactly where and sure changed the subject fast."

Fong shook his head. "I never see tractor. I only see horse and plow. I will ask. Reservation small. People know everything."

"Not everything," Sage said grimly. The other three looked at him sharply and he added, "They don't know who murdered Inspector McConnell. And, unfortunately, neither do we."

Mae left the infirmary first, by the back door, moving along the wall hidden from the school windows. Reaching the corner, she studied the grounds and saw no one. Looking up at the school, she confirmed that every window was a dark blank. Barnhart's house, like those of the teachers and Sage's, was on the other side of the school. Glancing up, she saw a huge black cloud scuttling in from the west. She'd wait until it blotted out the half moon's light.

As she waited, her thoughts strayed to Eich. She was a foolish woman—at her age she had no business being smitten by a man, and a ragpicker at that, for goodness sake. What was she thinking? Still, he was kind, thoughtful, wise, and he lived as he believed. He had a reason for everything he did and those reasons made sense and felt right. By now, he should have reached the Grand Ronde reservation. She hoped the folks there were as welcoming to him as the Elipeena had been. And, most of all, she hoped he'd find Charley Red Hawk safe and sound.

With a start, she realized the cloud had darkened the night. She hurried across the lawn toward the school's front door. Reaching it, she breathed a sigh of relief. She'd left the door unlocked and it opened silently. Once inside, she started toward the wide stairway leading to the upper floors only to halt, her heart freezing momentarily until she recognized the figure standing on the bottom step, blocking her passage.

"Mrs. Lofton, what were you doing out this time of night?" Barnhart demanded. There was a chill menace in his words.

Mae calmly removed her shawl and draped it over her arm. She also widened her stance like Fong had told her to do whenever she felt threatened. Still, the reservation agent was unlikely to attack her in a building full of people. She knew how to yell bloody murder and the girls' dormitory was just one floor away.

She sniffed at his intrusive question and snapped, "I couldn't sleep. I went for a walk and saw that Mrs. Adell was awake inside the infirmary so I stopped to visit. Not that it's any of your business."

Barnhart said nothing for a beat then he said, "Well, Mrs. Lofton, it so happens that it is my business because you left your charges alone and unsupervised while you traipsed about."

She nodded briskly to acknowledge the truth of his accusation and moved to pass him. Pointedly, he continued to block her way. Much as she twitched to give him a shove, she daren't do that. Sage and the others would be unhappy if she attacked their suspect this early in the game.

Finally, Barnhart moved to one side. As she started past he warned, "Don't let me find you leaving the children alone again. If you do, I will send you back to your son and his wife on the next train" he said, adding maliciously, "I can just imagine their overwhelming joy at your early return."

She raised her chin and steadily climbed the stairs, showing Barnhart neither anger nor fear. Only when she was back in her rooms, her back against the door and taking a deep breath to settle her nerves, did she ask herself the obvious question. "Why was that skunk Barnhart skulking around the school building in the middle of the night?" Then she remembered. The office door off the central hallway had been standing open.

SIXTEEN

THE WOODEN BUCKET THUMPED AGAINST his leg as Charley Red Hawk picked his way around ferns growing beneath the towering firs. Fetching water was to be his job—every morning and twice more during the day. He didn't mind. The stream was pretty, shallow, and so clear the rocks on its bottom seemed bigger than they were when he plucked them from its bed.

Yesterday, Uncle Jack had left him here and gone back to the Grand Ronde. He understood. For one thing, his uncle couldn't be found missing from the reservation. Not because he didn't have a permit, though he didn't, but because the tribal police would think he'd hidden Charley and they didn't want the police thinking that. Besides, Uncle Jack said he had to meet someone coming from back East.

So, Charley understood but that didn't stop him from feeling a hollow loneliness. He didn't know this place, he didn't know these people, and they lived different than he was used to. More than anything he wished he were leaning against his grandma's side, listening to her stories or standing in a stream next to his father, netting a silvery, speckled trout. Fear took over at the thought of never fishing with his father again.

It had been a quiet, drift downriver in a darkness broken only by the crescent moon and lanterns shining from farm windows. Only when drifting past Independence and Salem, did they see many lights and hear people sounds. After a long while, using swift, firm strokes, Uncle Jack sent the canoe onto the river's west bank

Clambering out, Charley realized they'd landed just south of a town. "Newberg" his uncle whispered. After concealing the canoe in shrubs as best they could, his uncle beckoned and they took off, walking through the darkest hours of the night, angling westward around the town. Minutes later, Charley stopped dead. Ahead stood huge, strange things, looking like the tops of cider jugs a giant had broken off and shoved into the ground.

Uncle Jack walked a few paces further before realizing Charley wasn't following. After turning back, he swiveled to follow Charley's line of sight. Nodding sagely and without any ridicule, his uncle said, "Do not fear. That is a brickyard and the tall columns are the chimneys of its ovens. The men who make the bricks harden them in those ovens."

Charley knew about bricks. Moolock had a single, small brick house. And, bricks lined the well the school used for watering the stock. He looked up at his uncle, trusted what he saw in his face, and started walking, though he stayed close to his uncle's side. Reaching the brickyard, Uncle Jack pointed out the stacked rows of bricks and the chimneys coming out the top of rounded ovens. Charley got over his fright but still thought the brick ovens spooky.

Once they'd passed Newberg, Uncle Jack led them into a stand of trees, and there they slept until the sun stood two fingers-widths above the horizon. After a quick meal of dried meat, they set off again, keeping to roads when the roads were empty, stepping into the brush or trees whenever they heard people coming.

As they walked, often in silence, Charley would sneak looks at this husband of his mother's sister. Uncle Jack didn't look like a valley or coastal Indian, even though he lived on the Grand Ronde reservation. He was tall and slender with a sharp nose, high cheekbones, and arched eyebrows. Charley figured that was because his uncle's people came from the Modoc and Rogue River tribes. They'd come north from somewhere in the far south of Oregon many years ago. There was a rumor that one of Uncle Jack's grandmothers had been a Chinook slave, though his grandmother refused to talk about it. "Sad times," was all she'd say.

Charley's grandmother, father, mother, and her sister, Uncle Jack's wife, looked like Elipeenas—shorter, rounder, with softer faces. They were strong and sturdy, perfect for climbing mountains and sneaking through woods. That's what his father said. Charley thought about how some ancestors warred against each other long ago. Now, they were mingling and marrying.

As they walked, his uncle told stories about the people who once lived on the land they walked on. Like his own father, Uncle Jack remembered the traditional ways and the history of the Indian peoples. "This is Kalapuya land, the band was called Yamel and other names but, today, mostly they are called 'Yamhills'. It means 'bald hills'," he said and pointed at a nearby hill Charley had noticed because treeless, smooth rock capped its summit. His uncle continued, "They kept this part of the valley rich in food by burning the undergrowth and by taking only the plants, fish, and game animals they needed to survive. They were peaceful Indians who did not make war on their neighbors—probably because they always had enough to eat. A few live on my reservation but most of them died in the early 1800s from white man's diseases.

He stopped and looked down at Charley with a sorrowful face. "Charley, nine out of every ten Indian people in this valley, and elsewhere in Oregon, died of white man's diseases. At the Willamette's mouth, there was a village where thousands of Multnomah people lived. Malaria swept through, and in a few weeks, it was a ghost town, home only to the dead."

His uncle squeezed his shoulder and started walking as Charley's imagination filled him with the Multnomahs' terror.

When the sun touched midpoint, they headed northwest, following the Yamhill River until it turned due west. At that point, his uncle led them along a smaller tributary flowing from the low hills lying directly north. They saw neither roads nor signs of human habitation as they began climbing. Some hours later, they reached the summit of the final hill. His uncle swept his hands in a wide gesture that encompassed the broad valley at their feet. "This was the land of the Atfalati, or as they are called today, the 'Tualatins'. They were another Kalapuya band."

He chuckled. "They liked the color red and wore beads hanging from their ears and noses. This is a rich valley. They lived more like white people. They had big family houses in at least 20 different villages. Smallpox and malaria, brought by sailors in the early days before white settlement, killed almost all of them." He heaved a sigh before saying, "They were a contented people."

They spent the night on the hillside overlooking the valley. As Charley lay gazing into the darkness, he imagined the happy, colorful ghosts of the long-dead Atfalati people floating above the plain below. Somehow, it was comforting.

The next morning, when they descended onto the flat, cultivated valley, dawn grayed the sky though the sun hadn't risen from behind the

Cascades. Uncle Jack led them across it at a fast pace. They aimed for the thickly forested hills of the coast range, walking along roads bordered by many farmhouses and fenced fields. It was during this march that Charley realized his uncle must have made this journey many times before because he never hesitated to consider the way ahead. He didn't need a star to guide him.

Once they'd crossed the valley and were in timberland, their pace slowed as they began following a rugged farm road deep into the mountains. There were a few crudely built houses in very small clearings. "And now," his uncle announced, "we are in the land of the Clatskanie. They were great hunters and makers of flint arrowheads."

"Were they Kalapuyans too? Like the Yamhill and Atfalati people?" Charley asked.

"No, they were from a different tribe and spoke a different language."

"Are they all dead?" Charley had noted the words his uncle had chosen.

"Only one lives. You will soon meet her. She is very old and is called 'Maria' but you must call her 'Grandmother' as is our way."

"Why did they speak a different language?" Charley thought his uncle sounded a bit impressed with the Clatskanie people.

His uncle gestured him to sit on a fallen log and, once they were settled and chewing on jerky, his uncle spoke. "There is a legend about the Clatskanie people. It may or may not be true. Grandmother Maria told me the story as she once learned it from her grandmother. All who know the truth departed many, many years ago." That said Uncle Jack cleared his throat and began.

Far to the north, in what is now Canada, there lived a great chief on the southern shores of a giant lake, called Great Slave Lake. His band was part of the Athapascan tribe and that was the language they spoke. This chief's wife gave birth to two twin boys. That tribe believed twins were a very bad omen and so twins were always killed at birth. The chief's wife knew this so she ran away with her babies to Indian people living far away on the ocean's edge. Only when the chief was dead, and her boys were young men, did she return.

But there was a problem. In the Athapascan tradition, a chief's eldest son became chief upon his death.

But standing before the tribal council were two sons, born at the same time. What was the tribe to do?

One of the chief's sons stepped forward and said he would leave the tribe and travel southward. Other young men, eager for adventure, said that they and their families would go with him. And so a band of Athapascan people began traveling south. Everywhere they went, they could not stay because other Indians had already claimed the land. Mostly, the Athapascans were allowed to pass peacefully. That ended when they reached the land of the Chehalis tribe in southern Washington. The Chehalis would not let them pass and made war on the Athapascans. Many died on both sides and many were injured.

The Athapascans who survived reached the Columbia River and traveled to its mouth. There they were taken in, nursed, and made healthy by the people of the Chinook tribe. Once the Athapascans were healed, the Chinooks gave them canoes and a guide. He led them upriver to land on the river's south shore.

The chief of the Clapsop band of the Chinooks came to drive them out of his territory.

As is the Indian way, the two tribes talked before battling. During this discussion, the chief noticed the Athapascans' very fine flint arrowheads. He was so impressed with the arrowheads that he offered to let the Athapascans live inland from the river, provided they gave the Clapsop people one hundred flint arrowheads each year.

This agreement was reached and the Athapascans moved into the hills above the river, to the place where we are right now. Later they became known as the Clatskanie. They were great hunters. The Clatskanie remained friends with the Clatsops who were famous fisher folk. The Clatsops would send their young Clatsop boys to learn from them about how to hunt in the Athapascan way.

Charley gazed around him at the thick forest, imagining that dangerous journey from the far north. They sounded like a strong people. "But what happened? Why is there only one of them left?"

His uncle sighed. "Some of them married people from other tribes and so maybe a bit of their blood survives. But almost all of them, except for a tiny handful, died in the 1830s when malaria infected the river mosquitoes. Grandmother Maria is the only Clatskanie left. Once she is gone, there will be no more Clatskanie. But, there are other Athapascans who now live on the Siletz reservation. Before that, they lived in Southern Oregon, some are called the 'Cow Creek' tribe and some are known as 'Rogue River' people. I am Modoc and Rogue River. So, maybe I carry Athapascan blood. The Navajo and Apache tribes who live down in the Arizona territory are also Athapascan. They were an adventuresome people."

His uncle stood, signaling his story was finished. Moments later they moved deeper into the forest along a deer trail that led away from the farm road and into wildness.

Rustling among the undergrowth jerked Charley out of his memories and back to the task of filling the water bucket. One of the camp dogs trotted up to sniff his ear. Charley sighed, scratched the dog's backend, just forward of its tail, and stood. If he didn't fill this pail with water and return to camp, someone would come looking for him. He was taking too long given that both bear and mountain lion roamed this forest.

Wading into the icy water to dip the pail, he thought about his Uncle Jack. On that hillside, above the valley of the Tualatin ghosts, Charley told his uncle what he'd seen happen on the path between the school and his father's house.

Silence had followed his tale as his uncle stared out across the valley. Finally, he'd turned to look at his nephew, his grave face sympathetic and kind. "Charley, my nephew, you will have to be very brave. The coming days will test your bravery. I wanted to stay with you but I cannot. I must return to the reservation as soon as possible. That means you must remain with strangers. They are good people who will care for you but they live differently from how we live on the reservation. They are very traditional. Will you promise that you will honor your father by respecting them and doing your best to be brave?"

Charley promised and now here he was, alone on the stream bank, in a strange, misty forest, with a full wooden bucket at his side. The faint sounds of the people he now lived amongst drifted to him. They spoke little English, forcing him to recall the few words of Chinook Wawa he'd learned from his mother before cholera took her away. He fought to hold back tears as he pictured his grandmother in her rocking chair and his father smiling proudly at him.

SEVENTEEN

Muted shouting snagged Sage's attention. Looking out the window, he saw Barnhart and a bearded man standing under the woodshed's slant roof. Barnhart's hands were punching the air. His stance was angry and aggressive. Earlier, Sage watched a loaded, high-sided fuel wagon back up to the shed. Barnhart was chastising the wagon's driver. Suddenly, the driver gave a two-handed shove to the center of Barnhart's chest. The agent stumbled backward and fell sprawling atop the pile of newly dumped wood. The driver leaned over and shook a finger in the cringing agent's face. After snapping a hand forward in a gesture of contempt, the man turned on his heel, strode to the wagon, and mounted the seat. With a jerk, the wagon took off.

Meanwhile, Barnhart clambered to his feet, dusted off his pants, and glanced toward the school. Sage quickly slid his chair back. He wasn't sure what had just happened or why, but he was certain Barnhart would not want anyone to have witnessed his humiliation.

Mae entered and closed the door. "I see that the swine is outside. You need to know that he caught me last night coming back from our meeting. I told him I couldn't sleep and stopped to visit Lucinda. I don't think he knew you or Fong were there but, he ordered me to stay in the building at night."

"Damn, that's going to make it harder for us to meet."

She nodded grimly. "I can legitimately visit Lucinda late afternoons when the children are supposed to be studying. That's how we'll need to relay information." She turned toward the door then swung back around. "I'm going to talk to Christine Many Feathers and ask her to check the names. Sage, I think the time has come to trust some of the people here. If she asks me what it's about, I'm not going to lie."

"Lucinda said the same thing about her doctor. Do what you have to do. Just be damned careful. Only tell her as much as you need to," he said. She nodded, opened the door, and stepped into the hallway.

He half rose from his chair when he heard her say sharply, "Weldon, shouldn't you be in your classroom boring the children instead of sneaking around peeking through keyholes?"

Sage didn't hear the answer but what he'd overheard was alarming. That damn Willingham was a problem.

Lucinda was quietly tossing used eye swabs into the infirmary's pot-bellied stove. Defler said that trachoma was highly contagious so he wanted her to burn everything it touched. She'd again assisted him with the eye clinic. Many of the same people had returned and she was dismayed to see very little improvement in their reddened eyes. Still, they reported that they felt less pain and seemed to see a bit better so she hoped the copper sulfate was preventing the condition from worsening. She suspected their positive responses had more to do with the Elipeenas' innate courtesy than with any improvement.

Gazing around the infirmary, her eyes lit upon Patty Blake busily drawing at the kitchen table. The little girl was much improved which meant she was also livelier, though she seldom smiled and never grinned. While both Lucinda and the doctor were glad she was recovering, it posed a problem. How were they to keep her improved health a secret from Barnhart?

Lucinda wondered if Patty was afraid of Barnhart. Every so often, she'd nervously glance out the window. Whenever she spotted the agent approaching the infirmary, she ran for her room, jumped into bed, and hid under her covers. Only after Barnhart left, could they coax her out. Lucinda wondered about the girl's fright. Still, their subterfuge couldn't last forever. She was afraid of Defler's reaction if Barnhart demanded Patty be returned to the boarding school.

Lucinda heaved a sigh that Defler noted. He was sitting at his desk, finishing up his reports on the morning's patients. "You must be tired,

Mrs. Adell. I am so sorry that I kept you but you are such a great help and our patients have taken to you."

Lucinda crossed the room to sit in the chair across from Defler. She studied the doctor, saw the deep worry lines etched in his face, and thought about his unfailing kindness to his patients. She took a deep breath but only said, "I've burnt all the swabs. We're nearly out of the new ones. And, we're down to our last bottle of copper sulfate solution. Shouldn't we order more?"

"I've asked and asked," Defler said, dropping his pencil onto the desk. "I don't know how the Indian Service expects me to doctor these people when we lack even the most basic supplies."

Lucinda took another deep breath. "Maybe the Indian Service doesn't expect you to do without."

His look sharpened. "What do you mean?"

She pulled the piece of paper that Sage had given her the night before from her apron pocket. "Two weeks ago, the Indian Service sent you two cartons of swabs, 1000 count in each carton. At the same time, they sent you five bottles of copper sulfate solution."

As she spoke, Defler was vehemently shaking his head. "No, they sent none of that. We never received any of it."

She raised an eyebrow and let the silence lengthen. An expression of dawning comprehension crossed the doctor's face. "Your husband, he's doing the agency books. You told him we didn't have supplies and he looked into it."

She nodded but said nothing as Defler continued following through on his thought. "That son of a gun Barnhart is selling my supplies, isn't he?" Atop his desk, Defler's two hands were white-knuckled fists. Doubtless, if Barnhart entered the infirmary that moment, the good doctor would launch himself at the agent's throat. "What else? What else was delivered that I don't know about?" he demanded through gritted teeth.

Lucinda began reading from the list in her hand: sterilizing equipment, forceps, suturing thread. It was a long list and Defler's face darkened at each item until it was a dusky red. When she'd reached the end, he jumped up from his chair and started for the door.

"No, wait!" she cried, panic raising her voice to a near shout. If he alerted Barnhart now, they might not find out who'd murdered Inspector McConnell. He froze at her alarm, halted, and turned around, "Don't worry," he said, misunderstanding her fear, "I'll say I got the information from someone I know in the Indian Service. I won't involve you or your husband."

She shook her head, "Please, no. That's not it. There's more. Come, sit down."

His reluctant steps telegraphed that he doubted anything she said could stop him from confronting Barnhart. Still, he returned to his desk and dropped heavily onto his chair.

Lucinda looked over at Patty. She was staring at them, her little mouth an alarmed 'o'. Lucinda smiled at the little girl. "Patty, honey, could you please draw me a picture of your favorite toy?"

The little girl nodded eagerly and bent her head over a fresh piece of paper. Lucinda turned back to Defler and began speaking in a low voice. "This involves much more than just the medical supplies. My husband and I agree with you that Red Hawk had nothing to do with Inspector McConnell's death. John has been carefully studying the agency's records whenever Barnhart is gone from the office. He's convinced that Barnhart is stealing much more than your medical supplies and equipment. He thinks Barnhart is robbing the Elipeenas, the school, and the Indian Service in numerous ways. John's trying to gather the proof. We think that corruption is what's behind the inspector's murder. If you confront Barnhart now, before we get that proof, he'll cover his tracks and do whatever he can to stop John."

Defler's mouth opened in speechless shock. When he saw that she was finished, he shook his head from side to side like a stunned bull. "My God, what kind of mess have I gotten my wife into? I knew things were bad on this reservation but I figured the Indian Service was stingy and Barnhart was incompetent. This is far worse than anything I could have imagined."

"Yes, it's bad, alright," Lucinda agreed lamely.

"Barnhart can't be doing all this on his own. Who else is involved?"

Lucinda hesitated and finally said, "It is easier to say who isn't involved. Right now, we think you, Christine Many Feathers, Louise Lofton, and Virgil White Cloud, aren't involved. Otherwise, we assume, until proved differently, that the rest of the staff are part of it, including the two who were temporarily transferred out, Barnhart's sister and nephew."

Defler narrowed his eyes. "There's even more to this than you're telling me, isn't there?"

"Dr. Defler, it is safer if you and your wife don't know anything more. Please trust me. And, please don't confront Barnhart or give any indication that you know that he's dirty. We need just a little more time to prove George Red Hawk innocent."

Mae Clemens sat on an outside bench beneath the leafing branches of an ancient white oak, watching the girls she supervised shaking blankets and beating rugs. Beside her sat Christine Many Feathers. She had quickly agreed to Mae's suggestion that the girls get out into the sunshine. Knowing Barnhart would object to the children being idle, the two women had created chores he'd find acceptable—beating rugs and shaking blankets.

"Mrs. Lofton, I worry about the girls. At their last weighing, every one of them weighed less than when they arrived at school last fall. That is the opposite of what should be happening." Christine's wrinkled brows emphasized that worry.

"You said you attended an Indian Service boarding school. What was it like there?"

The young woman gave a rueful laugh. "Well, it wasn't wonderful but at least nobody went hungry and the food was a lot better. My school was away from the reservations, far away. The students were taken from all over the country and never allowed to go home." She went silent, momentarily lost in memory.

Her tone was subdued. "They did everything they could think of to drive the Indian out of us: eliminating our clothes, hair, language, family—everything Indian was ripped from us. You know, that ole Indian Service plan to 'Kill the Indian to save the man.' That's why I wanted to teach at an Indian boarding school and, thankfully, President Roosevelt ordered the Indian Service to hire more Indians like me. So, here I am, doing my best to make it a little better for these Elipeena girls. When we are alone, we talk about their lives as Elipeenas and what it means to them. I tell them about being a Cherokee. We find common ground and experiences."

She turned to look straight into Mae's eyes. "I know about your late-night storytime. I've also heard that you have the boys teaching you the Elipeena and Chinook Wawa languages."

At Mae's startled look, Christine laughed. "You think the boys and girls don't find ways to talk to each other? Barnhart might think they're kept strictly separated but that's an illusion. Kids always find ways." She took a deep breath. "I told you this because the children trust you and, the one thing Indians are good at, is spotting liars. Good Lord, we've certainly had decades of experience."

Mae cleared her throat and looked around to make sure no one was within hearing. "Well, my Irish mother had a saying: 'There are three things we should never break: Promises, trust, and someone's heart.'"

She took Christine's hand and looked into her eyes as she said, "I promise I won't break your trust because I know it would break your heart. And," she paused to breathe before taking the plunge. "And, I must ask you to promise the same."

Christine squeezed Mae's hand. "I promise," she said.

"I have been working with Mr. Adell to uncover irregularities in the school census."

Christine looked puzzled. "I don't understand. What 'irregularities'?"

"We believe that Barnhart's reports to the Indian Service list more children living at this school than actually live here. I've compared the census names of the boys to the children in the dormitory. There are five names on the boys' census of children who do not live in the dormitory—in fact, one died over a year ago."

When she saw Christine hadn't made the connection she said, "The Indian Service pays Barnhart $167 per month for each child at the school. That comes to over $10,000 per year for just those five phantom children. Barnhart's salary is around $14,000 a year, you're making $6,000. So, his phony census brings in a healthy $10,000 bonus for somebody at this school. We just don't know who all is getting it—besides Barnhart."

Christine's dark eyes had grown huge. "Do you think he's charging for fictitious girls as well?"

Mae shrugged. "I don't know. I have no way of knowing because I don't know all the girls in the school," she said and hoped for the best.

Christine didn't disappoint. "Well, I do and if you give me that census list I can tell you right off who isn't at this school."

Mae glanced up at the school and spotted no one standing at a window. That sneaky Willingham was supposed to be in the classroom displaying his stunning incompetence as a teacher and belittling his students. She turned to Christine. "I was hoping you'd say that," she said, pulling the list from her pocket and handing it over.

EIGHTEEN

Eich's gut clenched as he headed toward C. Jackson's house. He'd spent his first night on the reservation in the buckboard's bed, under the tarp, between two crates, rolled up in blankets. If he didn't find Charley's uncle today, he'd have to make different arrangements for the coming night. He was getting too old for rough living. Everything hurt when he woke up and first moved.

Fortunately, the day dawned clear and he soon began his second day of rounds. This time there were more takers and fewer doors that stayed shut. Word of his incredibly cheap goods had spread. When he reached the Jackson's, he slowed. There was a buggy sitting in the front yard with a sleepy horse between its shafts. Hoping it wasn't Dr. Duncan's buggy, he climbed down from the buckboard. Despite the doctor's seemingly sincere ministrations, Eich didn't trust him.

He waited beside his buckboard and the door soon opened. A tall Indian man he'd never seen before stepped onto the porch and then down into the yard. He said, "I am sorry but we cannot talk with you today. We have a guest who has just arrived." The man spoke English well with a courteous undertone.

Eich shook his head and stepped closer, "No, I am not selling anything. Are you Mr. C. Jackson?

"Folks around here call me Captain Jack." At Eich's puzzled look, the man added, "Private joke, I'm Modoc. You can call me 'Jack.'"

"And, my name is Herman Eich, please call me 'Herman.'" Eich lowered his voice to say, "I have a message from George Red Hawk and I must speak to you."

Jack glanced around and then stepped closer so that he could speak softly, "What does the husband of my wife's departed sister have to say?" he asked.

Eich repeated the code words and saw that they struck home. The man's posture relaxed and he said, "Please come inside."

Eich shook his head. "No, I must first speak with you privately."

They moved beneath a tree and Jack listened as Eich told him their suspicion that Charley Red Hawk had witnessed something. He warned Jack that Barnhart had the Elipeena police searching for Charley. He could tell from the man's lack of reaction that nothing he said was news. Still, he persisted. "The trial is in just ten days. If Charley saw something, he has to testify. That is why I am here. I need to find Charley, learn what he knows, and get that information to Mr. Red Hawk's lawyer."

The man's considering look said he was pondering whether he should trust this itinerant trader. With his head, he gestured them toward a nearby bench. Eich began to hope that the man knew where Charley was.

That hope was both met and dampened. "My nephew is not on this reservation," were the first words Jack said once they were seated.

Disappointment pierced Eich. Still, the man had left a tiny opening that Eich took. "But, you know where he is?"

The Indian gave a slow nod. Eich felt encouraged. "Do you know what he saw?" Again that slow nod. "Would it help Red Hawk's case?" This time, Jack said, "Yes. Maybe."

Eich paused, wondering how he could get from these somewhat encouraging answers to being allowed to talk to the boy. Charley's uncle read him correctly because he said. "You came at the right time. Tomorrow, we go to the place where Charley is. But, the trip is long and it will be difficult to get there and back before the trial.

Eich gazed idly across the yard at the horses standing quietly between their respective shafts. Then he understood. "What if we take trains, would that be faster than the buggy and buckboard?"

Jack shook his head. "It would but I do not have that kind of money. Besides, we would also have to hire horses for part of the journey."

Thinking of the wad of bills Sage had pressed upon him, Eich persisted. "But, if we had the money to catch a train in the valley and then we hired horses, could we get there and back in time?"

That question brought a cautious nod. That was enough for Eich. He stood and said, "Money is no problem. Time is. When can we leave?"

Across the yard, the front door opened and a well-dressed man stepped onto the porch. After glancing at the two of them, he went to the buggy, removed a suitcase, and carried it back inside.

Jack looked at Eich. "We will go, but first, we will eat and plan our journey. It is too late to start today. We will leave early in the morning. I must sneak off the reservation because no one can know I am gone. You are right, Herman. The Elipeenas' boss man has his men and our tribal police looking for Charley. They have been here many times. They came early this morning, thinking to catch Charley asleep." His lips twisted. "When they came before, my daughter told them I was in the mountains, which they assumed meant I was hunting. Still, it was lucky I was back when they came today. I let them search. Maybe they'll stay away for a while. I was already planning to leave with my guest. Now the three of us will go."

Eich had no inkling why a "guest" would be going to where Charley was hidden but he merely nodded and told himself to be patient. All would come clear in time.

Eich followed Jack inside. The first thing he noticed was the shelves holding woven baskets and carved wood. He had to resist crossing the large room for a closer examination because the work was stunning in its skill and intricacy. Jack saw his interest and said with pride, "The weaving is my wife's work. The carvings are mine."

A man had stood at their entrance. He was the one who'd removed the luggage from the buggy. Holding out his hand, he said, "Hello, I am Gabriel Conteur." He wore a well-cut suit, tie, and vest. His round face looked intelligent with deep-set dark eyes beneath heavy brows. A small mustache with twisted ends grew above a firm mouth. He had neatly barbered black hair and smooth, tawny skin.

"Mr. Conteur is an ethnologist from the Smithsonian Institution," Jack explained and there was pride in his voice when he added, "He is the first Indian to hold that position."

Eich reached out a hand, saying, "I am Herman Eich, but I do not occupy such an exalted position in the world."

Conteur's eyes twinkled as he shook. "Let me guess: You are from the tribe of Israel, raised in New York City, and you attended Columbia University."

Eich laughed delightedly. "Got it on the nose," he said. He glanced around the room and saw the three of them were alone.

Jack correctly interpreted the glance and said, "My wife, the sister of Charley's mother, and the children, are staying with her parents. We can talk freely. I have already told Mr. Conteur about Charley's situation. We were discussing what to do when you arrived."

Eich was relieved. Charley's Uncle Jack's forthrightness made him instantly trustworthy. If he trusted this man Conteur, then it was all the better. His experience with Sage, Mae, Fong, and the others, had convinced him that the more minds tackling a problem, the more workable the solution.

The three of them sat around the kitchen table while Eich shared what he'd learned about the murder, the corruption on the Elipeena reservation, and his belief Red Hawk was completely innocent. The only thing he kept back was the fact that there were others involved in the investigation. These two men did not need to know that. If they didn't know, they wouldn't have to lie or, worse, tell. Jack was also reticent about sharing all his information. He'd only say they needed to make their way to the town of Clatskanie on the Columbia River.

The result of their talk was that the next morning before dawn, Eich's buckboard trailed Gabriel Conteur's buggy as both headed off the reservation. Near its border, the same two tribal policemen stepped into the road and stopped the buggy. Eich edged his buckboard around the buggy while waving a friendly hand at the policemen, both of whom had benefited from his generous goods pricing. He kept on going until he'd traveled half a mile off the reservation. Pulling to the side of the road he said, "As we figured, they stopped Conteur to search his buggy."

"Good," replied Jack from where he nested beneath a canvas tarpaulin they'd draped over the empty crates in the wagon bed. He made a small opening and looked at Eich to say, "It's best I stay hidden a while longer. We don't want to run into anyone coming from the outside. They'd notice an Indian and white man riding together, even if they didn't recognize me."

Hoof clomps and vehicle rattles sounded and Jack ducked back under cover. Eich glanced back and said, "It's Mr. Conteur." The ethnologist waved a hand as he rolled past, picking up speed. They'd left early. They needed to bypass the train station in the nearest valley town, Whiteson. Chances were too great that someone would recognize Jack.

At Sheridan, Eich and Conteur stabled the horses and vehicles before they boarded the train separately. Once Jack confirmed he recognized no other passenger on the train, he gave the signal and the three of them met in the dining car where Conteur finally explained why he was accompanying them.

"When U.S. soldiers ejected Oregon's tribal people from their ancestral lands and forced them onto reservations in the 1850s, some of them fled into the mountains. They are the people pulp fiction calls 'renegades'. There were renegades, like Geronimo, who fought back. Some others simply fled to remote places where they continued pursuing their traditional way of life. Can you see that, for an ethnologist like me, these renegades are a gold mine of information about the lifeways and cultural beliefs of the old times?"

Eich nodded he understood as Jack jumped in to say, "There are a few renegade camps in Oregon. Charley's hiding in one of them. Even before this all happened, Mr. Conteur was planning to interview that camp's people. His arrival is why I had to leave Charley and come back to the reservation. Also, I couldn't be found absent without a permit until I figured out what to do about Charley's situation."

Conteur took over again. "What I do is called 'salvage anthropology.' We're trying to memorialize the Indian history that disease, death, and boarding schools have all but eliminated."

"Who is the "we"?" Eich asked.

"Mostly, progressive Indians and our white allies."

"Progressive Indians?" Eich prodded, wanting an explanation.

Conteur sighed. "The purpose of the Indian boarding schools was to separate the children from their tribes and the culture of their tribes, to turn them into white-like citizens with no reservations. We believe the U.S. government intends to renege on all its treaty promises by claiming Indians are completely absorbed into the white culture. They call the process 'assimilation.' Once the Indians are all 'white' they can seize the reservation lands and ignore the treaty promises."

A smile crossed the man's face and he said, "But, it backfired on them."

Eich looked at the man across the dining table, thought of the harsh Elipeena boarding school, and wasn't so sure.

Conteur noted his skepticism and laughed. "It's true. I am a perfect example. They took me from my family in the Dakotas and sent me over a thousand miles away to a Pennsylvania school. For eight years, I never saw my family. You've told us about the Elipeena school. Well, mine was just as bad, except, I never got to go home. And, when I finally did, I had changed, I no longer fit in. I didn't fit in with my people and I didn't fit in with the white people either. One of our progressive Indians,

Charles Eastman, graduated from a highly ranked medical school. As a doctor, he fought corruption on the Rosebud Sioux reservation in South Dakota. The Indian Service fired him for those efforts. When he tried to be a doctor in Chicago, no white person would use his services, and the Indians there were too poor and too few to sustain his medical practice.

"As for me, fortunately, one of my school teachers got me a scholarship to a college in New Hampshire. Later, I acquired a white sponsor who helped me get the job with the Smithsonian."

Eich recognized the pain in Conteur's recitation but said nothing.

Conteur continued, "But, back to the reason boarding schools backfired on the white man's assimilation plans. I was educated in the white man's language, learning to read and write. I also saw the white man's hypocrisy, how time and again he ignored the written words of his god whenever it was convenient, or he wanted something that was morally wrong."

He leaned forward, eagerness infusing his words, "You don't think Roosevelt is changing the Indian Service because of white people, do you? Sure, some of our white allies have his ear but it is our words, our experiences, and our ideas they are putting into that ear. And, we progressive Indians plan on becoming much more vocal. We're going to establish a national society dedicated to furthering Indian rights. Most everyone involved with the Society spent time in an Indian boarding school. Those schools made us suffer but they also gave us the weapons with which to fight them. Plus, we got to learn that we had more in common than we had differences."

"But how does your study of the traditional Indian ways further your goal of Indian rights?" Eich asked.

"Because our work makes our people proud of where they came from, in who they are. It will give them the courage to stand up and demand their rights. They will see that, before the white invasion, it was the Indian people who were advanced and it is the greedy whites who were the savages. Extreme poverty, death, and the unrelenting and power-hungry contempt of the whites stole that awareness from our people."

He paused, drank some coffee, and then added, "And, whites need to see that their red brethren have something to teach them, something they need to learn. As my fellow student, Luther Standing Bear said, 'White men seem to have difficulty in realizing that people who live differently from themselves still might be traveling the upward and progressive road of life.'"

Conteur wasn't through. "Our traditional lives were without hypocrisy and truthful. Can the white society say that? Chief Black Hawk of the Sauk and Fox people once said, 'How smooth must be the language of the whites, when they can make right look like wrong, and wrong like right'. We Indians have been brutalized by the hypocrisy that cloaks the white man's greed."

"Do you think you can reach the hearts and minds of the whites with that message? After all these years, is not that a futile hope?" The question Eich asked was the one that frequently bedeviled his own heart whenever he, Sage, and the others launched yet another mission against the rich, greedy, and powerful.

Conteur seemed to understand because he gave Eich a sympathetic look. "Well, how we deal with the whites is a choice each of us must make. For now, my choice is reason and compassion," he said. "Let me tell you another story told by that same Chief Black Hawk about making that choice." Conteur's gaze momentarily turned inward as he gathered his words. Clearing his throat he said:

> An Indian grandfather was talking to his grandson about how he felt. He said, 'I feel as if I have two wolves fighting in my heart. One wolf is the vengeful, violent one. The other wolf is the loving, compassionate one.' The grandson asked his grandfather, 'Which wolf will win the fight in your heart?' The grandfather answered, 'The one I feed.'

Eich sat back in his chair, marveling at the grandfather's answer. In that pause, Conteur took another drink of his coffee and added, "In 1938, when wise Chief Black Hawk died, a white man stole his bones to exhibit in a carnival sideshow."

CHAPTER NINETEEN

LITTLE TIMMY QUIRT CHATTERED AWAY in Elipeena as his nimble fingers attached a wriggling worm to the handmade fish hook. Matthew smiled at Joshua over the boy's head. Their plan had worked. For the first time, the little boy was smiling and speaking in something other than whispered monosyllables. Of course, Matthew hadn't a clue what Timmy was saying but his happy chatter was gratifying.

Joshua wanted Matthew included, because he quickly translated, "Timmy says that he and his grandmother went fishing many times and that she taught him how to bait the hook. According to him, they caught a lot of fish."

After the obligatory Sunday religious service, the three of them set off across the fields and into the woods. Once there, Joshua led them to a small brook. They'd quickly found sticks to use as poles and Joshua had pulled both hooks and string from his pocket. Matthew doubted they would catch anything but it was peaceful sitting in a patch of sun, the clear brook at their feet, the birds twittering overhead.

Suddenly Joshua stiffened. "Did you hear that?" he asked, sharply.

Matthew had heard nothing but now he held his breath and listened hard. The words were faint but clear, Mr. Adair was yelling his name. He stood, faced the direction from which the call came, cupped his hands around his mouth, and yelled, "Over here!"

"No," Joshua said and jumped up. And, when Matthew turned to look at his new friend he was surprised to see the other's boy's face suffused with anger. At first, he was puzzled then he realized, this was another secret place—one known only to the boys. No adult was to know of it.

He rushed to reassure. "That's my uncle. He would never tell anyone about this place, I promise. We're, we're . . ." Matthew hesitated and then finally decided to take the plunge. At their last meeting, the others had told him he could use his judgment as to whether, and what, to tell Joshua. This was after Mae had sung the Indian boy's praises.

Matthew glanced down at Timmy, remembered that the four-year-old couldn't speak English, so no danger there. "Look, Joshua. My uncle and I are working on something together. He must really need me or he wouldn't have come looking."

That was not a satisfactory explanation for Joshua because his face stayed stormy as he spat out, "What something? You two are building something?"

Matthew gave a decisive shake of his head, only to think better of that denial. "Well, in a way, yes. What we are trying to build is a case against Barnhart that will cost him his job, maybe even send him to prison."

Joshua's mouth fell open before it snapped shut. He stared at Matthew for a beat as if carefully weighing the truth of Matthew's words then asked, "What can I do to help?"

It was at that point Sage stepped out of the woods. He took in their tense stances and the little boy sitting on the ground between them staring upward and open-mouthed into their faces. He shot an inquiring look toward Matthew.

"Uncle Adell," Matthew quickly responded, "I went ahead and told Joshua that you and I are trying to get evidence of Barnhart's corruption. He wants to help us," he said, hoping Sage would catch on, from his words, the limited nature of Matthew's revelations to Joshua.

Sage directed his attention to Joshua "Is that true? You're willing to help me and my nephew with this?"

Joshua nodded, saying "I'd be honored to help. My mother tells me hate is a wolf I should not feed but, if I did, I would hate Mr. Barnhart."

Sage gestured toward the little boy who continued staring at them. Glancing at Timmy, Joshua was quick to reassure. "Timmy has only lived at the school for a few weeks. The poor kid speaks only Elipeena and a tiny bit of Chinook Wawa. No English." He said something in Elipeena to the boy who nodded and turned to drop his worm-dangling hook into the water.

Once they were seated on a log lying beside the brook, Sage said, "Joshua, you understand that you must keep secret whatever we tell you? We don't know what Barnhart will do if he learns we are trying to prove he's corrupt."

"You think he has something to do with that Indian inspector's murder, don't you? You don't think Mr. Red Hawk did it?" Mae was right; the boy's mind worked lightning fast.

"Do you?" Sage asked.

"I am positive no Indian killed that inspector," the boy said. He bit his lip as he weighed what he wanted to say next. "But what chance has he got with a jury of white men?" he finally asked.

"Why are you certain he isn't the killer?" Sage wanted to know.

"Mr. Red Hawk is one of the most respected and powerful men on the reservation. We all knew that he was trying to make things better and that he was helping that inspector. Why would he kill the man who was trying to fix things for us?"

"Are people willing to come forward and say that in court?" Sage asked.

Joshua heaved a sigh. "They are afraid of Mr. Barnhart and what he will do if they try to help Mr. Red Hawk. He already keeps a lot of their money and supplies the Indian Service sends for them. Who knows what else he will do?"

"What about the Indian policemen? Are they afraid of Barnhart?" Sage asked.

Joshua's lips twisted. "Barnhart is the one who hired them. Nobody trusts the younger one, Ulysses, especially since his wife seems to spend more money on fripperies than anyone else. The other one, Victor? We're not so sure. Barnhart probably picked him because he's the best tracker on the reservation. If Barnhart is paying him extra, we've seen no evidence of it."

They'd left Joshua and Timmy fishing after Joshua said that he'd promised they'd catch a fish and didn't want to disappoint the boy. Yet another point in Joshua's favor, Sage thought.

As they headed back toward the school, Sage said, "Barnhart took the buggy out, saying he was going to Salem. That should give me time to really search his office but I need someone in the central hallway, making sure he doesn't return or that someone else doesn't come along."

"What about that sneak, Willingham? Mrs. Clemens says he's always creeping around."

Sage smiled. "Lucinda and Mrs. Clemens are going to picnic within sight of his house. If he leaves and heads to the school they'll let us know. Mae will claim she needs to fetch mustard from the school kitchen and she'll make a lot of noise when she comes in."

Sure enough, as they got closer to the school, they saw that the two women had a blanket, covered with various consumables, spread over the lawn between Willingham's house and the school.

Once inside the school, Sage posted Matthew in the central hallway to keep watch by peering out the front door's side windows. He entered the office and closed the door into the hallway. Matthew was to rap sharply on the door if he saw someone coming.

Sage used his thin, flexible piece of whalebone to slip the latch on the inner office door. He studied the small room. There was the desk with two chairs before it, a small filing cabinet, bookshelf, and, of course, that snug little safe in the corner. He tried the safe's handle and, as expected, found it locked. If Barnhart's corruption scheme included others, there'd be a second set of books showing payouts. They'd show different numbers than those in the ledgers Sage had seen. Maybe that safe was where Barnhart stored his ill-gotten gains.

He turned toward the inbox on the desk. Quickly thumbing through, he found what he wanted, the invoice for the recently delivered firewood. The school got charged for ten cords. Ha! He'd watched the boys stack the wood. There couldn't have been more than five cords. Good trick. Deliver one-half, charge for the full. The invoice heading said "Torben Fuel".

Sage crossed to the filing cabinet. The Indian Service required bids for supplies and services. The lowest bidder was supposed to win the contract. He'd searched the outer office without finding a single bid. That meant they had to be in this file cabinet. Sliding the drawer open, he said, "Eureka" upon seeing file folders, each one neatly labeled with the name of a supply or a service the school bought through contract. He'd just pulled the one marked "fuel" from the drawer when he heard a sharp rap on the outer door and Matthew's raised voice.

Quickly he shoved the folder back in its place, shut the drawer, and headed for the outer office. He wasn't fast enough. Before he could close Barnhart's door, the hallway door swung open and the teacher strode in, a red-faced, protesting Matthew trailing behind him.

"Ah, Mr. Adell," said Virgil White Cloud, "I see you are doing some snooping while Agent Barnhart is away."

Sage didn't try to deny the accusation. How could he? He looked at Matthew who'd fallen silent. White Cloud intercepted the look, "Your nephew is not to blame. He was keeping an eye on the front. The problem was, I came from the classroom upstairs. He had no way of knowing I was already in the building when you two arrived."

Sage waited. At this point, the Indian school teacher held all the cards. He and Matthew could only wait to see what hand the fellow was going to deal. The man's eyes danced as he grinned. "Who do you think helped get Inspector McConnell sent here in the first place?" he asked.

Sage pulled Barnhart's office door shut, tested to confirm it latched, and then stepped closer to White Cloud, holding out a hand. As they shook, Sage said, "Please call me 'John,'" before saying, "It looks like we're on the same side. You think Barnhart's corrupt?"

White Cloud's grip was firm. "And, I'm Virgil. I know Barnhart is corrupt. Red Hawk, McConnell, and I were working together, trying to find proof of it when the inspector was murdered."

"Do you know who killed him?"

"I wish I did. The three of us met the night before George went up to Portland to meet his lawyer. That would be on Saturday. He was to meet the lawyer and return the same day. It had to be a quick trip because George couldn't ask Barnhart's permission to leave the reservation. You have to explain why you want to leave. He couldn't do that.

"Besides, he and Barnhart had had too many heated arguments. Barnhart would not have given permission no matter what the excuse. He's a petty, vindictive man. George came back the night before McConnell was murdered. McConnell was on his way to see George. He hoped to learn what the lawyer had said."

"Do you think Barnhart knew George Red Hawk was helping McConnell?"

White Cloud heaved a sigh. "I don't have proof but George told us that he thought he'd seen one of the tribal policemen lurking near our meeting place."

"The one who seems to have a lot of extra money?" interrupted Matthew.

White Cloud sent a sharp glance at him, "It looks like you two are better informed than I thought possible. But yes, that one, Ulysses."

"What angle were the three of you looking at?" Sage asked.

"McConnell had only been on the reservation a few days. We gave him a list and he'd looked at the books. The last thing he told us was that he'd studied the ledgers Barnhart gave him and that everything looked on the up and up. He'd taken some notes and was planning on matching the numbers to what he found from talking to the school staff and the people on the reservation."

"So, he'd made a list of things to inspect but he hadn't started investigating them before he died?" Sage asked. When White Cloud nodded, Sage followed up, "Did he say what was on his list?"

White Cloud chuckled. "Well, I know he found some leads when he looked at Barnhart's paperwork but most of what he wanted to investigate came from what George and I told him. So, let's see, that'd be: medical supplies, food purchases, equipment purchases, school supplies, school farm products, the annuity, and lease monies."

He took a deep breath. "Actually, I'm here today because I planned to search Barnhart's office to see if I could find something helpful."

Sage grinned. "How's that for a coincidence? Before you came in, I found the fuel invoice. It looked to me that the school pays for twice the amount of wood that is actually delivered."

White Cloud nodded. "Since the school was deathly cold all winter, that doesn't surprise me."

"What about the school census?" Sage asked.

"What do you mean?"

"It looks like Barnhart is charging the Indian Service for more students than live at the school."

"Well, that wouldn't surprise me but we hadn't thought of that." White Cloud was silent as he considered that angle.

"Where do you think Barnhart was making his biggest haul?" Sage asked.

"George was sure it was the annuities and lease payments. That's one reason he wanted to talk to the lawyer."

Sage asked the most important question. "Do you think Barnhart killed Inspector McConnell?"

There was regret in White Cloud's headshake. "I know he didn't. When McConnell was killed, Barnhart was in Moolock, having a long luncheon with a number of his suppliers. I had followed him there. Besides, like all bullies, Barnhart is a coward. He wouldn't have the guts."

"What about ordering it done, then?"

This time White Cloud nodded. "Most assuredly, he could do that without a qualm."

Sage silently wondered how much he should reveal to the teacher. Matthew shot Sage an intent look before giving a slight nod. Sage knew

White Cloud only through casual mealtime conversations that revealed the man to be intelligent and well-spoken. Still, he knew White Cloud went out of his way to be kind to the students. Matthew, on the other hand, sat in White Cloud's classes and talked to the boys about their teacher. He decided to trust Matthew's instincts about the man.

"Actually, I was in the lawyer's office for that meeting. I met George Red Hawk. That meeting is why Matthew and I are at the school," he said.

Before White Cloud could respond, the door swung open and Mae Clemens poked her head in to say, "That little snake is slithering this way." Then she spied White Cloud. "Oh dear," was all she said before pulling the door shut. Matthew jumped to the door and quietly turned the key in the lock as Sage looked at White Cloud and put a finger to his lips. White Cloud raised an inquiring eyebrow but Sage said nothing about Mrs. Lofton.

They could hear her out in the hall, asking someone where the cook kept the mustard. The three of them held their breath as they listened to her chattering while she led the man towards the kitchen.

White Cloud said in a low voice, "George planned to ask everyone on the reservation for firm numbers on how much money Barnhart gave them for their annuities and leases. Then McConnell was going to match that up with what the ledgers showed. Now, with George gone, I don't know how to make that happen. Folks might trust me enough to talk but I can't leave the school to ask them questions. And, I doubt very much they'd tell you anything. Besides, you have the same problem I do. Barnhart would note your absence."

Sage's smile was grim. "Well, I know exactly who can ask those questions for us."

Before he could explain, they heard Mae's voice and footsteps returning from the direction of the kitchen. "Thank you for helping me find the mustard. I would have had to open every single cupboard. I didn't mean to interrupt whatever you were planning to do. Anyways, why are you here?" They heard a low murmur in response and then she said sprightly, "Oh, you know, I've never seen those classrooms. Since you're just picking something up maybe I'll come along and take a peek."

Sage chuckled as he imagined the look on Willingham's face. "He better not turn his back on her. She might bean him one just for the pleasure of it."

TWENTY

ALBERT RED HAWK AGREED THAT they'd get better answers if Albert asked the questions. Fong's job was to write down the numbers next to each name and keep the list safe, just in case.

They had visited most of the houses and, while people cast curious glances at Fong, they obviously trusted Albert because they answered readily enough. The sunlight was angling sideways through the tree branches as they walked a well-trod path to an unpainted hut surrounded by alders. An old woman appeared in the open doorway when Red Hawk called. Her face wreathed in smiles, she graciously invited them inside and offered them tea she obviously couldn't spare. They declined the tea but took seats.

She reminded Fong of the elderly women back home in China: tiny, less than five feet tall, with black button eyes that nearly vanished into her wrinkles when she smiled. Fong saw that she'd lost most of her teeth.

A cot stood against the wall, with a thin, faded blanket tossed aside. She must have been lying down. A spring chill filled the unheated hut. She tucked the blanket around her shoulders when she sat on the cot's edge. Albert began asking questions. Her voice was breathy and weak. Frequently, a phlegmy cough interrupted her words. Tuberculosis, Fong thought. He glanced around the one-room hut. Little food stood on the open shelves in her kitchen area.

Just as he had at the other houses, Albert introduced Fong as his cousin. Inevitably she raised the same disbelieving eyebrow. Albert went on, explaining that Fong's grandmother had married one of Albert's

Elipeena cousins in Chicago. Like the others, she listened to his explanation with a knowing nod. After all, poverty forced many Elipeena to leave the reservation for work in the cities. And, once they were away from their people, who knew what strange things they got up to? This little old lady was no different than everyone else they'd met that day. She accepted the cousin story with a toothless grin.

Under Albert's careful prodding, her information was much the same as the others. In her case, she was supposed to receive a monthly annuity check. Earlier Albert told Fong that this money was payout from a trust fund the Indian Service controlled. The money came from the sale of land the Elipeenas had given to the government under a treaty negotiated in the 1850s.

"Grandmother, our people are concerned that you may not have received all of your annuity money," Albert said.

She gave a disgusted sniff, "That Barnhart. He miss payment day every time. This year, he cheat me out of one whole month." She got up and crossed to a nearby shelf. Pulling a paper from a pouch, she returned and handed it to Albert. "You see, I track. Barnhart tricky. See, dates are each month I get the annuity money. It comes later each time until one whole month missing. Also, before Barnhart is boss man, amount was $45. Now it is $35. He does not explain why I get less money and only get money eleven times in twelve months."

She sat on the cot again and crossed her arms. Her bottom lip stuck out and she said, "He think we Elipeena stupid people."

They were stepping from the old woman's path onto the main trail when two policemen blocked their way, one young and the other at least a decade older. The younger one spoke, his stance and tone belligerent. "Hold on a minute, you two," he commanded, his hand raised. He looked at Albert, "Who's this fellow you've got with you, Red Hawk?"

Albert went through his explanation. The man listened with narrowed eyes that studied Fong. Switching his attention to Red Hawk, he said, "What are you two doing?"

"I'm just showing my cousin around the reservation, introducing him to friends."

"Ha! You must think we're stupid," the young policeman said, a near echo to the old woman they'd just left. He turned to Fong. "What's your name and what are you doing on the reservation?"

"English too small," Fong returned and looked at Albert for assistance.

"What's your 'cousin's' name?" came the demand.

"Wong Tam. He is just passing through on his way to Seattle and stopped to say hello. Why are you giving us such a hard time, Ulysses?" Albert asked.

Fong could tell Albert was becoming uneasy. If anything, the younger policeman's agitation grew with each passing moment. Fong looked at the older policeman. He'd taken a few steps back as if he wanted to distance himself from the younger man's aggression. His face reflected embarrassment and his stance was tense.

Ulysses' tone was snide as he said, "Right, Albert. Now, how about you explain why you and your cousin are asking people about their Indian Service money?" He openly sneered as he added with heavy emphasis, "And why your cousin, who claims he doesn't speak English, understands enough of the words to be writing a list?"

Obviously, someone had told this Ulysses what they were doing. The policeman turned to Fong and held out his hand. "Give me the list Wong Tam, or whoever you are."

Fong stepped back as he shook his head. Their information was almost complete. Sage had written the names down alongside the amount the ledgers showed each Elipeena had received from Barnhart. In a separate column, Fong recorded the amount the person said he, or she, had actually received. Not only was there clear evidence of Barnhart's corruption, but the names were in Sage's handwriting. If Barnhart saw that handwriting, he'd know who wrote it.

The policeman stepped toward Fong, as expected. That step moved him further from Albert and positioned him in front of the other police-man. Fong glanced at that older officer, who said, "Ulysses, leave these men alone. We don't have a right to look at whatever list they are making."

The younger man snapped, "Agent Barnhart said I'm in charge, Victor, not you." Behind Ulysses the man, Victor, raised his hands in surrender and stepped back, signaling he wanted no part in whatever was to follow.

"I said, give me that list. Now!"

Ulysses' voice rose, but Fong detected a slight tremor. Whether it came from excitement or fear, he couldn't tell. He retreated another step and Ulysses followed, his face flushed with anger. What came next needed to happen so that no one blamed Albert. Fortunately, the two of them had prepared for this.

"Give him the list, Cousin Tam," Albert said to Fong.

Fong silently shook his head and again stepped back, again causing Ulysses to follow and increase their distance from Albert and the older policeman. Good.

Ulysses stood a good six inches taller than Fong and carried nearly twice as much weight. No doubt his size had helped him intimidate others on the reservation. Certainly, his movements were confident. He was a bully, which was probably why Barnhart picked him to police his fellow Elipeenas.

Fong took a deep breath and said in perfect English, "You may not have the list."

"Hah," exclaimed Ulysses even as he charged forward, his hands reaching to grasp Fong. Instead, he grabbed air and staggered from overbalancing.

Victor tried one more time. "Leave him alone, Ulysses."

"Shut up, Victor!" spat Ulysses as he charged again.

Although it was no trouble evading the clumsy oaf, it was time to end it. So, instead of sidestepping the grasping hands, Fong moved forward. When Ulysses' left fist swung in a roundhouse punch, Fong snapped his left hand down on Ulysses' elbow at the same time his right grabbed the striking hand and twisted the policeman's body so that Fong could deliver a powerful blow to the man's left ribs. Ulysses gasped and Fong gave him a hard shove that put him on the ground.

Albert began shouting, just as they planned, "Stop it Tam! Give him the list. Don't fight him!" Albert ran forward, jumping between Fong and the man on the ground. At the same time, Victor stepped forward, though not with great speed. Briefly, their eyes met and Fong suspected the older policeman enjoyed the sight of Ulysses' walloping.

Albert continued with his act, angrily shouting at Fong to hand over the list while effectively blocking the path so Ulysses couldn't start a second round.

Fong merely shook his head, said, "No" before turning to run away down the path. He got a good head start because he heard Albert trying to sound helpful and then apologizing for getting in the way of Ulysses's pursuit.

Fong lay on the nest of hay, a heavy blanket keeping him warm. The hay smelled fresh and sweet. He'd certainly slept rougher in days past. He let his mind drift. First, his thoughts landed on his wife, Kum Ho. She ran their provision shop while he worked at Mozart's and helped with Sage's various missions for the labor leader, Vincent St. John. Never did she voice a single complaint. She was a good wife, a great treasure.

Next, he thought of other rough times, like that long trek southward into Arizona, trailing the man who led a gang that robbed and murdered thirty-one gold-panning Chinese men on the Snake River. He chuckled softly. He hadn't found the fellow. Instead, the man turned up in Portland years later. But Fong hadn't exacted revenge, Sage had. Sometimes, Fong wondered whether the fellow had survived being shanghaied onto that rotted whaling ship. It had been heading to the deadly Bering Strait where many men died—especially shanghaied men.

Distant laughter disturbed his ruminations. No doubt Albert was once again re-enacting Ulysses' defeat, despite the fact he was doing so long after midnight. Apparently, Albert's fellow Elipeenas disliked the young policeman. Not so, the older one, Victor. Surprisingly, that fellow had sent word that Ulysses planned to conduct an early morning surprise raid of Albert's place. Victor also let Albert know he was suffering from a severe stomach ache and wouldn't be able to track the Chinese man who'd cracked the young policeman's ribs.

Fong smiled in the dark, gratified that he'd read the older policeman correctly. But Victor's information had sent Fong into the shed. Albert had removed a board at its rear so that Fong could disappear into the woods within seconds. He'd get plenty of warning because Albert had posted some of his friends in the surrounding forest. They'd owl hoot three times if Ulysses or any other policeman appeared.

Fong thought their willingness to help wasn't solely because of Albert's friendship. It seemed the Elipeenas held George Red Hawk in great esteem. During their investigations that day, he'd heard many praise the jailed man and vehemently declare his innocence. He gathered that many considered George Red Hawk to be the Elipeena people's unelected chief. Like Sage's crew, many said they believed Barnhart's corruption was behind the murder.

His thoughts flicked back to Sage. Fong had slipped through Sage and Lucinda's back door before returning to Albert Red Hawk's. Lucinda was getting ready to leave for the infirmary. She greeted him with a hug and a cup of coffee.

"You practicing snake and crane moves?" he asked her.

"Every day, out behind the house. It's too small inside here." She gestured around the tiny house with its minuscule living room, bedroom, and kitchen alcove. The bathing room was a tin tub on the kitchen floor, and the toilet was a one-holer in the back yard.

Sage wasn't surprised when he stepped into the house to find Fong there chatting with Lucinda. Like any married couple, he and Lucinda kissed before Sage dropped into a chair at the table and accepted coffee from Lucinda.

Sage smiled. "Good to see you, my friend. Is George's brother treating his 'cousin' alright? Do you have any results yet?"

"Albert very kind. Happy to help. Good results, very good results," Fong answered. He handed the list to Sage who scanned it quickly.

Sage went over to the hooks by the front door, removed a piece of paper from a coat pocket, and handed it to Fong. "That's the list of Elipeenas and the kinds of blankets, coats, and other things they should have received from the Indian Service last fall. It'll be up to you and Albert to discover what Barnhart actually gave them."

Fong eyed the list and then said, "Might be hard, now. Police on my tail. We will try."

Sage shrugged, "Do what you can," he said and took his seat again. He smiled at them both before saying to Fong, "I've already told Lucinda but you need to know that we have acquired three very willing recruits. They now know that we're trying to get evidence against Barnhart and want to help. Matthew told Joshua, Mae told Christine Many Feathers, and I told Virgil White Cloud. That makes four since Lucinda already has Dr. Defler on board.

"It turns out that it was White Cloud's letter about the boarding school that Red Hawk gave to Dr. Lane. According to White Cloud, his letter is what finally got the Indian Service to launch Inspector McConnell's investigation. At least, that's what McConnell told him. White Cloud also said that he, McConnell, and Red Hawk, met and planned how to get the evidence. Since McConnell's murder and Red Hawk's arrest, White Cloud's been trying to do it on his own. Turns out, he was intending to break into Barnhart's office when he found Matthew on lookout, and me, red-handed, coming out of Barnhart's office."

Lucinda turned eagerly to Fong, "The three of them nearly got caught by that sneak. Weldon Willingham. Luckily, Mae saw him coming and was able to warn Sage."

Now, some hours later, Fong stared at spider-webbed roof beams overhead and thought about his own luck that day. If that Ulysses carried a gun, their confrontation might have turned out differently. He sighed, wondering just how long their luck would hold.

TWENTY ONE

SEPARATELY, THEY STRODE THROUGH PORTLAND'S cavernous, marbled train station. When they met on the sidewalk outside, Jack asked them to wait and hustled back inside, leaving Eich and Conteur to stare at each other. When Jack returned, he held a yellow telegram.

"A friend works at the reservation agency. I asked him to keep an eye on things." He handed the telegram to Eich who read it aloud. "Seen on Sheridan platform. Stop. Two following. Stop."

The telegram needed no translation. Someone had seen Jack boarding the train and told the tribal police who were now on his trail.

"We better not wait two hours to catch the train," Eich said. "At least, we better not catch it from this station," he added more slowly before turning decisive. "Come on, you two need to wait someplace safe while I go find us transportation."

They trailed him away from the station and along the tracks until all three stepped into a copse of alders and evergreens. Blackened fire pits spoke of hobo camps, though only birds and squirrels moved about the woods. Eich turned to them saying, "I know of a nearby stable and they know me. I'll come from that direction," he pointed east across an open field. "I'll be driving a closed van with the back door unlatched. Come across the field and jump in when you see me. We'll catch the train further down the river, at Linnton. If they ask around the station, no one will be able to say we boarded another train. With luck, that means they'll think Portland was our destination. "

In less than half an hour, Eich reined a one-horse transport van to a halt at the side of the nearby road. Gabriel and Jack trotted across the field, jumped into the van, and slammed the double doors shut. With Eich's "giddy-up" and a jerk, the van began rattling north out of the city.

Less than hour later, the hazy smoke of a sawdust burner drifted into the van's backend as Eich reined in the horse. When he opened the rear door, he said, "I have to deliver the van to the stable here. Someone is coming to fetch it. The Linnton train station is at the bottom of the hill, head on down there and I'll meet you."

The two men clambered out of the back, dusted off their clothes, and headed downhill toward the small railroad station while Eich clucked the horse into a trot.

It was late afternoon when their train made a quick stop in Clatskanie. They were tired but agreed two well-dressed Indians and a scruffy white man checking into a hotel would be too memorable. So, once again, they waited while Eich went off to hire three horses. It was dusk when he returned leading horses with rolled blankets tied behind each saddle.

Jack raised an eyebrow at the sight of their mounts. Eich had seen the pastured horses behind Jack's house. They'd looked powerful and well-fed while these three drooped and their haunches were bony. After a shrug, Jack jumped into the saddle like a teenager, Conteur was not quite as limber while Eich's struggle to mount was stiff and accompanied by grunts.

Mounted, the three of them headed south toward the hills, Jack leading the way. Once they came out of the woods at the base of a trail heading upwards, Jack said, "We'll have to go separately up the trail because it lacks overhead cover and can be viewed from the riverbank. The three of us together will draw too much attention."

He turned in his saddle to say, "Gabriel, you go first. Keep going until you are past the farmhouse at the top of the ridge. You'll see a stand of old firs. Wait there. Herman, you'll go after Gabriel and I'll bring up the rear. It'll be dark by then but I know the trail. We can't make our destination tonight," he told them, "So, once I join you, we'll find someplace to sleep."

It was drizzling the next morning when they unrolled from their blankets. Fortunately, they'd settled down beneath the dense boughs of a drooping cedar tree and stayed dry. They wasted no time, waiting until they were in the saddle before chewing their dried meat breakfast. Jack led them along obscure trails, down into gullies to ford small streams, and over thickly timbered ridges.

Eich's thighs began protesting the unaccustomed horseback riding. Just as he was about to request a halt, Jack raised a hand, and they stopped. He dismounted, tied his reins to a tree branch, and walked back. "Wait here. We are close. I will go first to make sure it is safe and we will be welcomed." With that, he turned, trotted down the faint trail, and disappeared around the shoulder of the hill.

Conteur and Eich looked at each other and then Conteur dismounted. "Ouch. I haven't sat a horse in years," he told Eich. "I hurt places I didn't know existed. You want to get down too?"

"I don't know if I'll be able to get down," Eich responded.

Conteur tied his horse, took hold of Eich's harness, and reached a hand to help him dismount. Once on the ground, the ragpicker rubbed his thighs, trying to revive their feeling. On every side, towering firs swayed and creaked as a brisk wind pushed against their crowns.

Jack was gone a long time. Once he and Gabriel had walked out their kinks, both took up posts on fallen logs. The squirrels had silenced their warning and the surrounding life returned to normal as the men became lost in their own thoughts. A movement on a nearby tree caught Eich's attention. Turning, he looked into the curious black eyes of a dark brown, light-striped chipmunk that quickly skittered out of sight, only to cautiously peek at him from behind the tree trunk's cover. Eich contemplated the chipmunk's ancient Douglas fir. It was enormous compared to those he'd seen on the Elipeena reservation, or anywhere else for that matter. This was an old, untouched forest. He wondered how long it would remain so. How it must have pained the Indians to see tall giants like this one chopped down, cut up in pieces, and shipped far away.

A Stellar jay dove between the tree branches, its shack-shack-shack call stirring a memory. He reached inside his coat and pulled out McConnell's notebook. He opened it to the last pages and read them yet again. Somehow, it seemed fitting to contemplate the words, a way to honor the man who was the reason Eich sat here, waiting to learn about the inspector's last moments of life.

Jack appeared on the trail and they both stood. To Gabriel, he said, "Grandmother Maria is willing to talk with you. But, she is very old and tires easily. Are you prepared to stay a few days?"

"I certainly am. Is she willing to talk about her people, their language, myths, and practices?"

"Well, I didn't put it that way. I just said you wanted to write down the old ways of her people."

Jack turned to Eich. "I've told Charley that he can help get his father out of jail if he tells you all that he remembers. But, I must warn you. His memory has holes. I haven't tried to force him to remember what he has shut from his mind. That will be up to you."

He led them, and the three horses, along the trail and into a clearing. There was a large, windowless house, with hand-hewn plank walls, and a roof of hand-cut cedar shakes. A wizened old woman squatted before a fire in front of the house. "These folks live in the Chinook style, all sleeping in the house together. It is best suited for the rain," Jack said in a low voice as they crossed the clearing.

Movement in the surrounding woods made Eich wonder whether others were watching from the shelter of the trees, as curious and cautious as that chipmunk. When they reached the woman, Jack said some word in what Eich recognized as Chinook Wawa, before saying Conteur and Eich's names. She dipped her head politely at each of them before fixing her gaze on Conteur. He stepped forward and also said a few halting words in the jargon. She smiled at his efforts and patted him on the arm as if encouraging a child. Then she said a few words and gestured toward the open door behind them. The two soon disappeared inside the house.

Moments later, a boy appeared in that same doorway. He was small but sturdy, his face softly rounded, his hair black and grown shaggy since his last boarding school haircut. His dark eyes took Eich's measure before he looked towards his uncle. At Jack's nod, the boy's jaw tightened in determination and he stepped toward them.

"Mr. Eich, may I introduce you to my nephew Charley Red Hawk," Jack said with formality. "He is the son of my sister who has departed and George Red Hawk."

Eich reached out a hand to shake and, after some hesitation, the boy took hold with a slim hand that held some firmness. Eich began to hope.

"I thought we would go sit by the stream to talk," Jack said as if asking permission from the young boy who still had not uttered a word. Even now, the boy simply gave a silent nod, turned away, and crossed the clearing to a path. As they trailed him down the path, the rushing sound of a stream grew louder. Charley led them to a big leaf maple, its unfolding leaves already providing shade from the spring sunshine.

Its exposed, mossy roots stretched a good distance out from its huge trunk. Charley sat on one of the roots with his uncle close beside him. Eich sat on the moss-covered ground, his head level with the boy's, in the hope he'd seem less threatening.

'Charley," he said quietly. "I am trying to help your father. We think that you may have seen something that can help us do that."

The boy nodded but what he said was, "Mr. McConnell was a nice man. He gave me candy. My father liked him." The boy's eyes filled with tears. And Eich let him sit with his grief. Once Charley had swallowed his emotion, Eich said. "Joshua wants you to know all the boys miss you. They worried when you didn't come back to the school."

"I miss the fellas too. But I couldn't go back to the school."

"Why?" Eich asked.

"Because the grizzly bear would get me."

That was an unexpected conversational turn but Eich didn't show his surprise, instead he gently prodded, "Grizzly bear, what grizzly bear?"

"The grizzly bear that killed Mr. McConnell."

"Didn't a man kill the inspector?"

Charley paused before saying, "The grizzly bear wore clothes like a man but he had red eyes and fur all over his face. And he made blood, blood fly into the sky. It fell all over the bear." The boy shaking and his uncle put an arm around his shoulders and held him close.

Eich pondered Charley's description. Maybe it had been a bearded man the boy saw. He had to try. "Charley, could it have been a man with a big beard, this grizzly bear you saw?"

Charley's eyes blanked as he gazed inward at the memory. He shuddered and said, "Maybe."

"What happened after you saw the grizzly bear?" Eich asked softly.

That question started the child panting. He turned and buried his face in his uncle's shoulder. From there came his muffled response, "The grizzly bear roared and chased me."

His uncle gently turned Charley's face back to Eich's and said, "Be brave, Charley. Tell Mr. Eich everything."

Charley gulped, nodded, and continued, "I ran and ran and ran. I went into a cave and the grizzly bear didn't find me. I heard him crashing in the forest but he didn't find me." The boy began sobbing as that remembered terror took hold.

Eich and Jack exchanged a look. That was all Charley was going to be able to tell them.

When they returned to the camp, Eich heard laughter coming from the house. He waited in the clearing while Jack escorted his nephew inside. Although he was very curious about these "renegade" Indians, he had no time to waste. He had to talk to Gray and get back to the Elipeena reservation as soon as possible.

When Jack came back outside, he said, "I got no more out of him than what you did. Do you think his testimony will be any help at all to George?"

'I don't know. Maybe. It's obvious he's telling the truth and that it wasn't his father that he saw kill McConnell. But, his claiming he saw a grizzly bear presents a serious problem."

"Among our people, the grizzly bear is the animal most feared. We tell many stories about the grizzly bear. Many believe that a man with grizzly bear power can shift his shape into something else. It could be that Charley saw the man's true spirit—a man with grizzly bear power he cannot control."

Jack led Eich and the three horses to the start of the trail that descended down to the river at Clatskanie. The Indian went no further. The plan was that Charley and his uncle would immediately set out for a location closer to Salem where they'd be holding Red Hawk's trial. Jack made it clear he'd be keeping Charley's hiding place secret. He assured Eich that, if Red Hawk's lawyer wanted to call Charley as a witness, the boy would appear within twenty-four hours. Jack would communicate with Eich by telegram. They parted after agreeing on certain coded words. Jack returned to the camp while Eich trudged down the trail, leading the three surprisingly frisky horses out of the hills.

TWENTY TWO

MAE HURRIED ACROSS THE LAWN, her cheeks hot from Eich's intense embrace. He'd arrived late that night, after driving his buckboard down the valley from Sheridan and across the valley to Moolock. Despite his exhaustion, he'd hugged her hard before announcing to the group: "I found Charley."

The six of them crowded the infirmary. Fong had come from the reservation, Sage from his house, Matthew and Mae from the school, Eich from his buckboard parked out on the town road. Instead of midnight, they were meeting at three a.m., hoping that it was too late for Barnhart or his lackey, Willingham, to be prowling around.

They kept Eich's report for last. Sage spoke first, quickly describing their evidence that proved Barnhart's corruption. "We've got a list comparing the delivery invoices with the supplies that Dr. Defler actually received. A comparison between the census record names and those of the children actually present is also complete—Barnhart's charging the Indian Service for twelve phantom children. I also took the wood contract and compared that to an actual count of delivered cords. I still don't have any evidence regarding the sale of the school's food but we'll have the testimony of Christine Many Feathers, Virgil White Cloud, and Dr. Defler. They'll be able to talk about the inadequate food and food crates disappearing into the back of Barnhart's buggy. So far, we haven't discovered the whereabouts of the new tractor. Of course, thanks to Mr. Fong and Albert, we know that Barnhart's biggest haul has got to be the difference between the lease and annuity money he's supposed to be paying the Elipeenas and what they say he's actually been paying. I've written a full report detailing everything we can prove and what we suspect."

Fong said, "Albert Red Hawk ask about tractor. He positive it not on reservation. But, one man say farmer five miles south has new green tractor with yellow wheels."

"That could be it, but how do we prove it?" Sage wondered aloud.

Matthew jumped in, "Me and Joshua talked about that tractor. He said that right after it arrived, Albert Brunner went to town. While he was away, the boys climbed all over it. One of them was showing off, walking along the front axle without holding on. His foot slipped and the hobnail in his boot made a deep scratch on the back of the axle. Brunner didn't notice it and the tractor was gone the next day. I bet Joshua could identify that scratch."

"Great! I'll add that to my report. I think we have enough useful evidence for Dr. Lane to get the Indian Service to act." Sage said. He turned to Eich. "Well, Herman, now that those preliminaries are out of the way, tell us about Charley. Did you learn anything that can help George Red Hawk's case?"

Eich cleared his throat and launched into the tale of his journey. A gloomy silence fell over them once he finished telling about Charley's "bear."

"I know what Philander will say," Sage said. "He'll say he can't put Charley on the stand and have him say McConnell was killed by a grizzly bear dressed in men's clothes."

"Yes, that is essentially what he said when I stopped to see him before catching the train south to Sheridan," Eich said.

Everyone felt frustrated. The corruption offered a motivation for McConnell's murder but what was the likelihood that the white jury would overlook the physical evidence against Red Hawk? Especially since they couldn't produce the actual killer?

For a good while, they tossed out one idea after another and grew increasingly dispirited. Just as they were about to give it up for the night, Lucinda said the five small words that sparked an idea. "Wouldn't Charley recognize the bear?"

Even as she now hurried toward the school, Mae smiled to herself. Because, after Lucinda said that, suggestions flew until they had a plan of sorts. When the group disbanded, Fong and Sage headed to Sage's because they'd agreed Fong's usefulness on the reservation was at an end. Hiding out in Albert Red Hawk's shed served no purpose. And, with the tribal police hunting for him, Fong couldn't go about the reservation. Instead, he would deliver their evidence and Sage's report to Philander Gray.

Matthew left for the school ahead of Mae, obviously trying to give her and Eich a few private moments together. "Silly old woman," Mae softly chided herself as she entered the school. All was quiet inside. Matthew would already be abed. She climbed the stairs, unlocked her door, and slipped inside where no light burned. Only the moonless night's faint glow guided her.

She locked the door, and headed to the bedroom where she quickly undressed and climbed into bed. Sleep remained elusive. Her thoughts kept scurrying around like mice in a cupboard, touching on Barnhart's shenanigans, the dear boys in her charge, and Eich. My Lord, what was she to do about Eich? He wasn't about to give up his rag picking life and she wasn't about to move into a lean-to. She'd spent too many years living that close to the bone. She didn't want luxury but she did appreciate simple comforts. A strange noise snapped her eyes open and halted her ruminations. A huge figure blocked the doorway's faint light and began moving toward her.

She snatched the small ormolu clock—one of Matilda Daley's innumerable gaudy treasures—from the bedside table in the frantic hope that its gilded knight with his uplifted sword might serve as a weapon. Seconds later the black hulk landed on top of her, his strong thighs on either side of her legs, pinning her down. She smelled cigarettes, boozy breath, and rotten teeth as hands encircled her throat and started squeezing. A voice whispered, "This'll teach you to wander about." The fingers tightened until a tiny squeak was the only sound she could make.

Panic washed through her but anger quickly followed. With the anger, came clarity. Fong had prepared her for just this situation. She slammed the knight's sword into the man's head. Shock lessened his grip and shifted his weight. Good, the blanket loosened just enough that she could raise her left knee. Grabbing his left wrist with both hands, she shoved his arm further left as she pushed off the mattress with her left foot.

Her maneuver caught him off guard. To stop from toppling onto his side, he had to take his left hand from her throat to brace himself on the mattress. One ragged gasp of air and she let loose a scream that traveled up from her toes.

It took forever before the hallway door to her rooms crashed open and a running figure hurtled itself onto the back of her attacker. The man's hands dropped from her throat as he reared backward, flinging her rescuer off the bed and onto the floor with a thud. Shouts began filling the front room. The man began moving, apparently deciding escape his best option. But, as he slid off the bed another, bigger defender charged through the doorway, seized the man's shoulders and slammed him against the wall, sending a shelf of porcelain figurines crashing to the floor.

Her attacker charged out the bedroom door and more crashes and yells sounded. Then heavy feet were thudding down the stairs. Moments later, the outer door slammed against the downstairs wall and the footfalls faded into the night.

With shaking hands, Mae lit the bedside oil lamp that had miraculously escaped damage. She wasn't surprised when the light fell on Matthew's pale face, but the sight of White Cloud caused her to gasp. He was helping Matthew to his feet. He turned and smiled at her. "Sorry about the breakage," he said.

"They aren't mine," she said automatically, adding, "Far as I'm concerned, this place can do without all her fussy knickknacks."

He chuckled but held up a hand as he looked over his shoulder toward the front room. Shocked faces peered in from the parlor. "Good lord," she exclaimed. "Is the entire dormitory in my front room?" Then she called in a calm voice, "Boys, thank you for coming to my rescue."

Matthew got up from the floor, reached her side, grabbed her hand, and whispered, "Are you alright, Mrs. Clemens?"

She patted his hand, "Yes, dear. Thank you. You saved me jumping on that rascal's back like you did. Go on back to bed and take the other boys with you. Mr. White Cloud and I need to talk."

Matthew reluctantly left her bedroom, though not without a searching backward glance. Mae waited for the outer door to close and then said, "Mr. White Cloud, if you would kindly go into the parlor, I will make myself decent so I can brew us some tea. I'd like to know a few things, including how you came to be in the school at this hour." She looked down at the ormolu clock and saw that the gold knight astride its top was holding a severely bent sword. Looking closer, she saw blood. "Good," she said and pointed to the blood. "It looks like I nailed the scoundrel."

White Cloud nodded and said, "Yup. Let's hope your sword stabbed him in an obvious place."

After donning robe and slippers, she headed into the front room where she stirred the coals and set a teakettle to boiling. At first, they simply drank tea. When Mae's hand started shaking, she set the cup in its saucer and said, "Well, Mr. White Cloud, how does it happen you were here? A happenstance for which I am very grateful, by the way. That fellow could have seriously hurt one of the boys if not for you."

"Sometimes, I can't sleep. When that happens, I roam the grounds. I saw all of you heading to the infirmary so I followed." He looked embarrassed as he continued, "One of the windows was open a few inches. So, I listened to your meeting. Very interesting. I knew about John's, Matthew's, and maybe your involvement, but Mrs. Adell, the Chinese man, and that itinerant trader? I was surprised."

Mae shifted uncomfortably, sipped her tea, and said nothing. White Cloud continued, "I watched Adell and the Chinese man leave, then Matthew."

She flushed, realizing that White Cloud must have seen her and Eich, but he quickly said, "I left when you and the trader came out. I figured it was a good time to slip away. As I headed home, I saw someone sneaking around the corner of the school. I ran across the lawn and reached the front just in time to see a man slip inside. I didn't recognize him so I thought I better see what he was up to. This is, after all, a building full of children.

"I thought maybe he wanted to steal food or something. So, I was in the kitchen when I heard you scream. As I was running up the stairs, I heard the boys rushing into your room. I was afraid you or one of them might get hurt." He shrugged. "So, that's the story of my night."

He set his cup on the side table and stood. "I better go tell Barnhart you were attacked. He'll think it suspicious if I don't. I'll stop at Mr. Adell's first."

She gazed up at him, a slight smile on her lips, "We never knew you were outside, listening."

He chuckled. "We Indians can move real quiet."

He waited in the dark for the knock. When it came he crossed the room and cracked open the door. "Did you do it?" he asked, only to have the door shoved open as the sweaty man pushed his way inside.

"No, damn it. A whole passel of people came to her rescue. I was lucky to get away with my life."

"Who? Who came to rescue her?"

"Well, all the boys from the dormitory. And, a big fellow."

"A big fellow?" he repeated dumbly. There shouldn't have been another man in the school, not at this hour. "Who was it?"

"I think it was that Indian teacher, or it could have been your clerk, that Adell fellow. Anyway, it was someone about their size."

"This just keeps getting worse and worse. Can't you do anything right?"

"Look, all she knows is that a man attacked her. She'll probably think I was after her scrawny body."

"Don't you realize she's going to wonder how you unlocked her door?"

"Nah, she'll just figure she forgot to lock it. Hey get me a cloth or something, I got blood dripping here."

When he came back with the wet towel, the wounded man said, "You know, it was strange. We planned that I'd just creep into her room. But, right after I got into the school, someone else came in and walked all around. I hid in a closet. When whoever it was, got far enough away, I went up the stairs. Then, by crikey, just as I got to the second floor, I heard that downstairs door open and close again. This time, whoever it was started climbing the stairs so I hid again. That person went up to the third floor." He shook his head and grimaced. "I swear more folks were running around that school tonight than rats in a cheese factory."

"Probably a couple of the older children snuck out for a little hanky panky. It wouldn't surprise me, the little heathens."

"I dunno, maybe," came the disbelieving response.

TWENTY THREE

FONG STUDIED THOSE STANDING ON the station platform from the shelter of the trees. He groaned when he recognized Ulysses. Sure enough, the tribal policeman climbed onto the train. There'd be no riding the cushions to Portland for Fong Kam Tong.

Why is he going north? Fong wondered, as the train hooted, picked up speed, and disappeared around the sharp bend. He crossed the open ground and sat down in the weeds at the platform's north end. It'd be a freight train for him.

An hour later he was running alongside the train as it slowed for the curve, his eyes fixed on an open boxcar door. He leaped, his fingers caught the floor edge, and suddenly, hands grabbed his wrists and pulled him up and inside. Once he gained his balance on the rocking floor he looked at his Good Samaritan. The scruffy white man's face registered surprise. "Blimey if you aren't a China man," he exclaimed in a British accent.

Fong flashed a toothy grin and said, "China man much obliged." The other man laughed and Fong knew he presented no danger. He glanced around. The boxcar was empty of goods, but three card-playing white men squatted in a corner. They stared at him and one of them said loudly, "Chinks ain't got no business riding this train."

Fong was bone tired. After receiving Sage's documents he'd returned to Albert's to say goodbye and then he walked the fifteen miles to the rail platform. All he wanted was to sit down, lean against the car's side, and close his eyes. He was not going to leave the moving boxcar to look for another one. Time was short; he had to get to Portland. Sometimes, like now, he was full up tired of stupid white people. "'Chinks' lay train rails. I have more right than you," he said.

The British man beside him gave a snort of laughter. The three men clambered to their feet, their spokesman snarling, "Just what are you laughing at, Limey? We don't like your kind neither."

Fong and the Brit exchanged glances and his new friend didn't step away. The three card players shuffled forward, aiming for a fight. Fong and the Brit raised their hands. "I not want to hurt you," Fong said to them. They only laughed.

Just then, the train slowed and the floor tilted as the train began chugging around another curve. If there was to be a fight, this was the place. Less chance of serious injury. Fong exchanged another glance with the Englishman before moving swiftly forward. After a few thuds and yells, all three men were outside the boxcar, strewn in a row alongside the rails like so many bad seeds. Fong snatched up their bedrolls and tossed those out as well. Only their scattered playing cards remained.

"Well, blimey," said the Brit.

"That's it!" Sage exclaimed. "You can't stay here anymore."

"Nonsense," Mae retorted. "He's not going to come back."

"You don't know that! He's already proven a locked door won't stop him!"

Her temper flared. "You think I'm an idiot. Of course, I know he has a key, but I'll shove the heavy armchair against the door. That'll give me plenty of time to yell for help. Matthew charged into my room lickety-split. He must have flown across the dormitory. And, Virgil White Cloud said he'll be on the prowl. Besides, unless I'm coming to see you, I'll stay with the children. No one is going to attack me with them around."

Sage seemingly gave in because he said, "Where is White Cloud anyway? I didn't get to a chance to talk with him last night."

"He's around somewhere, probably in his classroom." She stood up and gestured at the office door into the central hallway. "I need to get back to the girls. I left them without supervision. Who knows what they'll get up to? Although, these are such good children."

Reaching the door, she turned. "Where is Barnhart?"

"He's staying home today. Says he's sick. Do you think he's the one who attacked you?"

Her head shake was definite. "Nope, it wasn't him. He's too puny. And before you ask, it wasn't that good-for-nothing, Willingham, either."

"Can you remember anything about the man?"

"He was big. About your size but heavier."

"That's all you remember?"

"Sage, that room was pitch black. I barely saw his shape." She again began to leave, only to turn back. "You know, when I shoved his arm up and to one side, I think I felt long bristles on my wrist."

"You mean like a bushy beard?" They exchanged a look that said both were thinking of Charley Red Hawk's "grizzly bear."

White Cloud's students poured out of the classroom, heading for their noon dinner. Spotting Sage, the teacher gestured him inside and shut the door. Sage couldn't waste time. If Barnhart showed up for lunch, he'd notice that his clerk and a teacher were missing. Weldon Willingham was also likely to be slinking around.

"Thank you for coming to her rescue last night," Sage said. After a slight nod from White Cloud, he continued, "Mrs. Lofton told me you overheard us last night." Again, the teacher silently nodded.

"Look," Sage said, "We have to find the man that Charley saw kill McConnell. If we do, then we'll be able to prove Red Hawk's innocence." Sage grinned. "Of course, you know that, having listened and all."

This last observation caused White Cloud to shift uncomfortably but then he relaxed and returned the grin. Sage hastened to reassure. "Actually, it turns out that we're glad you did. We need your help."

"I want to help. What can I do?" White Cloud asked.

"As you heard, we suspect Charley's grizzly bear was a man with a beard."

"Or it was grizzly bear power controlling a man," White Cloud corrected gently. "Children sometimes see things truer than we adults."

Sage couldn't argue with that. "You're right. But, I think when he's not attacking people, the grizzly bear looks like a man with a beard. Is there anyone who comes to mind?"

"The industrial teacher, Albert Brunner. He wears a beard. He's about the right size. And, he is despicable."

"Why? Because he's involved in Barnhart's corrupt schemes?"

"Not only that. He treats the children badly. He whips them, ties them to the barn posts, works them way too hard," White Cloud said, adding, "I'd like to tie him to a barn post."

"Well, you may get your chance. We've got to identify the grizzly bear man right quick. We have only six days before Red Hawk's trial begins.

Philander Gray flung his door open at the sound of his secretary berating someone in the anteroom. Catching sight of a scruffy and tired-looking Fong, he sent her a questioning look. She quickly responded, "I told this gentleman," the way she bit off the last word said she considered Fong the opposite of a gentleman. "That he must have an appointment but he won't leave." She folded her arms across her chest, clearly expecting vindication.

Instead, Gray said gently. "Mrs. Clark, how about you take a break? Go have a cup of coffee?" He pulled some coins from his pocket, put them in her hand, and ignored her shocked look. After angrily gathering her wits, coat, and hat, she gave a disapproving sniff and left, banging the door shut behind her.

Gray turned, "I'm sorry Mr. Fong. She's never seen you here before. She's very protective of my time and acts the bulldog on occasion."

Fong chuckled. "Yes, I see that. Her words sharp, like teeth of bulldog."

Once seated, they discussed Eich's finding Charley. As Eich had warned, Gray doubted that he could put the young boy on the stand to testify about a hatchet-wielding grizzly bear.

"You and I might understand the whole grizzly-bear-power-takes-over-man thing but I can guarantee that jury will roll their eyes if we try to give that explanation."

Fong nodded his understanding. He said nothing about how his comrades hoped to deal with the jury's skepticism. Instead, he handed Gray the paperwork he'd brought.

Gray quickly scanned Sage's report before studying the lists. "Good, good. Dr. Lane will want to use these. I'll have my secretary type up duplicates and put the originals in my safe. She types fast. She might act the harridan on occasion but when it comes to my cases, her lips are clamped tight as a cobbler's vice."

Fong didn't doubt the lawyer's assurances so he asked his group's most pressing question, "Will corruption evidence help trial?"

"I'll try my best. This information should make the jury wonder if there wasn't another motivation for the murder. It might cast doubt on the prosecution's story but, I am afraid it won't be enough to counter the hatchet, gloves, and witness."

"Who is witness?"

Gray pawed through the papers spread across his desk before stopping to read one. "His name is Heinrich Brunner. He lives down near the reservation. I plan on going down tomorrow to see if he'll talk to me."

"I will go hide on reservation," Fong said. He went on to explain about the tribal police and seeing Ulysses board the passenger train.

"Do you think the tribal police discovered where the uncle hid Charley?" Gray asked anxiously.

Fong hadn't thought of that. He mulled over what he knew. Eich said someone told the Grand Ronde agent about Charley's uncle boarding the train north and that the agent sent two people to follow him. Maybe the agent's men had discovered the uncle had taken the Astoria train and telegraphed that information. The agent, in turn, likely telegraphed that news to Barnhart. That would explain why Ulysses boarded the train to Portland.

Seeing the concern on Gray's face, he said. "Uncle Jack and Charley not in renegade camp now. They safe from Ulysses."

It was Charley's first experience outside the Willamette Valley. Now, in these last few days, he'd seen a river so big. The opposite shore appeared and disappeared behind the mist drifting above its surface. At the river's wide mouth, he saw the wild clashes of water and could not believe it when his uncle told him how Chinook Indians had paddled their canoes through its churnings. But the wild river was nothing compared to the undulating water stretching far beyond the western horizon. They stood atop a bluff feeling the sea pound the cliff beneath their feet and, to its rhythm, his uncle recited stories of Chinook Nation fisherman paddling their gigantic cedar canoes far beyond the Pacific's crashing waves.

Then, they'd turned south, following a trail over the top of cliffs and along sandy beaches. Whenever they rested, his uncle told him about the people who first lived on the lands over which they walked. "None of this land was ever a 'wilderness' to them as it was to the white man," he said. "How could it be a 'wilderness' when our people knew every inch, every tree, every stream, every hill; each and every place that offered rich gifts of fish, roots, seeds, nuts, fruits, and game?"

The tales began with the Chinook Clatsops, who'd once lived at the river's mouth. They had been the wealthiest of all the Oregon tribes. They had lived in towns full of big plank houses that held several families. Their land was so rich that they could walk out of their houses and hunt, gather, and fish for everything they needed. Uncle Jack looked down at him and said, "I am sure you heard stories about your Modoc great-grandmother. She was captured in war and ended up a Chinook slave. She was freed after the whites forced the Chinooks onto our reservation and the civil war freed the black people. Slavery was bad for many but some Chinooks treated their slaves like family. That is what happened with your great grandmother."

Charley was grateful to finally have that family mystery solved. But now there was another, more recent mystery. They'd stopped to eat some dry meat when Charley asked, "Uncle, why do you know so much about all the Indian tribes?"

His uncle chuckled. "That is a somewhat long story. But we will sit in the shade of this grandfather tree and I shall tell you. When the whites took me away to attend boarding school, they sent me south to a California school. At first, it was very scary because there was no other child from the Modoc tribe in that school. The whites thought that, by mixing us up, we'd be easier to boss around."

"Were you?"

"Well, we were all afraid and we'd been raised to respect our elders, so except for running away, we were obedient children."

"You ran away?" Charley repeated wonderingly.

"The first time was from a school here in Oregon. That's why they sent me to California; they figured the great distance would discourage me from running away."

"Did it?"

"No, because I made friends with boys from nearby California tribes. So, I could run away with one of them and stay with his family. They always welcomed me. Unfortunately, I always got caught, eventually."

Charley thought about his uncle's story. He remembered the terror of being chased through the woods and the fear he'd felt when he'd snuck across the dark valley fields. He shuddered. "So, the white peoples' plan didn't work—them putting a Modoc in a school with kids from other tribes?"

That question made his uncle laugh, "None of us spoke the same language so it might have worked, except for one thing. They forced all of us to learn a common language, English."

"So knowing those other kids got you interested in other tribes?"

"It got me interested in history. That school only taught white peoples' history. But I knew Modoc history from my grandmother. I knew how we fought and died defending our land. She told me how the soldiers had driven us north like cattle from Northern California until we ended up on the Oregon coast. Many Modocs died from exhaustion, illness, and white settlers' bullets along the way. The Cherokee sing about their Trail of Tears, when they were forced marched from the east coast to Oklahoma. Well, Oregon had its own Trail of Tears and my people were on it, as were people from many Southern Oregon tribes."

Uncle Jack gazed into the distance, painful thoughts etching sad lines on his face as he continued, "At the California school, the other boys told me similar stories about their own tribe's history. The Tolowa people lived in Northern California. One Tolowa boy said that white vigilantes swooped in and slaughtered almost a thousand of his people during a peaceful prayer ceremony. They were murdered because the vigilantes wanted the land a federal treaty had set aside for Tolowa people."

"Did those vigilantes get the Tolowa land?"

His uncle heaved a sigh. "Yes. So few Tolowa people survived that the federal government moved them onto another tribe's reservation and sold the Tolowa's land to the whites who'd attacked. And, before you ask, not a single white vigilante died in the attack. And, not a single one was punished for murdering so many unarmed people. That was no surprise since California's governor had called for the extermination of all California Indians."

His uncle paused, picked up a small stick, and drew a symbol in the dirt as he whispered something Charley couldn't decipher though it sounded like a prayer. Uncle Jack continued, "Anyway, after learning many things like that, I wanted to know more about our history and about how our peoples lived before the white invasion. Once I graduated and returned home, I began talking to the elders living on the Grand Ronde and Siletz reservations. They come from over forty different tribes and more tribal bands than I can count or name.

"The more I learned, the more I realized that we have many, many things in common: our beliefs, our history, our values, and our way of living in harmony with Mother Nature. I want to balance history. I want to share what I've learned with our people, with all Indian people, and even with the whites. That is the same thing Mr. Conteur wants to do. That is why he is staying with Clatskanie Maria and writing down her stories. She is the last of her people. When she leaves her life, there will be no more Clatskanie Indians."

Charley thought about what his uncle said and it made him think of Teacher Willingham. "My teacher always makes us say that Christopher Columbus discovered America and that Robert Gray discovered the Columbia River, but that can't be right, can it? I mean, if Indians were here for thousands of years, doesn't it mean that Indians discovered America?"

His uncle glanced down at him and squeezed his shoulder. "That's right Charley. You are one smart boy. It was Indians who discovered America."

They spent the night with a Nehalem elder. As they sat in her small house, she told Charley how her people had used fir pitch to attach feathers to baskets, put the feathered baskets over their heads, and then waded out into the water to snare ducks and geese. She had laughed loudly at the memory, saying, "We were funny looking but, we were also the most successful trappers of the water birds."

The next day they traveled through what had been Tillamook territory. His uncle told him how the Tillamooks caught and dried tons of fish every season. They would journey over the coast range and into the Willamette Valley to visit the Kalapuyans and Elipeenas to trade dried fish for wapato roots and other things.

South of the Tillamook lands, Charley and his uncle entered Nestucca territory. His uncle said that most of these peoples' history was lost. Still, people remembered the Nestuccas for their sturdy houses and their love of horse racing.

Finally, as the sun began its fall into the ocean, Charley and his uncle crossed into the land of the Salmon River people. His uncle said that, like all the other tribes, these peoples' original name was something else, "Nachesne." Uncle Jack was somber as a friend of his, a Salmon River man, rowed them across a bay. The man stopped rowing and pointed at the bay's south shore. "Once we Nachesne people rested our dead over there in beautiful, strong canoes. We hung the canoes between two sturdy trees growing beside this water."

Charley looked at the shoreline and then back at the ferryman. "But now you bury them in the ground like white people do?"

The man nodded. "We had no choice. The white people kept tossing our ancestors' bones on the ground and stealing the canoes."

TWENTY FOUR

DESPITE GEORGE RED HAWK'S WHITE-KNUCKLE grip on the cell bars, his normally calm face was joyful. "My boy Charley is with his Uncle Jack? He's safe?" he repeated in an unbelieving whisper.

Gray nodded, happy to be giving Red Hawk some good news before having to temper it with bad. "Unfortunately, I don't think he's going to be any help to your case."

"He didn't see Inspector McConnell's murderer?"

Gray hesitated and then realized that what he had to say might not be all that strange to Charley's father.

"He did see the murder. And, you were right. The murderer chased him. Charley hid for a day before heading to his Uncle Jack's on the Grand Ronde reservation. He didn't get there. His uncle intercepted him and took him someplace other than the Grand Ronde. That's because Agent Barnhart alerted the Grand Ronde's agent and that fellow had the tribal police watching the uncle's farm. So, the uncle slipped away and found Charley."

"If my son saw the murderer, why can't he testify about who he saw?"

Gray sighed. "Because he would testify that he saw a grizzly bear attack Inspector McConnell with a hatchet—a grizzly bear wearing men's clothing. We think Charley saw a man with a beard but, he insists it was a bear."

Red Hawk dropped his hands from the bars, stepped back, turned, and gazed out the dirty window set high in the wall. No comforting words came to Gray though he'd known Charley's evidence would deliver a blow to his client's hopes.

When Red Hawk turned around though, a rueful smile twisted his lips. "I've always known Charley was special," he said with pride. "His mother and her grandmother both had strong spirit guides. Those women saw and knew things the rest of us couldn't. They would have become tribal healers in the days before the whites forced our people to use only white medicine."

Gray considered his client's acceptance of the fantastic. He wondered what it must be like to live in a world where men took animal shapes and women saw the invisible. Though, now that Gray thought about it, his own ancestors' world hadn't been all that different. They'd lived in one peopled by fairies, sprites, elves, leprechauns, trolls, and, like the Elipeena, believed in tree, water, and sky spirits as well as witches and demons. The Scandinavian, Greek, and Roman god beliefs were just as fantastic.

Red Hawk's calm voice pulled him back into the present. "I think that my son did see a bear's essence. But, I also understand that it won't help to have him say that to the jury."

"Unfortunately, I have even more discouraging news. There's a witness who claims he saw you head into the woods about the time McConnell was killed. He said he thought you were carrying something that could have been a hatchet."

"He is lying," Red Hawk said flatly. "What is this man's name?"

"Heinrich Brunner." Gray watched recognition harden Red Hawk's face. "Who is he? Do you know him?"

Red Hawk gave a thoughtful nod. "His sister is the wife of the farmer who wants to lease my allotment. His brother is the industrial teacher at the boarding school. Heinrich Brunner is also a friend of Agent Barnhart."

"Oh boy," Gray said.

Red Hawk's look pierced as he said thoughtfully, "And, like his brother, Heinrich Brunner wears a beard."

"Heinrich Brunner? Is he related to the industrial teacher, Adolph Brunner? What does Gray know about him?" Sage wondered aloud.

Fong shrugged. "Mr. Gray know nothing about witness. He was going to ask George Red Hawk. But, after long walk from train, I go sleep in shed of Albert Red Hawk. When I wake-up, I ask Albert. He say, Heinrich brother of Adolph."

"Oh boy," Sage said. "Well, maybe that's a good thing for us. I wonder if Heinrich is bearded like his brother, Adolph"

Another shrug from Fong before he said, "I stay on reservation," he gestured around the woods in which they were meeting, "I maybe have to fight Ulysses, again."

"So, where do you plan to go?"

"I think I visit Heinrich Brunner farm. Sneak around. See what he doing. Also, check tractor axle for scar made by boy's boot."

"Maybe we'll send Herman down there to talk to him and take old Heinrich's measure. He's been coming around a lot ever since Ma was attacked. It's becoming a little too obvious. Besides," Sage added, "I think I overheard her threatening to swat him with her broom if she saw him again."

Fong laughed. "Mr. Eich like her pretty much. Good idea he go far from broom. He can give me ride part of way. My legs wobble like limp noodles. Too much walking."

"It's Thursday, we've just four days before the trial starts," Sage said. Frustrated, he ran his fingers through his pomaded hair only to look at his greasy fingers in disgust and reach for a handkerchief in his pocket. He'd done it again. His John Miner persona never wore pomade in his hair, while John Adair and John Adell both wore their hair slicked down close to their scalp.

He looked up from wiping his fingers to see White Cloud grinning. "Maybe you should try my hairstyle," Virgil said, waggling the end of his shiny black braid at Sage."

"Believe me, it's damn tempting," Sage said. "But, getting back to our problem. We have to get Adolph alone, scare the heck out of him, and do it in a way that he can't warn Barnhart."

"How about, we do it Indian-style, take him captive?"

"Where the heck could we keep him?" For the first time, ever, Sage wished he had the underground jail cell handy. Once they'd broken Portland's shanghai ring, Sage intended to demolish the brick cell in Portland's underground. Fong objected, saying that as long as they made sure no else tried to use it, the cell might come in handy. And, so it had. More than once. "Besides, how could we get our hands on him without the whole school and Barnhart knowing about it?"

"Christine Many Feathers."

'Christine could do it?" Sage let the incredulity sound in his voice. How could the girls' matron catch a man twice her size and age?"

Virgil shook his head in mock disappointment. "Really, John? You have to ask that? Have you seen her?"

Of course, he'd seen her practically every day since he'd gotten to the school. Then he understood. "You mean because she's beautiful?"

"I mean the beautiful Indian maiden can lure the nasty old white man into the woods. Haven't you seen him looking at her? I finally gave her a wolf charm for protection."

Sage squinted at White Cloud, unsure whether he was joking about the charm but the fellow's blank stare left him clueless so Sage moved on. "Okay, but, will she do it, and is it safe for her to do it?"

'I'll ask but I'm betting that yes, she'll do it. We natives are fond of the gamble but there's no risk in that one. As for keeping her safe, we can be close by. We'll just have to keep Brunner captive until the trial—three days."

Sage looked at the handsome man and thought about the suffering he'd endured just to get his education and a job teaching at a reservation boarding school. "Tough" didn't begin to describe White Cloud's determination. "Virgil, I guess you and Christine Many Feathers are in the same boat. Snatching Brunner could cost you your job and your freedom." Sage felt compelled to state that concern though he was certain that Virgil's commitment to ending Barnhart's corrupt reign was as strong as his own. Likely stronger.

Virgil waved the concern away. "After the trial, Brunner's not going to say anything. Either he's the murderer or, he was involved in selling the tractor off the reservation. He's going to flee the scene if he gets a chance."

Sage gazed around the small house and felt regret. This could have been a wonderful interlude—him and Lucinda living together in this small space. Instead, they were deep in the problems of murder, corruption, and danger, and hardly saw each other. He turned back to Virgil, aware he'd let the silence stretch on a bit too long. When their eyes met, Sage thought he'd seen a flicker of sympathy in the man's eyes. What Sage said, however, was, "Well, in that case, I guess you better ask her, pronto quick."

With dusk's muted green surrounding them. Sage and Virgil stood in the trees, watching Christine Many Feathers flirt her way across the field. Sage almost felt sorry for the man, who looked dumber than an ox after a whole day of pulling. But the idea of that stolen tractor and the faces of starving reservation people squashed any pity flat. Adolph Brunner had earned what was about to happen.

"So, what was the lure she used?" Sage asked, "Besides the obvious?"

"Something about a walk, a bracelet, and a broken clasp. Oh, and needing to find it before dark. Packrats, you know." Virgil smiled, seeming to find Adolph Brunner's entrapment entertaining.

Sage gave a disbelieving headshake but then his attention snapped to the young woman and middle-aged man who were getting close. "You ready?" he asked.

Virgil stepped away, slipped behind a tree, and soon disappeared, intending to position himself on the industrial teacher's far side.

For a moment, it seemed to Sage that nature held its breath. There was no insect buzz, bird twitter, or breeze flutter among the leaves. Then Sage heard the young woman's chatter, sounding nervous to him but Brunner probably thought she was adorably shy.

Sage stepped onto the path, intercepting the two about fifty feet into the woods. Christine Many Feathers stopped immediately but it took Brunner a few steps further to realize his private tryst would come to naught. His disappointment came out as irritation. "Adell, what the hell are you doing here?" he demanded.

Over the Brunner's shoulder, Sage saw Christine turn and tiptoe back down the path.

Noiselessly, Virgil White Cloud stepped into her place behind Brunner. Like an immovable forest Colossus, he stood, his arms folded, his feet apart.

Sage smiled benignly. "Why, I am waiting for you, Mr. Brunner."

"Why aren't you releasing the children from the table? They are getting restless." Barnhart's tone was querulous.

Mae tamped down a snappy retort. "I'm waiting for Christine. She's going to help me supervise the end of the dinner hour and the clearing of the dishes," Mae meekly explained.

Barnhart scowled. "What do you mean? Miss Many Feathers left a long time ago with Adolph Brunner. Something about a lost thingamabob."

Mae made a show of looking puzzled. She glanced at Joshua who stood nearby. He would certainly know that what she was about to say was a lie. "Oh, she found that bracelet in her pocket. She's been helping me the whole dinner hour. She's just gone to the necessary but she'll be back momentarily. Do you need her for something?"

Barnhart looked disbelieving but Christine Many Feather's entrance forestalled whatever he was about to say. She looked flustered. "Oh, I am sorry Mrs. Lofton, for taking so long in the restroom," she began, only to shoot a surprised glance at Oswald Barnhart upon catching sight of him. "Oh, Mr. Barnhart! Were you looking for me?"

From under lowered brows, he said, "Last time I saw you, Mr. Brunner was going to help you find something you'd lost in the woods."

She rolled her eyes as if acknowledging her stupidity. "Just as we were leaving the school, I found it in my pocket so we didn't have to go look. Mr. Brunner said he had some things to do at his house. I heard the children being noisy and came to help Mrs. Lofton." She said this somewhat breathlessly but Barnhart probably thought she was merely anxious that he not consider her a slacker.

Barnhart waved a dismissive hand, "No, no. I just wanted to know why the children were still sitting at the supper table." He turned toward the children who were quietly watching the scene before them as if it were a theatrical performance. Barnhart made a big show of waving his hand at them and saying in a raised, hectoring voice, "See that these children practice exiting the dining room as if they were ladies and gentlemen."

Mae and Christine watched as he turned and left the room. Both women bristled at the implied insult to the children and their eyes met in agreement. Then as one, they turned to face Joshua. The boy's dancing eyes said he'd not missed a word of their lies but the rest of his face was placid as he meekly asked, "May I ring the dismissal bell now?"

TWENTY FIVE

Eich's buckboard rattled down the farm road. Fong sat in the open bed behind him, ready to duck under the trap should anyone appear.

After the two friends finished discussing their plans regarding Heinrich Brunner, Fong changed the topic. "Attack on Mae scary."

"I knew something like that would happen. I never should have left her."

"How could you stop it?"

Eich couldn't think of an answer. If he'd been at his post in the shed, he could not have reached her as quickly as Matthew and White Cloud did. But, the image of that man's hands around her throat haunted him, day and night. At first, he'd resisted Sage's request that he and Fong go to Heinrich Brunner's farm. He agreed only after Sage pointed out that Brunner might be Mae's attempted murderer. Besides, Mae did not want him hanging about, she had shooed him away. He smiled, remembering the reassuring twinkle in her dark blue eyes. She still cared for him. "Ah, I could not have done anything," he admitted. "I probably would have slept right through the whole fracas."

Despite that admission, Fong understood, saying "Someone attack Kum Ho, I want to kill him. Maybe I would."

The two men then rode on in agreeable silence until Eich reined in the horse. "I see the farmhouse through the trees. The driveway to Brunner's farm is probably beyond that wooded bend. Maybe this is the best place for you to dismount."

Fong slipped out of the buckboard and into the woods. There he waited until Eich clucked the horse forward. Once horse and buckboard disappeared around the bend, he began cautiously making his way through the woods, angling toward the farmhouse visible through the trees.

Eich rolled up the drive and halted before the barn. A man in overalls stepped from the barn about the same time as a middle-aged farm woman stepped onto the farmhouse's covered porch. Eich had studied the farm as he approached. Neatly plowed fields flanked the driveway. Two sleek horses trotted up to their corral fence to observe his arrival. The house and barn were substantial with the farmhouse looking newly painted white with bright blue trim. Everything said "prosperity". It was a setting markedly different from those he had seen on the Elipeena reservation. He wondered how much of this prosperity was due to thefts from them.

There was restrained curiosity in the faces of the man and woman who approached. Eich climbed down and said, "Greetings, my name is Herman Eich. I have little bits of this and that that I'd like to show you if you are interested in buying."

The woman glanced at the man. At his nod, she stepped forward. "Mayhaps I need a few things for the house. What might you be offering?" Her voice held a faint trace of the Irish brogue that Eich sometimes heard in Mae's words. He mentally shook himself. He didn't need to be thinking of Mae Clemens right now.

"Well, ma'am, I sell sewing notions, fabrics, cooking pots and utensils, toys, and storybooks for children and such."

The woman eagerly drew closer and soon Eich was spreading his wares across the buckboard's tailgate. He laid out more than usual because he wanted to delay his departure and keep the farmer out of the barn and looking on. The woman selected a few things, glanced at her husband who again nodded. With a thank you to Eich, she picked up her purchases and returned to the house. The farmer moved closer.

Eich turned to him, noting the bristly beard, the tall stature and arms made strong by physical labor. He could be Mae's attacker. Eich pasted on what he hoped was a congenial smile. Brunner didn't seem to notice the insincerity. "You got anything a farmer could use?" he asked.

Eich nodded and began unloading seeds, tools, overalls, and other useful items. After Brunner purchased a few things and paid for them and his wife's selections, he showed a tendency to linger.

Eich took advantage of the man's friendliness. "Mighty nice place you have. Have you lived here long?"

Fortunately, Brunner was a man prone to chattiness. Eich soon learned he'd inherited the farm from his parents who'd come across the country from Ohio in a wagon, many years ago. That he grew corn, alfalfa, and wheat and the coming year looked promising in terms of yield. Also that Brunner had hoped to pass the farm onto a son but, so far, "the wife" had delivered only girls. So, he was beginning to fear that he might have to settle for a son-in-law, provided he was a "good sort".

Eich expressed interest to keep the man talking. Finally, he edged the conversation somewhat closer to his purpose. "Those Elipeena Indians must have been here when your folks started this farm. Did they give any trouble?"

"Naw, by then, plagues had pretty near cleared most of them out. My dad said that at least ninety percent of them were already dead. Besides, the Willamette Valley Indians were mostly peaceable folks."

"Good lord, that's a lot of people dying." Eich's shocked reaction was unfeigned.

"Yeah, well, their loss, our gain. The government let us homestead here 'cause there weren't enough Indians left to hold all the land."

"So, your family's never had any Indian trouble?"

"Well, I can't say that. Sometimes they get liquored up and a little wild. They're not all that happy to have us white folks here. Some of them still think it's their land and that they can roam wherever they want. My shotgun's right near the door. It's hard to keep them on the reservation but Agent Barnhart does a pretty good job."

"Ah, you know Mr. Barnhart? I've spent many a pleasant hour with him," Eich lied—that time having been far from pleasant.

The farmer nodded eagerly. "I see him regular my own self. He likes to play cards with some of us."

"I heard that he's been gone lately," Eich prodded.

"Now, that I wouldn't know. Me, and the wife, we just got back from a month-long train trip to California. We were down there visiting her family and I was checking out some cattle I want to ship up here."

"Your trip must have been a nice change of pace. I know farming is a lot of work. When did you get back?"

"It so happens that you just caught us. We got off the train in Salem last night. After picking up our buggy we rolled in this morning bright and early. I was just in the barn checking on how well our handyman took care of things while we were gone."

Eich didn't know how he felt about that information. On one hand, he kind of liked the loquacious farmer and didn't want him to be a murderer. On the other hand, it meant the murderer and Mae's attacker remained unknown. That meant she was still in danger."

Over the farmer's shoulder, Eich caught a glimpse of a figure flitting into the woods. He turned to Brunner. "Well, I best be rolling along. I appreciate your business and enjoyed your conversation."

Eich was scowling when he rounded the bend and saw Fong leaning against a tree by the road. Fong climbed in the back and the buckboard jerked forward. "What happen?" Fong asked.

"It isn't him. He said he's been gone all the past month. He just got back this morning. I suppose he could be lying but why would he? He does not know me from Adam. I bet he doesn't even know about the murder yet. He didn't act suspicious and chattered away like a magpie. I don't think he's McConnell's killer or Mae's attacker."

"He may not be murderer but he is thief," Fong said with satisfaction. "Axle show hobnail scar."

Eich smiled, "Well, at least we accomplished something today. That is useful evidence. One more thing for a new Indian Service inspector to look at."

After they rode on a bit farther Eich had a worrisome thought, "One problem could be that Brunner will get wind of what we're doing and hide the tractor. He could move it to another farm or something."

"No, that not happen," Fong said confidently.

Eich turned on his seat to look at his friend and found him smiling. Fong reached into his jacket and pulled out several wires and held them up.

"Tractor not start if it not have these," he said as his smile stretched into a grin.

Lucinda was scrubbing cupboards while Dr. Defler completed his monthly report. He'd agreed with Sage that, given the attack on Mrs. Lofton, Lucinda should sleep at the infirmary during the day. Defler was curtailing his reservation rounds, planning to leave Lucinda alone only if there was an emergency. And, in which case, he'd send for Matthew, leaving Joshua to watch over Mrs. Lofton.

Lucinda had unwillingly agreed to the safeguarding and chafed at her lack of freedom. Unable to sleep longer than a couple of hours, she'd re-emerged from the vacant bedroom determined to be helpful. The infirmary air felt thick with anxiety. Both of them were thinking of Monday's trial and about how much hung in the balance. Defler had told them that, if Barnhart's corruption remained unexposed, he and his wife were packing up and moving to Portland. He found the restrictions on his ability to practice good medicine intolerable. Little Patty was up and about, blissfully unaware of the tension surrounding her. She was paging through a storybook Eich had given her that morning.

Lucinda glanced out the window and stiffened. "Barnhart," she said urgently. Within seconds, Patty jumped to her feet, she and her book disappearing into the back room. Defler raised an eyebrow but stayed at his desk. Lucinda went back to scrubbing. Both pretended surprise when Barnhart opened the door abruptly and stepped into the infirmary, slamming the door behind him. He put his hands on his hips and glared at the doctor. Lucinda froze in the hope the agent would ignore her presence. She would not leave the doctor alone when the agent was in such high dudgeon. He looked hitting mad.

"I have it on good authority that the child is fit as a fiddle and that you are keeping her here when she could be back in the school!"

"Patty is not . . ." Defler got no further because Barnhart stormed past and reached the bedroom before the doctor or Lucinda could move. The agent flung open the door and Patty began shrieking in terror. Lucinda knew what that shriek meant. She'd heard it enough growing up, sometimes coming out of her own throat. Before Barnhart could step into the child's room, Lucinda was at his side, grabbed his arm, and yanked him away from the doorway and out of the terrified child's sight. "You leave her the hell alone," she said and gave Barnhart a shove.

Barnhart stumbled, regained his balance, and raised his fist, "How dare you!" he shouted, only to find his wrist caught in the doctor's firm grip.

"You will not raise your hand to Mrs. Adell," the doctor spat out. "And you will not remove that child from this infirmary."

Barnhart wrested his arm from Defler's grip. "That child is healthy and belongs in the school. She will return to the school whether you like it or not!"

Lucinda stepped forward until she was inches from Barnhart's face. "I know what you have done to her. You will only touch that child again if it's over my dead body."

Barnhart involuntarily stepped back, whether to escape her fury or her words, she couldn't tell. He glanced down at her clenched fists. He turned on his heel and went to the door. Once it was open, he turned back. With an arctic chill in his words, he said, "Come Monday, Defler, I am sending a telegram demanding your termination for insubordination and malfeasance. You'll never work in the Indian Service again." His cold eyes raked across Lucinda as he pointed and said, "And you, you are a temporary employee that I can fire at will. Your job here is over!" Barnhart was gone, with the door slamming behind him before either of them could reply.

Patty's sobs sounded from the bedroom. Defler looked dismayed. "She's not safe here. He'll come back with reinforcements."

Lucinda's smile was grim. "We need to gather her toys and whatever else she needs. Patty and I will be gone before he can return."

TWENTY SIX

THE OFFICE DOOR OPENED AND slammed against the wall knocking plaster loose. Sage looked up to see Barnhart lunge inside. The agent stood panting, wild-eyed with sweat running down his face. Sage jumped up. "Sir, what is the matter?"

"Have you seen Adolph Brunner today?"

"Why no, last time I saw him was after supper yesterday. He was walking to his house. His lamps were lit last night so he must have been home," Sage lied. He knew why Barnhart was so upset. The agent had entered Brunner's house to find most of the man's possessions missing. Sage and White Cloud had seen to that. Satisfaction flashed through Sage but he cautioned himself against cockiness. They had only two days before Red Hawk's trial and Brunner wasn't talking, yet. They'd expected that but hoped his tongue might loosen after a day of solitude.

"Well, he isn't home now and I have twenty unsupervised boys running amok outside," snapped Barnhart.

"Do you need me to go out there and supervise?"

Barnhart let go of enough of his panic to give Sage a suspicious glare. "Do you know what your wife just did?"

Sage shook his head. He really didn't know why Barnhart was upset. Lucinda was living at the infirmary and he and White Cloud had returned very late from their futile attempts at questioning Brunner. Sage had been too tired to stop and visit.

"Well, obviously you do not control her as well as you should."

Sage was genuinely perplexed. "What do you mean? I haven't talked to Lucy since yesterday morning."

"That damn woman shoved, grabbed, and tried to hit me! She and that doctor have conspired to keep a child away from school. I found out, went to retrieve the child, and your wife attacked me!"

"Good Lord," Sage said, but he easily imagined what happened. Lucinda had shared her belief that Barnhart had sexually used the little girl. If anyone knew the signs, it would be his Lucinda. She never spoke about what she called "the monsters" of her childhood but he knew she'd been sold to a brothel at a young age. With a struggle, he kept his face straight and said, "Well, I will certainly talk to her. That is unacceptable, of course."

"Good luck finding her! I went back with Willingham to retrieve the child and both the child and your wife have disappeared. Defler is gone too. They locked the infirmary. She's not at your house either."

"Maybe they're at the doctor's house in town."

Barnhart's headshake was adamant. "No, I went there too. He was home. Willingham and I searched the place but the child wasn't there."

Sage thought and then said, "Do you suppose she took the child to Portland?"

"That was my thought, so I sent one of the tribal policemen to the train platform. He'll be bringing her and the child back."

Barnhart didn't move, clearly pondering his next move. Finally, he said, "I'm going back out to look for Brunner. You go watch the boys. Have them mow the lawn or something useful."

As Barnhart reached the door he turned around. "I fired Mrs. Adell and, come Monday when I'm in Salem to testify, I fully intend to send a telegram to the Indian Service demanding Dr. Defler's termination and the return of my regular clerk and matron. This chaos has gone on long enough! Plan on departing by the end of next week, regardless!" he said, and banged the door shut.

Sage allowed his face to relax into a smirk, "Oh, we plan on leaving but you will too!" he muttered as hope and fear knotted his gut.

Lucinda shifted on the single bed, trying not to wake the child who lay curled against her side. She glanced around, grateful for this hideout. She'd run across the field into the woods, Patty growing heavy in her arms.

Panic made it hard to remember what Eich and Fong had said about the location of Albert Red Hawk's farm. When she'd stumbled far enough into the woods, she crawled beneath a cedar tree's concealing boughs to think. Defler said he'd buy her some time by leaving himself. He hoped Barnhart would assume the girl was hiding at the doctor's home in town.

Once Lucinda caught her breath and calmed herself, she set her mind to recalling the reservation's roads. If she walked straight through the woods, she should intercept the road to Red Hawk's house. The dense forest began at the road's far side. If she heard someone coming, maybe they'd have time to disappear among the trees. She shivered. She didn't want to stay out past dark. There were grizzly bears and mountain lions to worry about, as well as Barnhart and the tribal police.

All that was behind them. Safely lying on the small bed, Lucinda fought the chuckle bubbling in her throat, fearing it would disturb the little girl's slumber. No one could be more surprised than Lucinda about where the two of them had ended up. When she'd knocked on Red Hawk's door, he'd quickly pulled her inside. When she saw who else stood in the neat front room, she turned to run. Red Hawk caught her arm, rushing to reassure, and introduce her to the other man.

"I am afraid you can't stay here. That Ulysses, the tribal policeman, is likely to turn up at any time. Fortunately, Mr. Fong had already left before Ulysses found his nest in the shed. But he's suspicious and we don't know if he's returned from his train trip north," Red Hawk explained.

She smiled. No one would think of looking for them here. Just then, there was a knock on the bedroom door. "Come in," she called and gently nudged Patty awake.

The door opened and Albert Red Hawk's guest of yesterday entered the room carrying a tray holding toast, coffee, and milk. She saw that he wore his uniform and a big smile. No, she thought again, they would never think to look for her and the little girl in tribal officer Victor's cabin.

"This won't be easy," Sage said to White Cloud when they met up in the woods. It was dusk and he'd just watched Barnhart disappear into his house, a shaken man whose day had not gone well. He'd never found his farm instructor, Lucy Adell, or the little girl, Patty Blake.

The woods were quiet, with the birds and other daytime critters already settled down for the night. Reaching the reservation road, they continued straight across it. The dense forest, with its patches of long grass and bracken fern, closed in around them. Dusk sent small bats swooping across open areas as they gobbled mosquitoes and other insects.

White Cloud said, "John, Willingham said your wife attacked Barnhart and kidnapped Patty Blake. He said Barnhart's searching for them."

Sage chuckled. "She did, and I'm proud of her." He told White Cloud of their suspicions about Osborne Barnhart and little girls."

"I didn't know. But, I have seen him stroke their hair and shoulders. It made me uneasy but I never did anything," White Cloud said and Sage could hear self-recrimination in the teacher's voice.

Sage reached out and touched White Cloud's arm, halting him. "Look, Virgil, there is no way you could have known. Barnhart was very, very secretive about what he was doing. Patty Blake is an orphan. He knew she had no family members to watch over her. I suspect that not even that sniveling Willingham knew about it. At least, I hope so."

White Cloud looked unconvinced and simply turned around and kept walking. They reached the windowless hut deep inside the woods. Sage thought the choice of Brunner's prison cell ironic. It was the former house of George Red Hawk's friend, Jefferson Spencer. The elder who'd died during the winter.

Before capturing Brunner, they'd boarded up all the windows and strengthened the hut's weak spots. It had probably been cold during the night but they'd left Brunner a blanket. To Sage's mind, that was better than Brunner deserved.

As they neared the hut, a figure stepped out from behind a tree. They both shook Jeremiah Hunter's hand. They were grateful that Christine Many Feather's beau had been willing to stand guard over Brunner since late the night before. "Is everything alright?" White Cloud asked.

"Well, Virgil, he hollered for a bit after you fellows left last night until he finally realized no one would hear him, except for me. I heard him pacing and cussing all night long,"

"He didn't see you, right?"

"Nah, I never opened the door and disguised my voice when I had to speak to him. He wanted out to pee. I told him that was not going to happen. After a bit, he gave up on that idea."

"You best head home now, get some sleep," White Cloud advised. "You still willing to guard him tonight and tomorrow night? Those should be the last nights. George's trial starts on Monday."

Hunter assented to the plan and walked off into the forest. Once he was out of sight, the two men exchanged a look and Sage said, "Well, here goes something, I hope." He pulled a key from his pocket and opened the shiny new lock.

A wild-eyed Brunner jumped up from sitting on the floorboards when the door swung open. They stepped inside, studying their captive by the light coming through the doorway.

"Turn around," Sage ordered. Brunner complied and White Cloud quickly tied the man's hands. They guided him from the hut and onto a debarked log that once served as the deceased old man's outdoor veranda.

Brunner found his voice. "You are not going to get away with this. You can't just kidnap and imprison someone. Who the hell do you think you are?"

"Tell us about the inspector's murder," Sage said flatly.

"I told you, I don't know anything about no murder."

"I think you followed the inspector and clobbered him with that hatchet. He was getting too close to uncovering your corruption."

Brunner twitched but repeated. "I don't know anything about his murder. That Indian feller killed him. Everyone knows that. Hell, he's going on trial in a few days."

"No, everyone knows George Red Hawk had nothing to do with the murder. He was helping the inspector, that's why you framed him for the killing, isn't it?"

This time Brunner's brow wrinkled and he seemed uncertain as he repeated, "Red Hawk was helping McConnell?" From his widening eyes and the tone of his voice, Sage believed that Brunner hadn't known.

"Yes, he was. The net was closing around you and Barnhart and everyone else. You found out and you killed him."

The industrial teacher's face turned calculating, "Wait a minute, I couldn't have killed McConnell. I was in Salem, selling . . . ." He abruptly clamped his lips shut.

White Cloud's deep voice conveyed contempt, "You were in town selling the school's fall harvest. You sold hay that was meant for the Elipeenas. I know, because I saw you load it up and take it away. You white people force them to buy cattle from your friends and then you steal the feed of those cattle."

"So, who bought the hay?" Sage asked but Brunner remained silent. "If you don't want to be accused of murder, you better tell us the name. If you were in Salem, you can't be the murderer but we need the man's name."

Brunner evidently had no loyalty toward the man because he quickly said, "Alphonse Meyer."

White Cloud's tight-lipped nod said he'd heard of the man. Sage turned to his next topic. "Why did you attack Mrs. Lofton?"

Brunner huffed dismissively, "That nosy parker? Why would I attack her?"

"Because you thought she was looking into your and Barnhart's corruption."

He shook his head, "Look, I didn't have a thing to do with her other than sometimes she takes over watching the boys whilst I go into Moolock. I ain't said but ten words to her."

White Cloud's follow-up question caused Brunner to twitch. "If that's so, how come you called her a 'nosy parker'?"

"Barnhart's always complaining about her. He thinks she's suspects what we've been doing," came Brunner sullen answer.

Sage felt a tingle of excitement. They were getting close to breaking the dam. He decided to hit Brunner with the one thing they knew for certain. "McConnell found out that you sold the school's tractor to your brother and pocketed the money. We know that tractor's in your brother's barn. We know your brother's also going to perjure himself at Red Hawk's trial. Do you want to see Heinrich in the cell next to yours?"

Brunner looked away and, for the first time, regret swept across his face. He took a deep breath. "It's my fault," he said. "I talked him into it. He didn't want to at first, but Barnhart was insisting we sell it. I thought Heinrich's farm was far enough away, no one would find it."

Sage and Virgil exchanged relieved looks. Brunner was going to spill the beans. And he did. He confirmed that Barnhart was selling the school's food and farm products, that the tractor had been stolen but, other than that, Brunner seemed ignorant of Agent Barnhart's other money-making schemes. It seemed Barnhart only involved those he found necessary to carry out a particular scheme. Still, what Brunner had to say about Barnhart was condemnation enough.

"Okay, Mr. Brunner. Here's the deal. We tell the Indian Service inspector that you came to us and helped. You will still lose your job, your brother will lose the tractor, but I will do my best to keep both of you out of jail." Sage's words sent hope flashing across Brunner's face.

Sage raised a hand, "But, you have to write and sign an affidavit repeating what you just said and testify about it at the Red Hawk trial and at any Indian Service proceedings."

Brunner's resistance to that proposition was momentary. He finally said, "Okay, as long as you can promise that my brother won't get into trouble." Sage felt a twinge of respect for the miscreant. People sure were complicated; most were a mix of good in bad, with many mostly good unless temptation reared its ugly head. He'd rarely encountered a purely evil person, though maybe Barnhart fit the bill.

"Brunner, I promise to do my best to keep your brother out of jail. We need to keep you here until early Monday morning. I am sure you understand, we can't exactly trust you."

The man stiffened, opened his mouth to protest, and then thought better of it because his shoulders slumped and he said, "How about giving me something to eat?"

As they walked back through the forest, Sage felt a bit guilty. "Did I make that man a promise that I can't deliver on? Do you think the Indian Service will want the two Brunner brothers jailed?"

White Cloud turned around to give Sage a sardonic look. "The Indian Service will fire Adolph but never worry. The last thing it wants is a corruption trial. They'd think it would be the same as picking up a rock and exposing a termite colony. There is more corruption in the Indian Service than I can shake a spear at. Roosevelt's promised to get rid of it by enforcing civil service regulations. I doubt he'll be able to do that. Even if he does, they'll still find ways around it. There are too many fat plums for the politicians to hand out. They're already complaining because Roosevelt's demanding the Service hire more Indians. Imagine that, Indians working for the Indian Service."

Sage thought White Cloud's sarcasm justified given what he'd seen of suffering on the Elipeena reservation. Sage had a mixed reaction to Brunner's information. The extent of the corruption saddened him but he was elated that they'd secured another witness against Barnhart. But a sobering thought squashed his momentary elation. They were no closer to finding McConnell's murderer. He gave voice to that glum thought. "I'm afraid we've run through all the beards on the reservation. Neither one is Charley's grizzly bear, I'm convinced of that."

"We will find Charley's grizzly bear," White Cloud said confidently.

Sage studied his companion's strong back, wondering why the man sounded so confident.

Virgil seemed to sense Sage's thought because he glanced back over his shoulder and said, "We Indians know things."

Sage didn't know if White Cloud was pulling his leg or stating a fact. He decided it was better not to ask.

TWENTY SEVEN

SAGE ROUNDED THE FRONT CORNER of his house to find Barnhart standing on his porch. The agent saw him and demanded, "Where have you been?"

"I was in the outhouse," Sage lied.

"I came an hour ago and you weren't here. Are you trying to tell me you spent an hour in the outhouse?" Barnhart's tone was suspicious and hostile.

"No," Sage said. "An hour ago I was out looking for my wife who you ran off." Since Barnhart had already announced his intention to do away with Sage's services, he saw no need to suppress his hostility.

"Did you find her and that girl?"

Sage set his mouth in a grim line and gave a terse, "No."

That was another lie. He knew exactly where Lucinda was. Eich was back roaming the reservation. He'd learned from Albert Red Hawk how that tribal policeman, Victor, had switched sides and was protecting Lucinda and Patty. He could imagine Lucinda's amusement at being hidden by a policeman.

Deciding increasing Barnhart's anxiety would be a good thing, Sage asked. "Did you find out what happened to Adolph Brunner?"

Barnhart scowled. "No, it looks like he's left the area for good. Even his brother doesn't know where he is."

"Mr. Barnhart, what was it you wanted to ask me?"

"Ah, nothing. Just wondered if you found that wife of yours."

❀   ❀   ❀

Sunday dawned as a perfect spring day. The sky was blue, the air sweet, and every plant looked rain-washed and newly green. Sage had slept easy knowing Lucinda was safe. Eich and Fong were also staying nearby. Virgil White Cloud had insisted they both sleep at his place since Barnhart and Willingham never visited him.

The day before, Sage had walked to Moolock and asked the doctor to send a coded message to Philander Gray. They thought the doctor sending a telegram would be less noteworthy than Sage. They didn't know whether Barnhart had a confederate or two among the townspeople. Afterward, the two of them had waited at Defler's house for the reply which came quickly and satisfactorily. By nightfall, Brunner would be confessing his sins to U.S. Marshal Reed. Come Monday morning, Reed, Fong, and Eich would escort the industrial teacher to Salem.

This morning, Sage sat on the front porch, wallowing in what his mother would call a bad case of the "drearies." No wonder. It was the day before the trial and they still didn't know who had murdered Inspector McConnell.

Suddenly, his mother was rounding the corner of the school building and crossing the lawn with angry strides. She looked ready to bite somebody. He stood when she reached the porch.

"Well, it's official, I've been fired. By week's end I'm to go back to my son and that awful wife of his," she declared before grinning at him.

"I saw that look on your face and wondered."

She waved a careless hand, "That was for the benefit of that weasel Willingham. He's watching out the window. Will we be able to dump him in the stew as well?"

Sage shrugged. "We're certainly going to try. I suspect his bank account will be unaccountably large. Barnhart must pay him to keep his lips buttoned about all the corruption. I guarantee he'll spill the beans in two seconds flat if he thinks he's in danger."

"I agree. It won't take a sledgehammer to crack that nut. If 'ole Weldon's staring at jail time, he'll squeal like a pig. Anyways, I came over here because he's been following me around, trying to overhear whatever I say. Why, in church this morning, I sat next to Christine and darned if he didn't plop himself down on the bench right behind us."

"Made it hard to talk?"

"Nah, we whispered. He liked to fall off his bench trying to hear. Even if he did, it meant nothing. I was just whispering nonsense to make him crazy."

"You certainly have taken a dislike to the poor man," Sage observed.

She sniffed. "Two rotten peas in a pod—Barnhart and Willingham both. I can't wait to see them get their comeuppance. Anyways, I'm here because I want to know what's been happening and whether our Lucinda got someplace safe."

He told her about Brunner and what Eich and Fong had learned at the brother's farm. He also reassured her about Lucinda. A few minutes later, she left to relieve Christine of her supervising duties, promising to hang a kerchief out her window if she needed him at the school.

It was nearing noon and he was still sitting on the porch, mulling over everything they knew when his eye caught the flutter of a kerchief. Less than a minute later, he was running up the school's porch steps. His mother stood outside the front door.

"What is it?" he asked.

"Barnhart came into the office a while ago. It sounds like he's tearing the place up."

"Okay, I'll handle it. Wait on the landing above. If you hear anything, run for White Cloud's house to get help."

"Humph," she responded.

Not pausing for her agreement, he brushed past her and entered the school. The office door was locked but Sage still had the key. He looked over his shoulder. Mae was standing right behind him. He tried to shoo her upstairs but she shook her head, stepped to the side of the door, and folded her arms.

Barnhart is right—I can't control the women in my life, Sage thought as he turned the key. He stepped into chaos. Papers lay strewn across the outer office floor and the file drawers were pulled out, canting the entire cabinet forward. He heard Barnhart's frantic curses coming from the inner office. That door was open and Sage saw that the paper storm had hit that office as well.

Crossing to the inner door, he saw Barnhart at his desk, sitting with his head in his hands. "Good grief! Has the office been burgled?" Sage asked.

Barnhart's head jerked up. "No damnit. I can't find anything. There's papers missing—letters, invoices, receipts. You must have misfiled them somewhere."

"Maybe I did misfile them. What exactly is missing? Maybe I can help you find them." Sage felt a surge of hope. Maybe the missing papers were a clue to the murderer. Barnhart's next words quickly dashed that hope.

"Some delivery receipts from the Indian Service, the school's fuel contract, some of Defler's letters to me, copies of correspondence I sent to the Indian Service, and a few other papers." Barnhart squinted at Sage. "I don't suppose you remember seeing those items?"

All paperwork Fong had carried up to Portland, Sage realized with an inward smile. But, he shook his head and said helpfully, "I'm happy to look for them, maybe tidy up a bit."

"Not in here you don't," Barnhart snapped and then softened his tone. "Go ahead and straighten up the front room. And keep an eye out for those documents." He got up from his desk. "Lock up when you're done. I have to go pack and leave for Salem. The Red Hawk trial is tomorrow. I'm spending the night in Salem because I'm to testify in the morning."

Barnhart left after carefully locking the inner door. Sage heard his mother and Barnhart exchanging words in the central hallway. He stuck his head out to make sure that there were no problems only to glimpse her skirt disappearing up the stairs and the front door closing behind Barnhart.

Sage turned and began picking up, ordering, and putting away the papers Barnhart had flung about. As he did so, he was hoping that Barnhart would never return to his office and that, instead, an Indian Service inspector would arrive to take over. That was what Gray's coded message had promised. A federal marshal and an inspector should arrive tonight. He didn't mind tidying up since they'd be inspecting Barnhart's paperwork.

Sage was reluctant to leave once he was finished. He was certain there was a clue to the murderer in the office. He sat at the desk, idly running his mind back over the list of things that Barnhart had been hunting for. He'd never seen the agent that shaken or angry. He was willing to bet that fear drove the agent's anger. Most likely, Barnhart was terrified he'd be tied to McConnell's murder. That would explain the agent's increasingly irrational behavior.

"Darn," he exclaimed aloud. "Something has to be here!" He was tempted to search the office himself but then, Barnhart would have found it if it was in the office. The mess said the agent had conducted a thorough search for something. A thought flashed through his head. Suppose the document Barnhart wanted was one of those taken by Sage? His mind skittered down that path for a few minutes as he gazed unseeingly out the window. What had he taken? Most of what Barnhart said was missing, that's what.

He put his head in his hands, mimicking Barnhart's earlier posture. A yell from outside drew his attention back to the window. The boys were playing a game of baseball on the lawn between the school and the woodshed. Playing games was one of the few times the children acted carefree. He watched as Joshua hit the baseball so hard that it sailed up and over the woodshed to the cheers of his teammates. Home run!

Woodshed. Why did the thought of that structure send a tingle up his spine? He honed in on that feeling, grasping it with all his mental force. Then he remembered the one other time he'd seen Barnhart spitting angry. The agent had been haranguing the fuel contractor. Sage remembered something striking—that man hadn't acted the least bit intimidated. Odd that. The man's fuel contracting business depended on Barnhart's goodwill. Sage replayed the image of that argument in his mind's eye. He sat bolt upright. Minutes later he was hurriedly locking the office door and running for White Cloud's house.

When he burst through the front door without knocking, he found Virgil, Fong, and Eich sitting around the kitchen table, playing some kind of card game. A closer look revealed that Fong was teaching the other two the fine points of fan tan. They startled at his abrupt entrance but he didn't apologize.

"Virgil, we've got to get to Salem as soon as possible!" he exclaimed.

That night, a caravan of wagons, buggies, and horses left the Grand Ronde reservation. A white farmer who'd bought one of the unassigned allotments eventually got word to the acting agent that every Indian seemed to be leaving the reservation. Duncan grumbled. He'd issued no permits. He struggled to dress in the dark, trying not to wake his wife. Once outside, he noted the clear sky glittered like a jeweled vault overhead. Tiredly he hitched the horse to his buggy and set out after the people who were leaving his jurisdiction without his permission. On his way, he stopped by the old army blockhouse now used as a jail and police barracks. He planned to enlist the aid of the tribal police in turning back the renegades. He found no one there.

Across the valley and to the south of Salem, the Elipeena people were also on the move beneath the starry sky. Their caravan moved silently past the end of the school's driveway. That night no one tried to find Barnhart to tell him that most of his charges had departed the reservation without his permission.

TWENTY EIGHT

LUCINDA HELD PATTY'S HAND AS they climbed the tall cement steps leading into the imposing courthouse. They'd arrived in the dark and it wasn't until morning that the two hundred or so people camping on its grounds saw the building in all its white glory, complete with cupola, clock, and copper Goddess of Justice gleaming in the dawn.

Patty's hand trembled in hers. "Don't worry, dear. Your friends surround you. They won't let anyone hurt you, not even the bad man," Lucinda assured her. She'd wanted to leave Patty behind with one of the Elipeena grandmothers but Patty had cried hysterically and clung to Lucinda's leg. So, when Lucinda climbed aboard one of the Elipeena wagons, the little girl was with her. Fortunately, the night had been dry and people had been able to roll up in blankets and get some sleep on the neatly trimmed courthouse lawn. At dawn, there was generous sharing of dried meat and berries as well as coffee a few folks boiled atop small campfires.

The police arrived as expected, but they kept their distance, seeing the peaceful nature of the overwhelming numbers. "They're not going to poke a stick into a quiet beehive," Victor told her. He was wearing his full tribal police uniform, as were the policemen from the Grand Ronde reservation. The unperturbed presence of the tribal policemen had to be reassuring to the Salem officers.

The courthouse doors opened promptly at nine and she and Patty entered midst a protective throng of Indians. Within seconds, they'd filled the small courtroom to overflowing with even more standing in the hallway.

A courtroom clerk entered, took one look, and retreated. Minutes later the clerk returned to declare that the judge was moving the trial to a larger courtroom on the second floor. Everyone trooped up the inner staircase and into a much larger and more ornate courtroom. Even still, there was standing room only. Albert Red Hawk made sure that Lucinda and Patty sat close to the front behind the defense table. She had the pleasure of seeing Barnhart blanch when he caught sight of her on his way to his reserved seat, in the same row as hers but, across the aisle and behind the prosecutor's table.

The black-robed judge entered and everyone rose to their feet. After a steely-eyed look at the crowd, he sternly warned them to behave. Next, he ordered that George Red Hawk be brought into the courtroom. At the manacled man's entrance, the entire group of Indians silently rose in respect even as the judge fruitlessly banged his gavel. It was only after George took his seat beside Philander Gray that his supporters sat down.

Barnhart craned his neck around, anger suffusing his face when he recognized many of the Elipeenas. His lips tightened as he turned to stare straight ahead. Seconds later, he rose to push his way down his bench to reach the Elipeena tribal policeman who sat at the end of Lucinda's bench. Barnhart's fierce whisper carried, "You get these damn Indians out of here! They don't have my permission to be here!"

Victor looked up at Barnhart, his face set, and his voice steady as he said, "I suggest you take your seat, Agent Barnhart, the trial's about to begin."

Barnhart stared down at the policeman in surprise. He finally found his voice and hissed, "You are fired!"

"Maybe," was Victor's enigmatic reply. Barnhart stood a moment longer then turned and pushed his way back to his seat.

The judge banged his gavel and began speaking. He noted that, although the trial was taking place in a state courtroom, he was a federal judge and that this was a federal matter because a major crime had taken place on an Indian reservation and the alleged perpetrator was Indian. His statement concluded, he instructed the clerk to bring the jury in. Minutes later, twelve white men entered and took seats in the jury box, all of them looking appropriately somber.

Once the jury settled into place, there was a disturbance at the back of the courtroom. Three white men entered. They proceeded down the aisle, to take reserved front row seats directly behind the defense table. Lucinda recognized both Eich, now dressed in a suit and tie, and Adolph Brunner, similarly dressed. The third man wore a shiny brass badge prominently displayed on his suit coat. As they sidled their way along the row to take their seats, Lucinda caught a glimpse of Barnhart's horrified face. She couldn't resist. She winked when the agent's frantic eyes flicked towards her.

The prosecutor called Barnhart as his first witness. His direct testimony was what they'd expected but subdued, no doubt because the man was in shock over who was in the courtroom. Still, he testified Red Hawk had always been a troublemaker, a drunkard, violent, and frequently left the reservation without permission. The prosecutor offered the reservation's ledger book into evidence. The jury seemed to be lapping it up, believing every word.

Gray rose and announced that he had no questions which caused Barnhart to slump in evident relief. That relief was short-lived because Gray went on to ask the court's leave to recall Barnhart as a hostile witness during the defendant's case in chief. He further asked that the judge order Barnhart to remain in the courtroom until the close of all testimony. The judge granted both requests and Barnhart was temporarily excused from the witness box. He acted dazed and stumbled as he returned to his seat.

Lucinda smiled at the next worsening of the agent's situation. A large Indian man flashed a badge at Barnhart's nearest neighbor and gestured the man out of his seat. He then took that seat next to Barnhart. The wide smile he gave the agent was more wolfish than friendly. It was clear to everyone including, Barnhart, that the man was there to make sure that the agent stayed put. Lucinda figured that he must be the Indian Service inspector they had been expecting.

The prosecutor was clearly uneasy about Barnhart's behavior but he soldiered on, likely confident of his next witness. He called Heinrich Brunner, the man whose testimony was supposed to place George Red Hawk at the scene of Inspector McConnell's murder.

After the clerk swore in Brunner, and he had stated his name, the prosecutor began, "Mr. Brunner, did you find yourself on the Elipeena reservation on the day of Inspector William McConnell's murder?"

Brunner opened his mouth, only to catch sight of Herman Eich who was staring at him with raised eyebrows and his own brother, Adolph, who gave a negative shake of his head. For a moment, like a beached fish,

Brunner's mouth opened and closed. Lucinda had talked with Eich and understood the farmer's dilemma. He'd told Eich he'd been in California on that day—a fact easily proved. If he said what the prosecutor wanted, he'd be perjuring himself.

"Mr. Brunner, do you need me to repeat the question?" the prosecutor nudged, puzzled by the man's hesitation.

Brunner looked sheepish, licked his lips, and said, "No sir. I was in California."

Lucinda didn't see the prosecutor's reaction because she was looking sideways at Barnhart. The agent abruptly bent over, put his elbows on his knees, and hid his face in his hands. She and Albert Red Hawk exchanged grins.

Following Brunner's testimony, the prosecutor struggled to keep his case afloat, moving on to testimony from the doctor who'd declared the inspector dead. Next, he had the sheriff testify about how the tribal policeman, Ulysses, found the body on the trail, and then the items on George Red Hawk's property.

Gray's single cross-examination question to the sheriff was pithy and to point. "How do you know that hatchet and those partially burnt clothes were not planted on Mr. Red Hawk's property?"

The sheriff gazed at the Indian faces staring at him, some of which he had to recognize. Whatever the reason, he chose to answer truthfully while making no effort to bolster the prosecution's case. "I don't know whether they were planted."

"So, those items could have been planted?"

"Yes," came the sheriff's terse agreement.

The prosecutor declined to ask further questions and called his next witness, Ulysses. Despite repeated calls, the young tribal policeman neither answered nor appeared. Lucinda knew he wouldn't, no matter how many times they called his name. She'd seen the telegram from Mr. Conteur that Eich had received the night before. "TP U got lost. Stop. Broke leg. Stop. Recuperating in camp. Stop."

In Ulysses' absence, the prosecutor had no choice but to rest his case.

It was Gray's turn next. He called Charley Red Hawk as his first witness. There was a rustle as the small boy rose from beneath the shelter of his Uncle Jack's arm and calmly walked down the aisle toward the witness box. Lucinda saw George Red Hawk's face turn encouraging and proud as he looked at his son. The young boy climbed into the witness box and calmly sat on the chair.

Gray gently led the boy through the introductory steps. Patty softly squawked and Lucinda realized she was squeezing the little's girl hand too tight. She loosened her grip, shot the girl an apologetic look, and leaned forward to hear the next exchange.

"Charley, did you know Inspector McConnell?

"Yes. He was my father's friend. He was a nice man. He gave me a toy horse."

"Were you on the path to your house the day that Inspector McConnell was killed?"

"Yes," came the meek reply as the boy stiffened with the memory. "I wanted to see my grandmother."

"Charley, when you were on that path did you see someone kill Mr. McConnell?"

"Yes."

"Can you tell us what you saw happen?"

The boy gulped and then declared in a strong, clear voice, "I saw a grizzly bear, dressed like a man, hit Mr. McConnell with a hatchet."

Lucinda watched the men on the jury exchange disbelieving looks. Glancing behind her, she saw only a sea of calm, stoic faces.

Just then, the rear doors slammed open and three men began striding down the aisle. It was clear that strong hands were gripping the elbows of the unwilling man in the middle. That man was large, with heavy shoulders, broad chest, long dark brown hair, and a full, unruly beard. A white sticking plaster decorated his right temple. Sage and Virgil didn't hesitate as they propelled him down the aisle.

Everyone's eyes snapped forward at the sound of the witness chair falling over. Charley had jumped to his feet, his eyes wide in a deathly pale face. With a trembling finger, he pointed at the man tightly held by Sage and Virgil White Cloud and cried, "That's him! That's the grizzly bear that killed Mr. McConnell! I saw him and he chased me!"

Gray said, in a loud voice, "Let the record show that the witness, Charley Red Hawk, has identified Bjorn Torben, as the killer of Indian Service Inspector William McConnell.

"Through the testimony of Agent Osborne Barnhart and John Adell, a clerk on the Elipeena reservation, the defense will show that Bjorn Torben is the contractor who supplies fuel to the Elipeena reservation boarding school. And, we will further show that he is a willing participant in a criminal conspiracy headed by Osborne Barnhart. That conspiracy has defrauded the Indian Service and the Elipeena people of thousands of dollars and caused more than one unnecessary death. Moreover, through the testimony of Virgil White Cloud, a teacher at the boarding school, we will show that Inspector McConnell was working with Mr. White Cloud and Mr. Red Hawk to expose that criminal conspiracy when the inspector was foully slain."

These words triggered sudden action by Barnhart who leaped up and began pushing his way between bench back and spectators' knees, aiming for a side door out of the courtroom. The Indian Service inspector was close behind.

At the same time, Torben hollered, "Barnhart ordered me to kill him!" and gave a mighty jerk that freed his arms. He whirled toward the main doors. He never got there. An unmovable wall of Elipeena men stood between him and freedom. Lucinda swiveled her attention back to Barnhart and had to chuckle.

A small Chinese man stood before the side door blocking Barnhart's escape. Even though he was smaller than the charging agent, it must have been the malevolent grin on Fong's face that made Barnhart swerve toward the door into the judge's chambers. He didn't make it. The Indian inspector snagged Barnhart by the back of his pants, jerking him to a halt. Soon Barnhart and Torben stood before the judge, their arms gripped by the Indian inspector and the federal marshal.

The somber, well-dressed, Indian inspector stepped forward to address the judge. He spoke loud enough that the hushed crowd heard every word. "Your honor, I am Inspector Hayfield of the Indian Service. I am here before you to state that Mr. Barnhart has been relieved his duties pending an investigation. We anticipate that the Indian Service will be levying corruption charges against him. I have taken charge of the Elipeena reservation. With me is a U.S. Marshal, Charles Reed. I ask that you allow us to take custody of Osborne Barnhart for immediate transport to a holding cell in the Oregon State Penitentiary. Police officers from the Grand Ronde reservation will assist me." He nodded at two tribal officers who stood and walked forward.

The judge wasted no time. "Inspector Hayfield, Mr. Barnhart is hereby rendered into your custody. But, should Mr. Torben's declaration of Osborne Barnhart's participation in William McConnell's murder prove credible, he must be remanded back into state custody to answer a murder charge. While I understand the crime occurred on the Elipeena reservation, the alleged murderers are white men, and the victim was a white man, therefore such a charge is within the State Court's jurisdiction."

The judge nodded at tribal police officer, Victor. "Officer, please help U.S. Marshal Reed escort Mr. Torben to the courthouse jail cell. I expect a state court judge will arraign him, tomorrow morning, on the charge of murder." He flicked his hand and both prisoners were promptly hustled out the side door.

The judge next turned his attention to the defense table. "Mr. Gray, you need say nothing. Mr. Red Hawk, the court apologizes for the gross miscarriage of justice that resulted in your incarceration and this trial. Case dismissed," he added with a bang of his gavel. He immediately rose from the bench and left the courtroom. Cheers and hugs erupted as Charley ran into his father's open arms.

A small voice spoke at Lucinda's side. "Did the judge make that bad Mr. Barnhart go away like you promised?"

Lucinda picked the little girl up and hugged her tightly. "Yes, honey, that bad man is gone for good, just like I promised." Her answer triggered the first grin she'd ever seen on Patty Blake's face.

TWENTY NINE

"SURE WISH I COULD HAVE seen Barnhart's comeuppance. That must have been a treat," Mae said, only to have laughter erupt when she added, "Maybe I'll send him a sympathy card."

They were in the boarding school classroom. Those who always attended such meetings were there: Mae, Sage, Lucinda, Fong, Matthew, and Eich. But this time, the group was much larger because so many more people needed to be there: George Red Hawk, Albert Red Hawk, Charley Red Hawk, Captain Jack, Virgil White Cloud, Christine Many Feathers, Jeremiah Hunter, Joshua, Dr. Defler, and even the tribal policeman, Victor. They were there to hear from the two other people who were also present: Philander Gray and Inspector Alexander Hayfield.

Gray stood up to address the group. "As expected, Bjorn Torben is talking to the authorities since he's facing the noose. As you suspected, he grossly underbid the fuel contract so that Barnhart could select him as the contractor. Once he was awarded the bid, Torben shorted every delivery by a considerable amount. He and Barnhart split the overpayment. He claims Barnhart had that arrangement with most of the school and reservation contractors."

Gray turned to Sage to say, "You were right about the blankets and coats. The invoices show delivery of the highest quality goods but, instead, the merchant delivered the lowest quality goods. Once again, the merchant and Barnhart split the difference between the invoiced charge and the actual amount paid for the inferior goods.

"Inspector McConnell was here when Torben made one of his shorted fuel deliveries and asked to see the delivery receipt. Of course, McConnell reached the same conclusion as Mr. Adell: Barnhart paid Torben for more wood than he delivered.

"Barnhart told Torben that McConnell had to be gotten rid of. Fortunately, Barnhart didn't know that Mr. White Cloud and Mr. Red Hawk were working with the inspector. Had he known of their involvement, there might have been more murders."

Gray let that sink in, then continued, "Three days ago, the State Attorney General brought murder charges against Barnhart and Torben. We suspect those charges will take precedence over any Indian Service corruption charges. I'll let Inspector Hayfield explain the Indian Service's intentions." He turned to Hayfield, nodded, and took his seat.

When Hayfield stood his face was solemn. "I wish I could tell you that Barnhart's behavior was unique but it's not. President Roosevelt is determined to root out corruption on the reservations and in the boarding schools. At this point, he is putting more trust in the newly hired Indians, like me, than in the long term Indian Service employees.

"I am a member of the Seneca Nation in western New York State. For many years I was a tribal policeman. In this case, the Indian Service has ordered me to compile evidence and write a report detailing the corruption that has occurred on the Elipeena reservation."

The inspector paused and it was clear that he was reluctant to say his next words. "Barnhart's corrupt activities represent an extreme case. Unfortunately, the Indian Service has already seen every one of Barnhart's swindles on reservations elsewhere in this country. Corruption is a plague that infects the agency's highest levels." The inspector's words fell on his listeners' spirits like a sodden blanket.

George Red Hawk finally broke the silence. "What is going to happen to our reservation and our school? How does the Indian Service plan to right the wrong? Is it even going to acknowledge the harm that has been done?"

Hayfield shifted awkwardly. "Unfortunately, I can't answer that question. I am new to the Service and conditions within the Service are changing daily. If Barnhart is convicted of murder, that means the death penalty. I suspect the Indian Service will see no point in a public corruption trial. If there is no trial, then the agency could bury my report detailing that corruption. I'm told that is a common occurrence."

His face became thoughtful and he added, "One would think that the Elipeenas have the right to see that report because Barnhart stole their money and their resources. Again, I just can't say what the Indian Service will do."

He paused as another idea hit him and added, with a somewhat conspiratorial smile, "That Dr. Lane of yours' seems to have an inside track into the agency. Perhaps he will help you obtain the written report."

Sage glanced around the room and saw that no Indian face looked satisfied. He also saw no surprise. Doubtless, they were used to a bureaucracy that put their interests and rights last. "What is the answer to George's question about the Indian Service's plans for the reservation and the school?" he asked.

It was obvious from the smile on Hayfield's face that he was more comfortable with this subject. "First off, Brunner, Willingham, Matron Daley, her son, clerk Otis Daley, and the cook have all been fired and informed that they are now under investigation for corruption. None of them will return to this reservation nor will the Service allow them to work in any other position. I have received written confirmation of that decision. Furthermore, their replacements are on the way and should arrive by week's end."

Hayfield glanced around the room. "At my request, the Service has appointed Virgil White Cloud temporary headmaster at the school pending his acceptance. If his performance is satisfactory, I have also received a promise that it will be a permanent appointment. He will be one of the first Indians to serve in that capacity."

Everyone turned to look at White Cloud. At his solemn nod of acceptance, they began applauding. Hayfield smiled and continued, "Even though you have all done an amazing job of gathering evidence, there is still more to be gathered." He turned to Sage. "Mr. Adell, you were correct in thinking that Barnhart's office safe contained a record of his corruption payouts. I need to investigate the people he named in that ledger. Additional corruption charges will likely follow."

He smiled and added. "The safe also contained nearly fifty thousand dollars in cash. Thanks to Dr. Lane's intercession, the Indian Service has authorized me to retain that money and pay it out to the individual Elipeenas who were shorted on their allotment and lease monies. It won't cover all their losses but it will help."

There was a stirring of satisfaction and exchanges of smiles among his listeners. Hayfield turned his attention to Dr. Defler. "Sir, I know that this has been a trying experience for you. It is my sincere hope, and the Indian Service's wish, that you will stay on as the reservation's doctor and," here he paused before saying, "as the reservation's temporary agent."

The doctor began shaking his head. "I will certainly stay on as the reservation's doctor but I do not feel qualified to act as its agent."

George Red Hawk didn't give Hayfield time to respond. He stood, looked around the room, and saw agreement in the faces of his fellow Elipeenas. "Inspector Hayfield has already discussed his wishes with us and we agree. On behalf of our people, Dr. Defler, we ask that you take the position. Inspector Hayfield will not have the time to properly handle the job given the investigations he still must conduct. Dr. Defler, you have proven that you are trustworthy and that you genuinely care about the Elipeena people. That is the most important quality in an agent."

Once again there was applause. In its aftermath, Defler rose to his feet, his face flushed with embarrassment, his expression humble. "I don't know what to say. This is unexpected. My only hope was that we would finally get the medical supplies we need." He looked toward Lucinda who smiled and nodded.

Defler turned to Hayfield and said with firm resolve, "I will take the temporary agent position on three conditions."

Hayfield's eyebrows rose but he tilted his head to indicate that Defler should continue. "First, that it is temporary will be permanently filled by an Indian. Second, Joshua is due to graduate from the boarding school in a few weeks. Until that happens, and over the summer, I ask that he be assigned to the infirmary as my assistant." He turned to Lucinda and said, "Mrs. Adell, Lucy, I can never praise you enough or thank you enough for your wonderful work and for what you and your friends have accomplished."

Defler then turned back to face Hayfield. "Joshua has expressed an interest in working as my assistant and I believe he shows a genuine aptitude for medicine. Therefore, my second condition is that the Indian Service grants him full scholarships to attend both undergraduate college and medical school."

Joshua gasped and Matthew gave him a congratulatory light punch on the arm. The boys exchanged grins. Defler wasn't finished. "I understand that Dartmouth College, in New Hampshire, is particularly welcoming to Indian students and has programs to assist those students struggling against the deficiencies of their Indian school educations. Additionally, I want him to attend my alma mater, Boston Medical School. I can ease his way there because of my many contacts."

Hayfield gulped but said gamely, "I will forward your conditions on to the Indian Service. I suspect that they will agree given their desire to sweep this situation under the bureaucratic rug. I am sure Dr. Lane will help me convince them that acceptance is in the best interest of the Service."

Sage thought that, while the inspector was new to his job, he was quickly mastering the machinations of the bureaucratic life. He hoped Hayfield would stay in the Indian Service and rise in its ranks.

"What about Patty?" Lucinda asked, causing everyone to switch their attention first to her and then to Hayfield but it was Defler who answered, "Inspector Hayfield and I discussed the situation. We agree that, at this time, Patty is too mentally traumatized and physically unhealthy to return to living in the school. Therefore, the inspector has agreed to let her live with my wife and I until such time as a good Elipeena home can be found for her. She trusts us and we are very fond of her. She will continue to attend the school during the day." His words got a grateful smile from Lucinda and nods of assent from the Elipeenas in the room.

The doctor wasn't finished. "Additionally, both Inspector Hayfield and I agree that all the children would fare better if the school was converted into a day school." This time there were cheers. Once the jubilation quieted, Defler added, "Please understand that we must first get the Indian Service's agreement before that can happen. Fortunately, President Roosevelt seems to favor that approach, so we are hopeful."

Elation filled the room as the meeting ended and everyone headed for the cookies and cakes Lucinda and Mae had baked early that morning.

Later, once night fell, the Portland team met in Sage and Lucinda's tiny house. The six of them gleefully hashed over their mission's outcome. Still, an unsettled undercurrent ran beneath their celebratory mood. Sage finally gave it voice.

"Together, in the past, we've seen greed and ignorance's incredible ugliness. But I have to say, this experience has nearly brought me to my knees. If the Elipeenas' experience was unique, maybe I'd be more hopeful. But, as Hayfield said, the treatment of the Indians, the ignorance, the arrogance, and most of all, the greed, that assaults them—it's pervasive and continuous. So, I worry about the long term impact on them as a people. I worry about their future. I feel powerless to stop or change it."

Eich was the first to respond. "We should worry about ourselves as white people. Every harm done to the Indian people plunges a knife into our own souls. Much of what they could have taught us has been lost because of our greed, arrogance, and ignorance. Despite this, they still have much to teach us.

"And, there is hope. People like Gabriel Conteur, Captain Jack, and others have picked up the torch that whites knocked from the hands of the Indian people. They are determined that their ancestors will not remain invisible to themselves or to us. Our job is to support their determination and efforts."

Mae spoke up. As usual, her pithy words struck at the heart of the matter. "You mean white people need to shut up, listen, and try following for a change."

The End

HISTORICAL NOTES

THIS STORY IS FULL OF historical facts. There are a few preliminary bits you should know. For example, the Indian Service had many names over the years and was administered by a variety of different bureaucracies. The story uses "Indian Service" because that was the name its employees tended to use in their autobiographical writings. It is also descriptive and less confusing than its various other official names.

There is a tendency to portray the American Indian people as being interchangeable. This is an error. People's experiences living in settled towns along the seacoast were distinctly different from that of people ranging over the high plateaus. With few exceptions, tribal myths, practices, religion, and history differed—sometimes greatly. They do seem to share some common values: For example, an abhorrence of liars and elevating communal loyalty over individualism. One aspect of their differing cosmologies appeared to be the perception shared by aboriginal people worldwide, including the long-vanished European aboriginals. That is the perception that a god essence permeates everything in nature. This perception created a deep and abiding spiritual connection with the natural world that the current, individualistic, profit-oriented, mainstream culture does not possess in as strong a measure.

The country, and this story, owes a great debt to the initial Euro-American "salvage" anthropologists of the 1800s who traveled around the Pacific Northwest, capturing firsthand accounts of Indian life. Foremost among these were Franz Boas, Melville Jacobs, and Elizabeth Jacobs.

Without their early efforts, enormous amounts of Pacific Northwest Indian history would have been lost.

Overview

1. Scholars sharply disagree on the population numbers for the pre-Columbus contiguous United States (excludes Alaska, Hawaii, Puerto Rico, and other U.S. territories). Their estimates range from 2.1 million to 18 million. One estimate goes as high as 112 million. We will never know. We do know that the European invasion created the greatest demographic disaster ever seen in the world. Most scholars do agree that by the 1890s over 90% of the original population was gone with the 1890 census counting only 248,000 Indians. The 2010 census shows that Indian resilience increased that number to 5 million people who identify as Indian or Alaska Native.

2. Pre-Columbus, the contiguous United States was home to at least 273 tribal nations comprised of innumerable smaller bands. They spoke over 300 different languages and countless dialects among the bands. Today, the federal government recognizes a combined, tribal nation and band count of 333 but there are at least 245 existing tribal groups it refuses to recognize despite these people's continued existence. Today, approximately 175 Indian languages are spoken in the U.S.

3. As with the disputed national counts, estimates of the original Oregon Indian population range from 45,000 to 150,000 or more. That number dropped to less than 4,951 in the 1900s census. It is estimated that disease alone killed 90-95% of Oregon's original inhabitants. Malaria, brought by a visiting ship, killed many of them before any other white people arrived. Thus, Lewis and Clark and the first traders only saw the devastated remnants of the original population. The 2010 census shows 22,275 people who identified themselves as "Indian."

4. The original Oregonians lived in 32 different tribes comprised of approximately 95 bands. They spoke 21 languages that used 39 different dialects.

Story Characters

5. The letter from Inspector William McConnell that appears in the first chapter is mostly verbatim, changed only to include the fictional Elipeena reservation. The original letter was addressed to Harry Lane who was a U.S. senator serving on an Indian Affairs committee in Congress. The reservation McConnell was alluding to was unnamed. The story uses the inspector's real name to honor his efforts in trying to expose the corruption and wrongs occurring at the hands of the Indian Service. There is no evidence the real William McConnell was murdered.

6. As seen by the Lane quote at the story's beginning, Lane was a fervent defender of Indian rights. When he became a U.S. senator in 1912, he argued for stronger oversight and eventual abolishment of the Indian Service. He spent much of his boyhood in the company of the Kalapuya Indians of the Willamette Valley and developed a high regard for them and their cultural values. It may be that the stress their culture placed on communal responsibility is what led him to foreswear his status as a scion of an important Oregon family and dedicate himself to serving as Portland's "Poor People's Doctor", and then, as its progressive mayor and senator.

7. The Barnhart character is based on a former reservation agent of that name. He was a scoundrel placed in charge of the Umatilla Reservation in Central Oregon. Barnhart was temporarily removed from his position. In a three-part article, published in the 1904 *Oregon Historical Society Quarterly*, Barnhart's replacement detailed the corruption he uncovered. Despite this, Barnhart, who was a political appointee, was thereafter returned to his position. Only many years later was his employment terminated, "for cause". The real Barnhart did not commit all the types of corruption attributed to the fictional Barnhart.

8. The story character of Father Felix Bucher is based on an individual of the same name. He was the priest assigned to the Grand Ronde reservation during the story's time period. The description of his living quarters came from a letter written by

a white woman who visited him. People were concerned about his Spartan lifestyle and gave him gifts to make his life more physically comfortable. He was famous for giving those gifts away to the reservation people, including giving away a gifted bed more than once. Finally, someone thought to loan him a bed after telling him that, because it was a loan, he couldn't give it away. Bucher wrote of mystical and inexplicable experiences he had while serving the Grand Ronde people.

9. The character of Gabriel Conteur was inspired by the life of Francis La Fleche. He descended from the Omaha, Ponca and French peoples. His father served as chief of the Omaha. La Fleche was sent to Indian boarding schools and became the first Indian ethnologist attached to the Smithsonian Institute. He was supremely accomplished, earning degrees in anthropology and law as well as creating an opera based on Omaha stories. There is no evidence that he ever worked with Pacific Northwest tribes. Instead, his ethnological work focused on the Omaha and Osage cultures. His writings are still considered "seminal" contributions to the field. He became president of the Anthropological Society of Washington in 1922. One colleague wrote that Francis La Flesche "was, in every way, modest but none the less, was gifted with a social humor..." and "An instinctive kindliness which won the heart. Intellectually he was forthright and conscientious and fully alive to the quality of the work which he achieved."

10. All of the Indian characters in this story are imaginary. I do not know and I cannot know what it was like to be an Oregon Indian in the early 1900s. That said, I have tried to faithfully have these imaginary characters state what Indian authors and ethnologists have reported concerning the history and lifeways of the various Oregon Indian tribes and the actions of the early white settlers. In particular, the various snippets of the different tribal histories related by Charley's Uncle Jack come from the historical record. Unfortunately, an enormous amount of Oregon Indian history has been lost or remains to be discovered.

Pre-European Indian Life

11. The Chinook tribe, with its plentiful salmon and other seafood, was the wealthiest tribe in the Columbia River region. They traded widely. Because of them, Chinook Wawa, also known as Chinook Jargon, became the universal language used among the tribes in Northern California, Oregon, Washington, and British Columbia. It is based on Chinook and incorporates other tribal languages, French, and English. Later, Chinook Wawa was used by white traders and settlers when dealing with Pacific Northwest Indians. It is still spoken today.

12. The Chinooks were remarkable in their wealth and also in the fact that they lived in villages comprised of plank houses that held large extended families. Anthropologists note that they are one of the very few hunter-gatherer groups in the world to live in towns comprised of permanent dwellings.

13. Wapato, a tuber potato-like plant, fond of swampy places, was a staple of the Multnomah people. They lived in villages near the confluence of the Willamette and Columbia Rivers. In 2003, the Multnomah County government built a jail at this location. They named this new jail, "Wapato."

14. The Kalapuya people of the Willamette Valley practiced plant and animal husbandry to a greater extent than did other tribal nations. Whites were astounded by the valley's beauty and abundance. Only very recently has it been recognized that the valley's bountiful condition came about because of the Kalapuyas' deliberate planning, conservation, and labor. Among the Oregon tribes, the Kalapuyas had a reputation of being a peace-loving, agrarian people.

15. The Clatskanie were unique among the Columbia River Indians. They belonged to a completely different language group and were skilled hunters, not fisherfolk. By the early 1900s, only one Clatskanie was reported to be alive. Her name was Maria and she was living among the Chinook Nation people, along the lower Washington coast. There are different

stories about the origin of the Clatskanie. The book's Clatskanie origin story was taken from an early 1900s oral history given by a part-Clatskanie elder who said he'd learned the story from his Clatskanie grandparents. I chose to use the elder's version because it was the only one that purportedly came from the oral history of a tribal member. Other tribes, like the Northern California Yuroks, also viewed the birth of twins as an ill-omen and killed them at birth. The Clatskanie language establishes that they were related to the Navahos and Apaches living in the American Southwest.

16. The Chinook Clatsop band, in common with many Pacific Northwest tribes, institutionalized gift-giving which acted to equalize wealth among their people. Birth, marriage, coming-of-age, and a host of other celebratory events often included gift-giving that transferred possessions from the more wealthy to the less wealthy. Wealth transfers also occurred through a cultural love of gambling.

17. The Lewis and Clark diaries reference thieving by the Chinook Clatsops. These Indians saved the explorers' lives when they were wintering at the mouth of the Columbia by giving them food and other necessities. What these Euro-Americans did not know was that, in the Clatsop culture, when one received a gift outside of the celebration gifts, one gave an equal value gift in return. The Lewis and Clark group took far more gifts than they ever reciprocated in equal-value gifts. This created an imbalance that was unacceptable according to the Clatsops' understanding of how the universe worked, so their acts tried to restore that balance.

18. Certainly, not all Indian practices were admirable by today's standards. Many tribes engaged in warring raids. Certain tribes were mortal enemies. Sometimes slaves and women were treated in ways today's people would characterize as callous, harsh, and grossly unequal. Slavery, the result of war and raids, existed in Indian cultures across the country. Sometimes, slaves were ill-treated and murdered without censure. Other times, they were treated like members of the family. The treatment of slaves was as varied as there were tribes and individuals.

19. Charley Red Hawk's grizzly bear is the one part of the story that was not taken from Indian history, though the idea was inspired by an Indian myth. That myth names an individual with grizzly bear power that gave him the ability to change shape. As someone who has had mystical experiences and who has studied aboriginal beliefs, I cannot discount the possibility that people who live closely connected to nature might have spiritual experiences different from those of mainstream society.

Impact of European Diseases

20. As noted above, disease decimated Indian populations across the country and in Oregon. I found no evidence that Pacific Northwest Indians were deliberately infected with disease. At one point, in a ploy to stop attacks on ships sailing up the Columbia River, a Hudson's Bay Company officer shook a bottle containing a harmless fluid and threatened to let loose a disease if a band of Clatskanies didn't stop their attacks.

21. Deliberate infection was unnecessary because Oregon Indians lacked immunity to European diseases. Euro-Americans in the region died of the same diseases but their immunity meant they had much, much lower rates of infection and mortality. Historians believe the region's first devastating plague was malaria, brought by a passing Spanish ship in the late 1700s. Thereafter, the Pacific Northwest Indian population was devastated by wave after wave of the invaders' diseases: malaria, smallpox, measles, influenza, typhoid, diphtheria, scarlet fever, tuberculosis, and other diseases were all swift killers of the indigenous people.

22. Early explorers and settlers of the 1800s frequently reported seeing destitute and unhealthy Indians living in ramshackle villages. What these Euro-Americans failed to realize was that the people they saw had once lived in flourishing communities recently devastated by disease. In some instances, an entire tribe or band was so completely exterminated that only their bones remained scattered across the ground.

23. In the early 1900s, tuberculosis was rampant on Indian reservations. In 1916, Senator Harry Lane read a letter from the Blackfeet Reservation doctor in which he stated that 76% of the Indians had tuberculosis. People were contracting and dying from it at exceedingly higher rates than the white population. Boarding schools worsened the situation because children lived closely together and, often, were poorly nourished.

24. Dr. Defler's statement that boarding schools offloaded their TB-infected students so they could report a lower death rate appears in government reports and existing agency records of at least one Oregon reservation. These expelled children, in turn, infected their families who lived in impoverished and unsanitary conditions. One account noted that the pipe carrying the reservation's water supply ran very close to outhouses. Typhoid on the reservation was attributed to that situation. Although the Indian Service knew of the problem, it did nothing and typhoid continued to sicken and kill the reservation's people.

25. In that same 1916 letter, read into the Congressional Record by Senator Harry Lane, the Blackfeet Reservation physician reported that 90% of the Indians suffered from trachoma. Trachoma was the second most common disease on Indian reservations. It caused low vision and blindness among its victims—both conditions being ones repeatedly mentioned in an Oregon reservation ledger. First noted in Egypt, trachoma was virulently contagious and carried back to Europe by Napoleon's returning soldiers. Later, it was common among the European immigrants arriving at Ellis Island. Poverty and poor sanitation created the perfect breeding ground for trachoma. In the early 1900s, copper sulfate was the only treatment and it was largely ineffective. Only the later advent of antibiotics finally brought it under control on the reservations. It remains a serious problem in third-world countries.

26. The first Oregon outbreak of the 1918 Spanish Flu underscores the dangers inherent in Indian boarding schools of that time. The *Salem Statesman* newspaper reported on October 9, 1918, that the disease had "pervaded" the Chemawa Indian School

but remained "isolated". It reported that more than one-third of the students had already contracted the disease in the infection's first twenty days and sixteen of them died. Of course, that flu subsequently spread throughout Oregon.

27. An Oregon reservation ledger of the 1900s provided ongoing entries about individual tribal members. Frequently that ledger referenced "blindness" and "eye troubles." It also mentioned "lung disease" as being the reason that the individual was too ill to work. The other health issues appearing in the story also came from the reservation ledger.

28. One 1901 Oregon reservation census showed fourteen students as being removed from the census because they had died or were in ill health. Specifically, nine of them left the school because of tuberculosis, two because of "ill health", and two were dead. This was out of a school population of approximately 62 children.

29. Many Indian people believed that the spirits of their ancestors were present in their lives. They believed that desecration of their ancestors' graves harmed those spirits. The story's two instances of grave desecration come from the historical record. White trappers and settlers were notorious for their grave-robbing. The practice forced the Indian people to start burying their loved ones in the ground. Even then, Indian bodies were dug up by looters or plowed under by white settlers wanting to farm the land. Later anthropologists disturbed gravesites in the name of science. In recent years, a few of these stolen bones made their way back to their ancestral lands for proper burial. Most were lost.

Land Grabs and Forced Containment

30. Initially, the federal government's policy was to move and contain Indians on reserves. Many know of the Trail of Tears, where the "Five Civilized Tribes" of Cherokee, Choctaw, Creek, Chickasaw, and Seminole people were forced-marched from

the East Coast to a reservation in Oklahoma. At least 3,000 people died on the march.

31. What is little known is that Oregon had its own Trail of Tears in the 1850s. Tribal people were force-marched from their ancestral homes in Southern Oregon and Northern California under armed guard. Many died during the journey. They died from hunger, exposure, and because white settlers shot them even though captives were unarmed. When these people reached the Siletz and Grand Ronde reservations there was little shelter or food, such that many more of them died that winter. A few of them broke away during the exodus and disappeared into the coastal mountains. It is doubtful, however, that any of them were still living as renegades at the time of this story. But who knows? Ishi, a member of a Northern California Yahi band, lived hidden from whites until 1911 when he came out of the forest at fifty years of age.

32. The people of the Northern California Tolowa tribe, as well as other tribes, were viciously attacked, without provocation, by white settler vigilantes. Unarmed, peaceful, Tolowa men, women, and children were massacred while attending their annual prayer gathering. The vigilantes hoped to exterminate the tribe so that they could claim land that the federal government had reserved for the Indians. Ishi's Yahi band fled a similar vigilante attack and thereafter lived in hiding for decades.

33. After the civil war, President Grant wanted to avoid the treaty mandates that required the federal government to provide Indians with an education. His solution was to turn the responsibility for education over to various religious denominations. Oversight over each reservation was assigned to a specific Christian denomination. Only that denomination could erect a church on its assigned reservation. This was problematic for those Indians who wanted to belong to another church or to no church at all. Certainly, all of the denominations tried to squash every Indian belief or practice they considered contrary to their denomination's view of Christianity. Later, the U.S. government forcefully tried to suppress the Ghost Dance, Sun Dance,

and the practice of other Indian religions on the reservations. This happened in Oregon with the active suppression of the Indian Shakers and several other Indian-created religions. The Wounded Knee Massacre of nearly 300 Lakota Sioux Ghost Dancers occurred in 1890, just fourteen years before the setting of this story.

Forced Assimilation—"Kill the Indian to save the man" (and steal his land)

34. The phrase "Kill the Indian to save the man", was repeatedly used during the assimilation era. It originated with Civil War veteran, Lt. Col. Henry Richard Pratt who established the first Indian boarding school, the Carlisle Industrial Indian School in Pennsylvania. The stated intent was to strip Indian children of their cultural identity and their tribal and familial connections so that they could be inserted into the white culture and live like white men and women. Finding that parents would not willingly surrender their children, the Indian Service resorted to threats, violence, jailing, impoverishment, and lies to separate the children from their families. Often it transported them hundreds, if not thousands, of miles from their homes—oftentimes at very early ages.

35. In the early 1900s, Oregon had one off-reservation boarding school and six boarding schools located on reservations. Oregon's first boarding school was established in Forest Grove. It was modeled after the Carlisle school and administered by a man who revered Pratt and adopted his methodology. My initial interest in the history of Oregon Indians intensified upon reading an Oregon Historical Society article about Indian children who were forcibly removed from their families and sent to the Forest Grove School. They came from the relatively dry high plains of Eastern Washington and were sent to the Forest Grove school located in the much wetter Western Oregon. The article included a group picture of the children. It ended with the appalling declaration that, at the end of two years, every pictured child was dead.

36. Little Timothy Quirt's entry into the boarding school life at four years old describes the common experience. Countless personal stories relate how very young children's first introduction to boarding school began with the ripping away of their identity: Boy's heads were shaved, clothes were taken, possessions were seized, and they were given white names. The delousing process was particularly harrowing. A former student, Chief Luther Standing Bear, pointed out that, if hair lice were a problem, why did only the boys get their hair cut? Many schools punished children caught speaking their tribal language. Only English was allowed.

37. Dire poverty, with its accompanying starvation, forced many Indians to give their children and grandchildren to Indian boarding schools. They did so in the hope that, with more food and better clothing, their children would survive. These were necessity-driven surrenders that peaked during hard economic times, like in the 1890s and the 1930s depression eras. Countless first-person stories about being sent to boarding school mention the extreme poverty of the surrendering families. Others were orphans in a tribe whose members were so poor they could not support an orphaned child like they would have traditionally.

38. In many cases, however, Indian parents were forced to surrender their children. Some tribes and parents actively hid their children from the tribal police who would conduct surprise raids to seize the children. Pueblo men were imprisoned because they hid their children and refused to surrender them. In other cases, the reservation agent withheld allotment and annuity money and treaty goods, placing the parents in the position of either surrendering the child or watching the rest of their family starve.

39. Frequently first-time students ran away shortly after arriving at school, usually during the fall months. Tribal police were sent after them. Sometimes, these children died, particularly in the Midwest where sudden freezing weather caught them in the open. One former student wrote that was how two of his friends died.

40. Undoubtedly, some whites who engineered and implemented the assimilation scheme did so thinking they were doing the 'right' thing. They were dupes. In retrospect, it is abundantly clear that economic advantage motivated the federal government's assimilation policies. Whites wanted Indian land and the white federal government wanted to avoid the obligations required by the various treaties. The thought was that, if Indian people were incorporated into white society, then the need for their treaty rights and reservations was gone—leaving their land available to whites.

41. Reservation agents kept records in which they detailed the characteristics of various people under their control. The various descriptions mentioned in the story were taken directly from one such ledger. These white-centric, biased descriptions were passed on to subsequent agents who would use them in determining whether the person was "white enough" to get title to their land, receive benefits, employment, or even, raise their own children.

42. The fictional Agent Barnhart's demand that George Red Hawk cut off his braids was taken from an incident that occurred on the Umatilla reservation. A Umatilla left the reservation without obtaining written permission from the agent. He wanted to hunt on the tribe's traditional grounds. Upon his return, the agent charged him with violating the permit rule. The agent's rubber-stamp tribal court ordered the man to cut off his braids as punishment. He fled the reservation rather than cut his hair. Eventually, a court ruled, sometime after 1904, that such a punishment exceeded the authority of the Indian Service and was repugnant to American values of individual freedom.

43. Indian children and adults were ridiculed for using the slang and profane English they learned from native English speakers. Their English was considered evidence of the Indians' "inferior" intelligence. The reason they misspoke English, however, proved just the opposite. They used those English words because their languages contained neither slang nor profane words. Because the concept of idioms was foreign to them,

they did not know to differentiate them from other words in English. (Though, it is unfathomable why any mono-lingual speaker thinks he or she can criticize how someone speaks an adopted second language.)

44. The Indian approach to language education was effective and enlightened. Ethnologists of the time determined that Indian children never spoke in baby talk. Instead, they were taught their formal language as soon as they began speaking. As stated above, that language did not contain contractions, slang, swear words, or idioms and was strictly grammatical. Adults patiently corrected the children so that, by the time the child was ten or so, he or she spoke their language as well and as completely as an adult.

45. There is some conflict in the historical record regarding agency oversight at the Grand Ronde reservation. Some hold that all but one of the agents were either corrupt or indifferent to the plight of their charges. The "progress" detailed by the Dr. Duncan character appears in an annual report submitted to the Indian Service. It would be fair to say that regardless, few if any, Indian agents or boarding school superintendents or other white Indian Service employees, respected the Indian culture or declined to exercise control over the Indians' lives—most of them effectively functioned as "the boss man."

46. Any Indian who refused to live on his or her designated reservation was declared a "renegade." Not all Cherokees treked the Trail of Tears to Oklahoma, some hid in the Appalachian Mountains. Similarly, not all Oregon, Washington, and California Indians went onto reservations. In Oregon, the most famous of these were the multi-tribe Indians who settled in the Celilo Falls area on the Columbia River. They engaged in years-long legal fights with the U.S. government for the right to stay in their location and to retain their fishing rights. Another off-reservation group lived in Hobsonville along the Oregon coast. They also remained on their ancestral lands and are currently fighting the federal government for tribal recognition.

47. The story's scene of the Indians attending Red Hawk's trial is based on an actual event. A Grand Ronde man was charged with murder. The people of the reservation attended the trial and filled the courtroom. The event was unusual enough that it was reported by a white newspaper in a neighboring town.

Indian Service Corruption

48. Despite the adoption of the civil service scheme in the early 1890s, Indian Service jobs were still treated as patronage jobs usually awarded at the behest of politicians. When local whites wanted Indian land and met resistance from the agent, they resorted to political machinations to get that agent removed, despite civil service. This is what occurred in Tacoma. It was not until Theodore Roosevelt's appointment of a commissioner who'd fought for Indian rights, Francis Leupp, that significant emphasis was placed on hiring Indians for more than just menial tasks at the Indian reservations and boarding schools.

49. The positive impact of Indian Commissioner Leupp's appointment is reflected in the appointments on one Oregon reservation. In the 1890s whites filled all the positions. In 1904, there were six whites and six employees designated as mixed or Indian, filling reservation positions—including holding two of the three teaching positions.

50. The improper handling of allotment and lease monies by Indian Service personnel is detailed in numerous writings. Moreover, there seemed to be two kinds of reservation agents. One kind thought the whites around the reservation were rapacious and harmful to the Indian's interests. They resisted white efforts to sell liquor, steal property, and use their political influence to the Indian's detriment. The eventual disposition of the land upon which the Ft. Lewis army base stands, near Tacoma, is a case in point. White efforts to take that land entailed many years of lawsuits and political machinations. Ultimately, the whites were successful. Too frequently, however, the agent was corrupt and colluded with whites to steal from the people of the reservation.

51. Firsthand accounts and Indian Service reports provided the descriptions of corruption in the story—such as the selling of farm produce, reservation equipment, and supplies and the withholding of Indian lease and allotment monies. Not all 250 boarding schools in the country experienced corruption but many did. Even when there was no corruption, the living conditions were harsh. The schools were grossly underfunded and frequently, overseen by incompetent, ignorant, and/or cruel headmasters.

52. It should also be noted that the federal government commonly sold Indian land at far below market price. Often the sales occurred as a result of using fraud, coercion, and bribery to obtain tribal consent. The practice was so widespread that, occasionally and years later, courts stepped in to re-work the sale price in favor of the Indians.

53. In 2016, Elouise Cobell, also known as Yellow Bird Woman, of the Blackfoot Confederacy, was posthumously awarded the Presidential Medal of Freedom for her advocacy on behalf of Indian rights. She was a banker who founded the first national bank on an Indian reservation. In 1996, Cobell filed a class-action lawsuit alleging the federal government had mishandled over $100 billion of the Indian's trust funds. The lawsuit resulted in a settlement of nearly $6 billion and the return of some land to various tribes' control.

Red Progressives of the Early 1900s

54. During the Theodore and Franklin Roosevelt presidencies, federal Indian policy improved. Civil service was implemented to address corruption, the assimilation policy was discarded, day schools were instituted, and off-reservation boarding schools were mostly abandoned. There was growing awareness that Indians had artistic ability and that aspects of the various Indian cultures needed to be preserved and celebrated.

55. Credit for such improvements has gone to enlightened Euro-Americans. But I am convinced that their "enlightenment" was

the result of progressive Indians "educating" them. Historically, as is true currently, the words of whites belonging to a certain economic class were accorded much more weight than those same words coming from minority members of lower economic communities. Regardless, these whites did get the Indian perspective heard and change occurred.

56. The beginning of the twentieth century heralded the arrival of white realization that Indians were as intelligent, skilled, talented, and wise as whites and that maybe, Indians had some valuable insights about their situation. This was "old news" to the Indians.

57. Ironically, it was the Indian's reaction to the devastating reservation and assimilation policies that engendered their unified resistance. Putting children of various tribes together and then subjecting them to similar hardship emphasized their commonalities. Making them speak only English allowed for that communality to be discovered, often in the context of identifying white hypocrisy. Children from tribes that were traditional enemies banded together in the face of their common enemy.

58. Autobiographies about reservation boarding school life frequently mention the fact that the children created secret places where they'd meet to carry on their tribal rituals, eat their traditional foods, and freely speak their tribal language.

59. The early 1900s Pan-Indian movement was conceived of, and created by, people who'd had endured the boarding school experience. Dr. Charles Eastman, his brother, Rev. John Eastman, Rev. Sherman Coolidge, Chauncey Yellow Jacket, and Carlos Montezuma co-founded the Society of American Indians. It was the first national American Indian rights organization run by and for American Indians. The Society promoted the Pan-Indianism movement to unite Indians regardless of tribal affiliation. The Society's founders were the vanguard of what became known as the "Red Progressives." These Red Progressives were people who had succeeded in the white world by becoming prominent professionals in the fields of medicine, nursing, law,

government, education, anthropology, and ministry. Like the white Progressives, they also believed in progress through education and governmental action. One of their most noteworthy successes was the Indian Citizenship Act that was signed into law on June 2, 1924. This Act declared all Indians to be citizens, regardless of land ownership or whether they lived on or off reservations.

60. Events involving Charles Eastman, a Santee Dakota, are mentioned in the story. He was a physician educated at the Carlisle Indian Industrial School and Boston University. He was also a well-known writer, national lecturer, reformer, and reputed to be one of the most prolific authors and speakers on American Indian affairs. He was a co-founder of the Boy Scouts of America as well as of the Society of American Indians. While working as a doctor on the Lakota Pine Ridge reservation, Eastman went to the site of the Wounded Knee massacre where he saw the horrific slaughter while searching for and treating the few Indian survivors. Subsequently, he attempted to get the Indian Service to address reservation agent corruption. In response, the Indian Service terminated his employment. Thereafter, he attempted to work as a doctor in Chicago but no whites would use his services. It was common for boarding school trained Indians to find themselves unemployable in the white world and their training useless on the Indian reservations.

Miscellaneous

61. The town of Independence, Oregon, was briefly the hop capitol of the world when bacteria devastated hop fields in Europe and on the east coast. Farmers considered Indians to be the best hop pickers although they paid them less than white pickers. During the Willamette Valley's hop-picking season, Indians from many different tribes reunited with friends and relatives, found mates, and, joined in community games and celebrations.

62. Incredibly, despite an enduring, active, sizable, and continuous Chinook presence in the Pacific Northwest, the federal

government still refuses to recognize them as an Indian Nation. Ironically, the Chinook Clatsop band were the people who saved the Lewis & Clark Expedition during their wintering over at Fort Clatsop.

63. The National Archives in Seattle, Washington house the ledgers and other contemporaneous documents from the various reservations that were located in Alaska, Washington, Oregon, and Idaho. The Trump administration unilaterally decided to close and sell-off the Seattle archives building and disperse its contents to facilities far from the people whose histories it currently preserves.

Mainstream America needs to know Indian history. More importantly, it needs to know the contributions and concerns of contemporary Indians. Like many minorities, but perhaps more than most, Indians are given little voice or attention by the media or at high levels of government. That is a national shame. Arguably, at this time in history, our country needs to hear Indian perspectives most of all, both the historical and the contemporary.

ACKNOWLEDGMENTS

THIS HAS BEEN A DIFFICULT story to research and write. Not because the material was unavailable. The hard work of the people staffing the Columbia County Museum Association, the Oregon Historical Society, and the National Archives in Seattle, Washington, has preserved much Pacific Northwest Indian history. It was while researching in the National Archives, that a news reporter informed me of the Trump administration's plans to close it and disperse its contents to various archives far from the Pacific Northwest. This would be a disaster for Pacific Northwest Indians, Chinese, Japanese, scholars, and others who seek to understand and tell the region's unseen history.

Fortunately, there are a number of scholarly and autobiographical books, articles, and movies that tell the Indian version of U.S. history. Every day, more such material is being produced. So lack of information is not what made this story difficult to research and write. The difficulty lay in the fact that the horror and pain inherent in Indian history overwhelms. Worse, the majority culture's brutalization continues to this day. The Indian Nations are still fighting for recognition, the integrity of their culture, their ancestral lands, and the reparations that are long overdue them.

As for the story, it owes a huge debt of gratitude to Claudine Paris who labored mightily over the manuscript. Whatever satisfactory storytelling you find within its pages has much to do with her efforts. I also want to acknowledge Slaven Kovačević, whose skill and dedication make the book lovely to look at and easy to read. Their efforts aside, whatever errors exist are solely my own.

I also want to thank my readers, friends and family who continue to support and sustain my effort to tell stories about the people whose work made our present better than the one they endured. It's axiomatic that each generation stands on the shoulders of prior generations. No generation has created the perfect world, yet. But as a student of history, I do see that humans are evolving and that the world is moving closer to manifesting compassion through economic and social justice—in spite of the inevitable backsliding humanity endures along the way. I want to acknowledge and thank the people, and especially those of my friends, who continue pushing humanity towards a more moral and just future. Fortunately for all of us, they are too numerous to name here.

Closer to home, I thank the universe every day for my partner, George, whose desire for economic and social justice persists. And, who is always much kinder and more patient than I sometimes deserve.

Thank you for reading **Unseen**

We invite you to share your thoughts and reactions with
your library and on
Goodreads as well as on your favorite social media and
retail platforms. Your comments help and encourage
authors whose work you like and support.

Request for Pre-Publication Notice

If you would like to receive notice of the publication
dates of the next Sage Adair historical mystery novel,
please contact Yamhill Press at

www.yamhillpress.net.

Other Mystery Novels in the Sage Adair Historical Mystery Series
by S. L. Stoner

Timber Beasts

A secret operative in America's 1902 labor movement, leading a double life that balances precariously on the knife-edge of discovery, finds his mission entangled with the fate of a young man accused of murder.

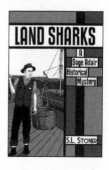

Land Sharks

Two men have disappeared, sending Sage Adair on a desperate search that leads him into the Stygian blackness of Portland's underground to confront murderous shanghaiers, a lost friendship and his own dark fears.

Dry Rot

A losing labor strike, a dead construction boss, a union leader framed for murder, a ragpicker poet, and collapsing bridges, all compete for Sage Adair's attention as he slogs through the Pacific Northwest's rain and mud to find answers before someone else dies.

Black Drop

In this ripping yarn, President Theodore Roosevelt has left Washington D.C., embarking on his historic train trip through the American West. Little does he know that assassination awaits him in Portland, Oregon. The words of a dying prostitute warn Sage Adair and his allies that they will be blamed for Roosevelt's murder. Since life is never simple, Sage also learns of young boys who need rescuing from a fate worse than death. As the presidential train and the boys' doom rush ever closer, every crucial answer remains elusive. Who is enslaving the boys? Who plans to kill the president? Can either tragedy be stopped?

Dead Line

Sage Adair encounters murder and mayhem midst the sagebrush and pine trees of Central Oregon's high desert. This captivating land of big skies, golden light and deadly secrets is the home of hardy and hard people–some of whom intend to kill him.

The Mangle

During a blistering 1903 summer, Portland's steam laundry women are working ten hellish hours a day. Exhausted and ill, they demand a nine-hour workday. Sage Adair, and his mother, Mae, join their fight until women begin disappearing. Desperately searching for the missing women, Sage and Mae face grave danger midst suffragettes, prostitutes, social workers, white slavers, arsonists and heartless bosses. Inspired by actual historical events, this is the sixth book in the award-winning Sage Adair mystery series.

Slow Burn

Arson, murder, kidnapping and false accusations abound in this seventh book of the Sage Adair Series. What begins as a simple assignment—helping the city's firefighters unionize, catapults Sage onto firefighting's front lines and into solving the deeper mystery of who is burning down the city and why.

Bitter Cry

Night fog drives a young newsboy into a seedy saloon where his appearance catapults Sage Adair into a world of painful memories, child exploitation and frantic searches for missing loved ones. In the series' eighth mystery, Sage and his colorful allies find collaboration to be the path to survival.

NOTES

Made in the USA
Columbia, SC
25 June 2023

18864536R00140